THE GODS WHO WALK

Book One of
The Antembra Trilogy

THE GODS WHO WALK

C.M.W. HAWKINS

Undead Avian Publishing

AN UNDEAD AVIAN PUBLISHING PUBLICATION

First Edition

10 9 8 7 6 5 4 3 2 1

Cover illustration by Justice Hopkins
Edited by Morgan Munro

Set in Palatino Linotype & Aara Regular

ISBN 13: 978-0-9952100-5-9

Printed through IngramSpark

Follow Undead Avian Publishing on Facebook or Twitter:
https://www.facebook.com/undeadavian/
https://twitter.com/undeadavian

For Isaac

PROLOGUE

150 Years Ago

THE SOUND OF footsteps upon cold stone echoed as a group of four figures dressed in hooded robes moved quickly through the dark catacombs. The one in the lead was also pushing a wheeled chair that held a man, chained and bound, with a crude crown of poorly fashioned tin upon his brow. He was desiccated, barely alive; his lips were cracked and his features were sharp and gaunt. The most striking thing about the man was that both his hands and his feet were missing.

"It's nearly time. We will begin here," the lead figure, a woman, spoke, motioning towards an antechamber. The procession stopped and moved through into a much larger room with the dead lining the walls. Torches were set into nearby sconces, bathing the room in flickering orange light.

Pushing her prisoner into the center of the room, the woman was thankful for the small sacrificial altar nearby which she could use for her purposes. Reaching under the chair she pulled out a mortar and pestle, a small scroll, and a vial of dark fluid.

Setting the mortar down onto the altar she opened the scroll and took in a deep breath. The incantation was complex, and casting the spell would require every bit of her concentration. A simple mistake, even a tiny falter in her focus, and it could go disastrously wrong; forty years of planning gone in the blink of an eye. She turned to the man in the chair. *I will not allow myself to fail.*

"Bring me the bone."

One of the men reached into his pack and pulled out an object that was about six inches long and stark white, even in the low-lit conditions. Taking it, she lowered her hood and ran her fingers through her long red hair. Keeping it stuffed within that hood was stifling, and she needed no such distraction. Looking over the scroll one last time she took another breath and spoke the first words.

"Et donga ut et Entranthas, yar les ay nok'lot."

She broke the bone into smaller pieces, surprised at how brittle it actually was in her hands. Starting to grind it to powder, she recited the second and third lines on the scroll.

"Ay nok'lot fet hux'ka fyr'gr. Slo'fyr tue yershalwa hux'ka ve!"

Satisfied so far, she opened the vial and poured the black fluid into the mortar. Mixing the two together formed a thick paste. The hair on her arms began to stand on end as she felt the energy in the room begin to increase. *It's working!*

Standing, she took the fluid over to the man sitting in the chair. His eyes were closed, but she paid him no mind. She was too close now for anything to stop her from this glorious purpose; her destiny.

"Komplux et zer'fy' Husticar ru et Ent'Tra wu fet ke vishe hu drosh dubl."

Once the words escaped her lips, the paste in the mortar lifted out and moved into the air. The inky, swirling mass was forming and reforming itself wildly, like a caged animal finally released after years of captivity. Her eyes grew wide and her lips broadened into a smile. The other three men had been quiet, but their collective gasp was enough to break the silence.

She continued to focus on the swirling mass; this part was crucial. The fluid had to be what killed the man sitting in the chair for the final part of the spell to take hold and achieve the desired effect. Not thinking of him as a man or a former king, but another reagent in her spell, she closed her eyes and drove all of her will into the ball of bone and blood. Something stopped her.

What? Why isn't...resistance?!

If she did not regain control immediately the spell would fail and they would not be able to replicate it. Her eyes opened, searching to find the cause of such a strong block to her mental will, and she was shocked to see the King before her, looking *down* at her. He was floating off the chair, his bindings disintegrating as he rose. The ball flew onto his chest and was quickly absorbed.

"Forty. Years."

His words were harsh, like metal raking across glass. The power behind them, however, was enough to push her back a foot before she was able to brace herself. How was such power possible from a withered shell of a man?

"Beaten. Broken. For...what?"

One of the men ran at at the King, attempting to subdue him before all was lost. She wanted to cry out to him to stay where he was, but the words refused to leave her lips. The King raised his arm, the stump where his hand would have been pointing at the leaping figure.

The man stopped, crying out in a way she had never heard a man scream before. He hunched over himself as a torrent of blood splashed out from under his hood. Without taking his eyes off of her, the King tossed the body to the other side of the room using some unseen force.

"For *WHAT?!*"

The words boomed and echoed throughout the catacombs, and she found she could speak again.

"To bring them back."

"*WHO?*"

"The Gods Who Walk."

His gave no outward reaction, aside from quirking an eyebrow at her. The other two men started circle slowly, trying to flank him. If she kept his attention long enough they cou-

Suddenly she couldn't move and found herself being lifted off the ground and brought towards the floating figure.

"Greyania!"

One of the men cried her name as they both lunged. Without looking to his would be attackers, both men were stopped mid-air and were thrown back with enough force for her to hear multiple bones crack upon impact. Neither got back up.

"There. No more distractions." His voice seemed less grating as he started to get used to speaking again. "The Gods Who Walk are legend. *Myth.* What makes you believe you can bring them back?"

"*You* were the key to freeing them."

The invisible force that was holding her up let go and she dropped the few feet to the ground, landing on her foot with enough force to hear a crack. Trying her best to not cry out in pain, she bit her cheek so hard it drew blood.

Not noticing or not caring, the King lowered himself to the ground and hovered just high enough that he would be standing if he still retained his feet. Turning away from her, he looked at the dead in their eternal slumber around the room with an air of reverence.

"I was tortured and kept at the edge of death's door...*for forty years*...so you could bring a myth to life."

"I told you, they are no myth. Their freedom would mean the return of all magic to Antembra, not just the paltry excuse that passes for it these days."

Being alive gave her confidence to deal with him. Even though she had been his jailor for the past forty years, his ultimate reason for being there, he had not killed her like the others. There had to be a reason, one she could possibly exploit.

She tried to keep him talking. "I have answered your question, now answer mine: how have you come to posses this power?"

He spoke to her as he would have spoken to a child. "Blood magic is powerful...primal, full of potential energy... *and* able to pervert and change existing incantations."

"Powerful, yes, but always with a terrible price."

Moving with unnatural speed she felt hands, though he had none, grab her and pull her to within inches of his face. His anger and fury were palpable.

"*AM I YOUR TERRIBLE PRICE*?! Was I to be the debt paid in full because you were too cowardly to tax yourself? *I WAS A KING!*"

The words caused her to tremble in true fear; never had she experienced such a powerful, malevolent presence before. His features softened for a moment, and he dropped her. Landing on her injured foot again, she was not able to keep the pain to herself and cried out loudly.

"It seems it worked. I can feel them now, stirring...*confused.*" His face broke into a wide grin. "The ritual has failed. They remain in their captivity."

"No!"

"Oh...oh this is wonderful. Know what terrible price *I* paid?" He knelt down before her, looking at her like a cat would a caught mouse. "My own life, before you could. Bit off my tongue and drowned in the blood. He said you wouldn't even notice. And now? I get what was promised me."

Who is he talking about? Her mind raced to try and figure out who of her inner circle could have betrayed them all, but the only three who truly knew what was happening besides herself were all dead in this room. The King stood and moved about, arms spread wide.

"Now, I am to be a *god*."

Horror spread over her face as the truth dawned on her. There were only two spells that could be cast with such a sacrifice. One was her spell of Unbinding, and the other...

"You cast a spell of possession."

"I had hoped it would have been one of those three," he motioned towards the bloody corpses, "but this is a far, *far* cry better. What he promised me is nothing compared to what I am now receiving."

The only other beings in existence who knew of what she was attempting were the gods themselves. It had to be one of them that conspired against the Unbinding, but for what purpose?

He looked down at his ruined limbs as they began to glow purple and fade into nothingness. He regarded this new event with no outward emotion.

"The new spell must be fully taking hold. It seems forty years of suffering expedites things."

He was fading more and more as the glow increased around his body. His features began to mutate and change, and she realized he wasn't just possessing the distant god, but *merging* with it. The last thing she saw before his body fully disappeared was a dark, sinister smirk.

"I won't kill you. *I should be thanking you!* Because of your actions, magic is fully released back into Antembra, and I not only am I a *god*, but the only *free* one."

She called after him. "No! Not like this!"

The ground quaked and the world shuddered as if it had been moving incredibly fast and now came to an abrupt stop. She and the corpses in the room, both new and ancient, were flung about like dolls. When everything finally lay still, she collapsed onto the floor. She had failed, and even worse, she had doomed the gods to an eternity of imprisonment.

Greyania.

A voice entered her mind and she panicked. *No, please. Not here. Not now.* She tried to block out her thoughts, to keep the voice from probing deeper into her mind, but it was no use. It brushed past her mental defenses easily.

It would appear things did not go as planned. I am disappointed, but there is no time for regrets.

Her mind felt like it was going to split into two and her whole body ached. Her foot, possibly her ankle, was certainly broken. She merely wanted to lie there in the dirt and join the dead around her.

"I failed. I failed all of you!"

Not even we could have foreseen the King's actions. He did much more than a spell of possession. It seems that interrupting the unbinding broke the world. Only we keep it from tearing itself apart. You will continue to aid us. Come. There is much to do.

It was not a request, but a command; one from her god. Taking a few moments to compose herself, she sat back up and brushed herself off as best she could. Finding a renewed strength, she began to crawl for the entrance.

"I serve those who walk."

ONE

"I'M GOING TO cram those words down your pale, scrawny throat!!"

The skin of the orc male bulged as he flexed his muscles in a show of force to try and intimidate the human he was arguing with. Shae, an elf sitting by herself watching what was happening, had to admit it was rather attractive. In a green sort of way. The human ripped off his own shirt, and while his skin was in desperate need of sun, his physique was also rather alluring.

Perhaps it was just the wine.

"Try it, and I'll shove my foot so far up your backside you'll have to lace your teeth!" the human retorted.

The orc was a good head taller than the human, with broad shoulders, thick muscles, a bit of a paunch, and a bald roundish head with dark gray eyes. Oddly enough he had no piercings, and one of his tusks was chipped. The human, on the other hand, was athletic and looked like he took his physique seriously. He had thick stubble that suited his square jawline, hazel eyes and short, dark brown hair.

"HUNTER, RHIKTER, BOTH OF YA! OUTSIDE, NOW!"

A dwarven barkeep hopped over the bar with surprising agility and stood between the two men, brandishing a nasty looking pair of daggers. Shae took a sip of her wine and continued to watch the encounter unfold from her table.

The orc scoffed. "Out of the way, Jorkt. Rhik and I have issues only getting bloodied can resolve."

"Blood it 'tis, den."

Jorkt moved quite fast, and before Shae could tell what happened, Hunter had fallen to one knee as blood began seeping from a wound on his calf.

"Ye both know these daggers're special, boys. Only way ta stop tha bleedin' is ta see a healer. Best be on yer way now, bef're I add more ta their bill."

Rhikter's body tensed, making it seem he was going to try and overtake the dwarf, but instead he tossed several gold coins onto the counter. What he did next surprised Shae, as he walked over to the orc and offered him a hand.

"Come, let's get you patched up so I can beat the shit out of you."

What followed was even more shocking; Hunter gave a deep, resounding belly laugh and took Rhikter's hand. Putting his arm around the man's shoulder, he walked with a slight limp as they headed out the door.

"This changes nothing, Rhik."

"Nor should it, Hunter. But I'd hate to hear you going on like a sow giving birth over how you had a disadvantage when I won our argument."

Both men had a hearty laugh as they made their way out of the tavern.

Curious. Orcs were a proud people, steeped in tradition and honor. A feud like that, especially with a human, would not go unmet unless the two were in good company. She'd been sent to try and find help for this mission, and perhaps she had.

Downing the rest of her wine in a single gulp, she wiped her mouth with the back of her hand and moved toward the barkeep. Jorkt was busy cleaning up blue orc blood off the floor, grumbling to himself all the while.

"Excuse me."

"If ya want ta pay yer tab, just toss tha coin on tha counter," he replied without looking up.

"Actually, I had a question for you. About the two who just left."

He spat on the ground with a curse and wiped it up with the blood, leaving a smear of blue. "Those two? Right as rain when dey ain't drinkin', dat's fer sure. But get a few pints in'em and it always ends in a godsdamned squabble. Last time dey broke two o' mah tables. Two!"

Now he looked up, squinting at her through one eye as if to assess her worth, and judge whether or not he should divulge any more information. Shae wore a hooded cloak, colored deep purple. Her wavy, black hair was cut to shoulder length, framing her oblong face. She also wore sturdy traveling leathers and had a crossbow and dagger at her sides. After sizing her up, he proceeded to end their conversation as he rose from the floor, meeting the gaze of her soft brown eyes with his own.

"If ya want ta know more 'bout 'em, ask yerself."

"Perhaps you can tell me exactly where they went, then?"

She took out several coins from her pouch, more than the single glass of wine was worth, and handed them to the dwarf. His eyes grew brighter and friendlier as he took her payment.

"They will've gone ta a healer. Der's one jes down tha road, takin' a left at tha fork. Kenna miss it." His eyes never left the coins as he turned back to the bar, a touch of pep to his step. "Just down the road, missy! Yer always welcome at Jork-t's!"

Without another word she turned to head out the door. *Dwarves. So predictable when it came to anything shiny and valuable.* Once outside she took in a breath of air. While it wasn't as stale as that within the tavern, it was hardly what one would describe as fresh.

Shae had never liked dwarven cities, and Aungermiest was one she held a particularly great disdain for. The city itself was housed within a gigantic underground cavern, deep below the surface. It's location had afforded it a great amount of protection from the change when the world froze in place and became stuck with one side facing the sun. It was a perfect sanctuary for all the refugees that arrived.

While she appreciated what the city meant for the races of the world, she wished it wasn't so...*dwarven.* Saying the city was planned was something of a stretch; it was a mass of dug out alleyways, roads, hovels, and artificial caverns that sprawled in every direction. Despite the fact the city was split into districts, such as industrial or residential, it was a virtual maze. Buildings of all shapes and sizes - tall, wide, short, thin - were thrown together with such recklessness that it was a wonder the city was able to function at all. She hoped she could find the two men...instead of getting lost in the twisting side streets and back alleyways.

*****

"Stop your fussing, we're almost there!"

"Jorkt must have put extra enchantments on those accursed blades of his. Not only is it bleeding, but it feels like fire gnats are crawling under my skin!"

"Probably. I wouldn't put it past the little miser. But, that doesn't mean you have to tell me about it every damned step of the way."

"It hurts, Rhik!"

"For an orc, you complain a lot."

As Shae spoke, both men spun around and tried to adopt a defensive stance, but they looked rather silly with the orc hopping on one foot, and the human carrying more than his fair share of the weight.

"Who goes? Friend or foe?" Hunter said.

"I didn't think people actually said that," she replied as she stepped into view. "Potential friend. I come seeking assistance with a task given to me by the Clan of Elemental Winds."

Hunter rolled his eyes and both men turned around to continue on their way to the healers.

"We want no part of whatever it is you are selling," Hunter replied.

"Last time we got involved with elves it ended poorly," Rhikter added.

Not surprising. Elves hadn't taken well to the change when magic suddenly burst back into the world. The sudden flood of energy during the change, the Unbinding of Magic, had lasting and powerful effects on her entire race. Those associated with her clan were far less affected than most.

"They *are* paying handsomely, and you two seem like you could fit the bill. As long as you aren't always trying to kill one another," Shae said.

"Can't promise that. Seems you're out of luck," Rhikter called over his shoulder as Hunter snorted in agreement.

Gods, these two were insufferable and she'd only just met them. Was it really worth her time and trouble to convince them? She hoped it was as she rolled her eyes and uttered a few words, aiming her hand at Hunter's calf.

A blue bolt of light shot out from her fingertips and struck him in his wound, causing him to cry out in surprise. Rhikter dropped the orc's arm and spun around, hand going for a dagger she had failed to notice. Before he could draw it, Hunter's hand was on his shoulder holding him back.

"Hm. She healed it," Hunter said as he looked at her. "I thank you, but I do not think we are the men you want. We are neither mercenaries, nor soldiers."

"Oh? What are you then? Please don't say drunkards. I'd hate to have wasted good magic on a pair of lushes."

Hunter smirked, his tusks gleaming in the artificial light of the city.

Rhikter answered, saying, "My friend and I are merely explorers. We go seeking what the world has hidden away. We then turn those items over to whomever may be interested in owning them. For a price."

Her jaw dropped. "By the gods, *you're tomb pillagers!*"

Rhikter made a motion for her to keep her voice down as they both moved closer to her and spoke in a quieter tone. "Pillage is such an ugly word. We *liberate* artifacts from their resting places and then make sure they find good homes. Like an adoption agency!" he said.

"It is not wholly illegal either, not since the change," Hunter stated defensively.

"It is to those of elven blood." Her words were like ice.

Rhikter narrowed his eyes at her for a moment and before she could react he pulled back her hood.

"You aren't working for the Winds, you *are* one! Well, half of one at any rate."

She cursed at herself for letting him see her ears. They were long, but the ends were stunted and rounded. She hated them. Her features were less pronounced as well, and much softer, like her human father's. Quickly, she pulled the hood back over her head.

"Let me guess...the last time things ended 'poorly' was when you tried to sell elves back their own artifacts."

"Hazard of the job. Since then, we've both decided that dealing with your kind is more trouble than it's worth. However, since you now want us out, we want *in*."

"Rhik." Hunter's voice growled as he eyed the human, voicing his disagreement.

"Fine, Hunter." He shot the orc a look and then turned back to Shae. "Tell us what you need us for, and I'll tell you if we're for hire."

She stood there, debating if she should even bother. Before she had learned what they were, she had been completely willing to hire them based on drunken bravado alone. Now that she knew they were pillagers, common grave robbers, she regretted ever following them in the first place.

The journey to the dwarven capital, Aungermiest, hadn't been as easy as she had hoped, and finding the bodies to accompany her on this mission had been even more difficult. Still going over her options in her head, an impatient voice filled her mind.

They will suffice, if they are willing. You know as well as I that getting able-bodied help is proving more difficult than we anticipated. Trying to find two others would take too long. Perhaps these rogues could be more useful than you think.

"But they rob graves!"

You're speaking aloud.

Hunter and Rhikter were both giving her a look that was a mixture of curiosity and concern. She swore she saw Rhikter take a step back from her.

"My employer and I are in communication right now," she said as a reply to their looks, "and she believes you might suffice, despite my reservations."

"I can't speak to your reservations, but I can attest that we are excellent at what we do," Rhikter stated.

"So you say."

"Look, half-blood, either you are going to hire us or not. Despite *my* reservations of working for the elves again after the last time, Rhik seems all too eager. Besides, we seem to need each other," Hunter said.

"Who said we need her?"

"You ripped your shirt to shreds in Jorkt's, and we are down to our last 30 coins."

Rhikter turned a deep crimson in embarrassment as the realization dawned on him that he was, in fact, without a shirt Clearing his throat he tried to compose himself. Shae found it amusing, if unnecessary.

"Uh, er...yes. Well. I guess we're in. What say you?" He extended a hand.

Introduce yourself and tell them to meet us at the Tavern in the morning.

You're coming here?

Yes. I need to oversee the rest of the journey directly.

Shae wasn't sure how to feel about that. She valued the guidance and advice from afar, but her coming in person? That was unnecessary and dangerous.

Taking his hand she gave it a single firm shake. "You may call me Shae. Meet me back in that tavern in the morning. My employer and I will be there to discuss exactly what we require as well as your payment."

"Perfect! We're staying near there as well. We can walk together."

Making no effort to hide her disdain at the prospect, she turned on a heel and disappeared down a side road. At least by morning they would both have shirts on.

*****

As day broke, she quickly gathered her things from the small room she had procured for the night, knowing she would not return. The tavern was one of those establishments that never really seemed to close, and she was pleased to see Jorkt busying himself with preparing breakfast behind the counter. Her stomach rumbled despite herself, and she realized the only sustenance she'd had since last night was the glass of wine.

She couldn't help but squint as daylight spilled into the tavern from the large bay windows at the front. Should she call it daylight? This city was at least a mile underground and the 'daylight' was derived from an artificial device the dwarves called Yormsun, named so in homage to one of the Gods Who Walk.

Originally, before the Unbinding, all dwarven cities that were under the ground like this one were dimly lit, and always seemed stuck in a perpetual twilight. Once other races came to the dwarves as refugees, the king at the time, Yemund Flinbat IV, decided to use their technology and magic to fashion a great ball of light to make their visitors feel more welcome. Or so the story went.

Getting lost in thought, she took the same table she had sat at the night before. There was no sign of either of the two men, nor her employer. This didn't bother her though; she was usually early to most meetings or gatherings. Her habit of always being prepared, ready with a plan of escape should the need arise, was a hard one to break. Not that she would ever want to lose such a vital skill.

After a few moments by herself, the smell of frying eggs and meat was too much to bear and she made a beeline to the counter. Licking her lips, she was about to get Jorkt's attention when she heard a familiar voice behind her.

"You may eat when we are finished, Shae."

"Yes, m'lady," Shae replied without turning around. Kicking herself for not getting a plate of food earlier, she backed away from the delicious smell and faced her employer.

The other woman was wearing a hooded robe, hers white instead of purple like Shae's cloak, but the hood was down which allowed Shae to see her. Obviously human, she had a heart shaped face and looked no more than forty. Her hair was stark white, except for a lock of shocking crimson on the left side, and cut into a chin length bob. Her violet eyes shone with deep wisdom, but there was a flicker of mystery that implied she kept much hidden.

"Come here child, let me get a good look at you. All these weeks of being in your head and I've nearly forgotten what you look like!"

"You act like my mother," Shae protested, disliking the doting attention the other woman was showering on her.

"I may not be her, but I knew her well enough to consider you blood."

Never one to enjoy being fussed over, Shae was actually pleased to see Rhikter and Hunter come into the Tavern.

"Ah," Shae said, moving so she could introduce the men, "these are the two...*explorers* you're here to meet."

She couldn't help but choke on the word explorer. All her life she had been raised in strict elven traditions and practices, and these two disregarded several, chief of which was never to disturb the dead, that her clan held sacred just to fill their pockets.

"Rhikter Coldfire and Hunter Rage, at your service." Rhikter was the first to speak.

"Interesting names," the woman said.

"Well, we can get some breakfast and tell you all about them, if you like."

Rhikter motioned to a table nearby and took the first seat, while calling over to Jorkt to bring a few platefuls of whatever he was cooking on the wood stove. Shae took a seat across from him, as Hunter showed uncharacteristic chivalry for an orc and held out a seat for the other woman. She nodded thanks, and Shae could have sworn she saw a twinkle in the woman's eye.

"Now then, to busine-"

Rhikter held up a hand, interrupting her, as he motioned toward Jorkt, who was bringing their food.

"I never discuss any deal over an empty stomach. Leads to bad choices."

"Your stomach being full doesn't stop you from making bad choices, Rhik."

He frowned as the orc smiled, just as Jorkt put the first platefuls down. It took the dwarf four trips, an extra one just for a lamb shank for Hunter, but soon they were all feasting. Shae was bemused that even the other woman was eating her fair share. In all the years Shae had known her, she had never seen her more than nibble at food. Perhaps the spell used to get here so quickly had taken a toll on her.

Rhikter sopped up the last of the bacon grease on his plate with half a roll and looked from one woman to the other before speaking. "Ok, now that my stomach is full, what do you need stolen, when do you need it by, and how much are you willing to pay for it?"

Shae saw red and leapt to her feet, leaning over the table as she started to yell at him for the audacity of such assumptions. The nerve of this oaf, to presume they had need of his unscrupulous talents!

"I knew this was a mistake! Thieves can never be trusted. You only seek riches, no matter whom you may hurt. Come, m'lady, we need not bother ourselves with their presence any longer."

Still seething, she grew more and more concerned as the other woman did not rise and join her as she thought she would.

"Shae, sit. Please. There are things that need to be discussed and clarified."

Slowly sinking back into her seat, Shae tried to figure out what she meant by looking into those deep violet eyes. When the woman broke the gaze by looking away, Shae knew that she had not been told the full extent of what this journey would entail.

"The elders knew that we were going to rob graves, didn't they? Knew we'd need men like this...*and still allowed it?*"

Her words were whispers, and she couldn't allow herself to believe such a thing could be possible. The only thing keeping her in that seat and not storming out was that her clan's elders had sworn her to a Judgement Pact.

For the Elemental Winds clan, a Judgement Pact was called on to ensure those you made an agreement with would keep up their end of a deal or task, no matter what. To fail in the pact was to be exiled.

"It was necessary, child. I was able to convince the elders that it would be unavoidable if we were to actually have any chance in locating what we sought. Also, the potential outcome of this journey we undertake far outweighs the taboo over breaking a few elvish laws."

Swallowing hard, Shae leaned back against the chair, pulled her hood down a bit further, and folded her arms.

"Fine. I stay only because of the sworn Judgement Pact," she stated begrudgingly

"As I knew you would," the woman replied.

Turning to face the other two, who seemed uncomfortable about what had just occurred, the woman spoke again, this time lowering her voice.

"I sent Shae here to find us able bodies, willing to work. I was also not wholly honest with her in what it was that we would be seeking. Are either of you familiar with dominion magic?"

Both men looked dumbfounded, which caused Shae to snort. Of *course* they would have no idea about it. The two of them looked barely able to understand the most basic of spells, let alone something as complex as dominion magic. The other woman shot her a stern look and continued.

"Using magic as a catalyst, you control something inanimate with your mind. Much like a temporary spell of possession, only not on a living thing."

As she explained, Hunter's eyes lit up and he slammed a fist onto the table, a wide grin appearing on his face. Rhikter jumped and the suddenness of it startled Shae as well.

"Rhik, this sounds a lot like-"

"The golem!" Rhikter shouted as he finished Hunter's sentence.

Shae's brow furrowed as she tried to piece together what they were talking about. Golem? Such constructs were not exactly common, but they also were not controlled with dominion magic. Could these two *really* be so ill-informed?

"No, you misunderstand," the other woman clarified, "we mean controlling it directly with magic and your mind, in congress. Not giving it a task or purpose with a spell."

"I think it would be easier to show you." Rhikter smiled as he replied.

"Very well, I concur. Child, would you please settle our tab? I'm most curious to see what they mean." The human woman turned to regard Shae as she rose from her seat.

"Yes, m'lady."

She had to admit, the concept had her curious as well. She frowned as she started to wonder what sorts of magic they could be using, or what forbidden artifacts they'd taken for their own nefarious purposes.

As the rest stood to leave, Hunter extended a hand towards the woman.

"You never introduced yourself," he said.

"My name," she responded with a smile, taking his hand, "is Greyania."

Two

THEY HAD BEEN walking through the city for about twenty-five minutes before Shae finally had enough.

"Are you leading us to this golem or are you just taking us in circles?! We don't have time for some foolish errand," she remarked.

"It is just around the corner, I promise," Rhikter said.

Giving an exasperated groan, Shae resigned to just follow them in silence. Greyania had spent the walk conversing with the orc and Shae had kept to herself, mostly because she was still trying to come to grips with what she was doing here and why.

If I was to eventually have to go against everything I was taught, why did the elders not trust me with that information right from the start? It was troubling hindsight. She had taken the Judgement Pact without a second thought; any of her clan would have done the same. Yet, they made her take one before she knew what the full extent of the pact was. Such a thing was not unheard of, but it was uncommon.

"We're here! It's right inside."

Rhikter's voice broke her out of her contemplation and she regarded the run down storage building they were standing before. There was a large bay door and a smaller door to the right of it. Both were secured with hefty padlocks.

The four of them stood outside for a few moments before Greyania broke the silence with the obvious, "Shall we go inside? I wish to see this construct of yours."

It had better not just be some pile of clay, either. Shae thought, projecting the sentiment towards Greyania. The smirk on the woman's face made it apparent her quip was received. Shae continued to send her telepathic messages. *Once we have a moment, m'lady, we need to have a talk about all this.*

All in good time, child.

I'm serious, Greyania. You may be like a mother to me, but your disregard for my beliefs...You know how I feel about such things.

We will talk, I promise.

Shae knew better than to push it beyond that. They had fought many times over the years, and she knew when pushing a point would only make things worse. Now was one of those times. They would talk, certainly, but it would be on Greyania's terms. That didn't sit well with Shae, but she was wise enough to accept it.

In the time it took to conclude her conversation with Greyania, Hunter and Rhikter had opened the large bay door, leading the way into a workshop that looked more like a junkyard than any place one could get work done.

There were several work tables pushed up against each wall, and pieces of metal, all sizes and shapes, were strewn about. Unlike the dwarves need for technology and mechanisms in their devices, each piece was solid and seemed to be armored plating of some kind. Even the most standard golems had a working mechanical heart, so this piqued her curiosity even more.

In the centre of the room sat the golem, unlike any she'd ever seen before. It appeared to be made of bronze, which seemed to be an unusual choice; most were made of earthy materials, such as rock or clay. It looked more like an ornate suit of armor than a construct, down to the decorative flourishes at the shoulders and joints, and it wasn't as bulky as most golems she'd seen. It seemed to be reinforced in several areas, and the left leg was steel below the knee. Perhaps a repair of some kind? Most startling was that it appeared to be hollow.

The helmet had a grated mouth and looked like it was supposed to carry a great crest across the top, but the crest was missing. Standing there in the shop, it appeared to glow softly in the dim light.

"Allow me to introduce Coldfire," Rhikter beamed.

"That's your surname. A bit narcissistic, don't you think?" Shae snapped.

There was venom in her words as she let them slip, and she didn't care. Even if she had to work with this lot, there was nothing in her pact that said she had to enjoy it.

"Sort of the other way around. We never got the chance to tell you more of our names. Hunter Rage is your standard orc naming ceremony, rite of passage, blah blah," Rhikter said.

Hunter frowned at Rhikter, but turned away, shaking his head and grumbling under his breath.

"Rhikter was always my given name, but Coldfire was my chosen surname, after finding this beauty on one of our jobs."

"So you stole it, and claim to have some understanding of it?" Shae asked.

If you can't be civil, still your tongue, child. Greyania's scolding tone invaded her mind.

Then I would never speak in their presence again!

Gods you are acting like a spoiled little girl. Fine. Keep to yourself then.

"Well...It isn't stealing if you take it from your own house," he continued, having no clue of the hidden conversation going on at the same time.

"I'm not following."

"As I said, Coldfire is my *chosen* surname. My family's ancestors *owned* this thing," he patted part of it affectionately. "I merely liberated it once I learned of its existence."

Shae was starting to get annoyed. All this exposition was dancing around the real reason they were there. She'd rather he just get to the point and be done with it.

"What makes Coldfire so special, then? Other than its construction being odd, I sense nothing special to set it apart from other golems. It doesn't even have a working heart."

Smiling, Rhikter grabbed something on the front of the prone construct, pulled open a small door, and crawled inside. Before either she or Greyania could react, the golem hummed to life, its eyes glowing with blue fire. As it stood to full height, at least ten feet, she noticed the same blue glow at each of its joints, and when the previously missing crest flared to life it was made of blue fire as well.

"Honestly, the energy is elementally based in fire, but with the blue color I couldn't help myself. Coldfire." Rhikter's words took on a metallic tone as they came from inside the machine.

He moved it out of the workshop and onto the street where they could get a better look at it. With the fiery blue glow and the bronze finish, it was hard not to be impressed. Shae had seen all manner of golems before, but never one worn like a suit of armor. It was uncanny.

"I knew sending her to this city was the right path to take," Greyania said, nearly too quiet for Shae to hear. Had she planned this all from the start? The more Shae thought about everything that had happened since last night, and how these men happened to be in possession of such a device, the less she felt this was all a twist of fate that their paths should meet.

"M'lady...you knew about these two and their golem, didn't you? Just as you knew I would never be party to this had I known beforehand."

Greyania never turned to look at Shae, her violet eyes sparkling as she kept them focused on the construct before her. "I had suspicions. Feelings. But never did I dare to imagine that we would find a Behemoth Vessel so quickly, let alone one that worked," Greyania responded.

"A *what*?" Hunter spoke up from behind them.

"A...Behemoth Vessel..." Shae let the words flow past her lips in disbelief. Her excitement was palpable as she explained the term to the two men.

Along with the myths and legends of the Gods Who Walk, was the tale of their vessels. Elemental constructs for their heralds to wear as they spread the gods' will. What made them more unique and special than any other armor or man-made golem, was the fact that they were imbued with essence from the gods themselves. A piece of the gods was in every vessel, and as such, they were as powerful as they were rare.

"I'm thinking about calling it Golem Riding," Rhikter interjected at the end.

"You may call it whatever you wish. That does not tarnish what this magnificent artifact truly is. Have you found a way to unlock its true potential?" Greyania queried him.

"The fists can become engulfed in blue flame. Does that count?" Rhikter's tone sounded perplexed.

"Hardly." Greyania shook her head. "According to the ancient texts and legends of the Behemoth Vessels, each had an amulet that was attuned to it. These amulets could only be passed down through familial bloodlines. By chance are you wearing it now?"

"No."

"The fact you are able to use it without such an amulet shows the strength of your bloodline," Greyania said in a pleased tone.

"I told you changing your name wouldn't erase your past," Hunter said.

"Not now, Hunter," Rhikter spat out.

Anger and a hint of shame colored his tone, and Shae grew concerned. These men were liars and thieves and Rhikter was hiding something; she didn't trust them. How Greyania could let her guard down so quickly, even in the face of such a discovery, was also troubling.

"Perhaps such conversations are left best to more private surroundings, m'lady? I am not comfortable with the vessel being out in the open," Shae said, pointedly.

"You may be right, child. Come, bring it back into the shop and we shall continue there."

"It's not like we keep it a secret," Rhikter protested.

"He is right. We use it as often as we are able and have developed something of a reputation because of it. Some even call him Tin Man," Hunter said as he chuckled.

"It is not some toy for you to gallivant in! This is a priceless piece of history and should be *regarded with reverence!*" Shae's outburst shocked even herself at the volume and intensity of it. The other three were silent a moment. Rhikter was the first to react by heading back into the workshop and calling out to Hunter.

"Shut the doors and grab the wine skin. I need a drink."

A few minutes later, Hunter had grabbed a skin of wine from a nearby cupboard and was placing down a few crude cups. After pouring wine in each, he took what was left of the skin for himself. By the time he was finished, Rhikter had climbed out of the vessel and joined them.

"Alright, according to you, this isn't some golem I happened to find, but something called a 'Behemoth Vessel'. I also overheard you saying to Greyania that it wasn't coincidence that you happened to find us." He took the cup and downed the liquid all at once, wiping his lips as he set it back down. He looked over at Hunter who remained stoic and said nothing at first. The orc eventually shrugged and nodded. Rhikter continued. "We'll take the job, but we do have some questions. First of all, how did you find us? *Why* us?"

"Did you really think taking something as wondrous and powerful as this out in public would go unnoticed? I had heard rumors of a strange golem, and I wanted to see for myself if they bore fruit. I am most pleased they did." Greyania smiled as she sipped her wine.

"I warned you, Rhik. From the moment we laid eyes on that thing I knew it would bring far more attention that it was worth."

"I don't know, old friend. From where I sit it's gotten us what promises to be a lucrative job offering." Pausing, his tone changed. "It *will* be lucrative, right?"

"Yes. Within reason." Greyania nodded.

"There, see? The extra attention *has* been worth it. Just how 'within reason' are we talking?"

As the two discussed the payments and what would be expected of Hunter and Rhikter in this endeavor, Shae excused herself to go look around the shop. It looked like any other dwarven workshop she'd seen, but the real reason for her exploration was to inspect the vessel.

Just moments before, as Rhikter operated it, it had seemed so full of life and energy. Now it looked like another inanimate golem, waiting for the magic words to be spoken that would breathe life into its husk. As she reached out to touch it a green hand grabbed her by the wrist and yanked it back.

"If you touch it without it knowing you, it gets defensive," Hunter warned.

"*Knowing* me? What do you mean?"

Releasing her from his grip, Hunter narrowed his eyes as he regarded the vessel. Shae got the feeling he didn't entirely trust it. Orcs were, by their nature, distrustful of most magics. Something about the way he looked at it, though, was deeper than that. Distrustful or not, there was an air of reverence towards it as well.

"When we first found it, it was barely functioning. I was the first one to touch it, and when I did it came to life with *purple* fire, immediately attacking us. Only when Rhik managed to touch it's helm did the fires turn blue and it turned docile. It took some doing, but we got it to a point where it accepts me."

"Preposterous. How can a machine *know* someone? It had to be a locking spell."

"No, nothing as simple as that. This...vessel as you call it...understands. Understands words, emotions, intent. It works in tandem with Rhik's will. It isn't just controlled by him like one would control a machine; it listens and learns."

"Nothing was mentioned in any of the texts of such a thing."

"Perhaps wiser men decided that fact should not be common knowledge. Imagine if the world knew exactly what this was capable of?"

The implications of his words flooded her mind, but it was merely speculation at this point. All that really mattered was they found what Greyania had been searching for and their journey could come to a swift close. That had to be why all this was occurring. Such a thing belonged in the hands of her clan, for they knew its true value.

"Shae, could you come back over here? There is something we need to discuss. Hunter, you as well."

"M'lady." Shae nodded and led the way back, taking her seat again next to Greyania. The woman seemed pleased, but slightly distressed. Had the scoundrel talked her into some exorbitant sum?

"Rhikter tells me they have no amulet for the Behemoth Vessel."

"Look, I know that's technically the name of it for you two, but would you mind calling it Coldfire? Got a reputation and all."

The audacity of this man was unfathomable. She could not wait to take the vessel and be done with their company.

Greyania continued, not bothering to respond to his request. "Without the amulet, the true power and potential of the vessel can never be realized. It is distasteful, but we must go through the graves of his ancestors to look for either the amulet or clues to its whereabouts."

"Is this the only way to make the vessel whole?" Shae asked.

Rhikter opened his mouth, about to protest the use of the word again. If it were possible to strike a man down with her gaze, Shae would have done so right that moment. He shut his mouth. *Good. He's not as stupid as he seems.*

"Unfortunately, yes. I know this is hard for you, Shae. But we *must* do this."

"The elders knew of *this* as part of our task as well?"

"Of course they did, child. They knew the mission and what it could possibly entail. We have their full support."

"Very well. I just hope the ends justify the means."

"If this works, then we will do so much more for this world than you realize, child."

A boastful claim, honestly. They were just going to deliver the vessel to the rightful hands of her clan. It would increase their power and standing among the other elven clans, and most likely the rest of the races of the world. How would it affect anything beyond that?

"Rhikter, we need to know your family name. Your *true* family name if we're going to research where your dead are buried and where the amulet may be," Greyania demanded.

He stood there, folding his arms while he looked at her, licking his lips as he seemed to contemplate whether or not to answer. *What could be so bad about one's name?* All her life Shae had been proud of her heritage, her family, and her clan. Turning her back on them was inconceivable.

"No. I have my reasons for not sharing, and I expect you to respect them. Besides, the amulet isn't with any moldering bones of some long dead ancestor."

"And how would you know this? You told me there was no amulet."

"I said I wasn't *using* an amulet. I never said there wasn't one. The amulet we found with it is damaged and seemed to be little more than decorative."

Greyania's eyes went wide and her brow shot up as she opened her mouth to yell. Shae couldn't help but shrink back from her, as she'd only seen her this upset twice before.

"You had it this whole time and didn't think to tell me? Do you have any idea how much danger this omission put you in? Put *us* in?!"

"Whoa, whoa, calm down...at first I had no idea it was part of Coldfire. Even so, it's *useless*. The clasp and setting have been melted around the gem. We were going to try and pry the jewel out, but gave up before we broke it."

Immediately her attitude changed, and her fury subsided. Her words, however, still rang with authority. "Melted? Let me see it. Now."

Hunter went to the back of the shop and pulled a small tool chest down from one of the shelves. Opening it, he pulled out a hunk of metal that had a gemstone wedged into the center. The gem itself was an indistinguishable color due to the scorch marks. Only the fact that a bit of chain remained attached to the melted lump betrayed that it had once been an amulet. Hunter tossed it onto the table.

"No clue what caused this much damage, but that is night silver, so the fire had to be hotter than hells. Even dwarven forges can barely *fashion* the stuff, let alone make jewelry out of it," Hunter explained.

As Shae looked at it, she felt a strange pull towards the gemstone; there was magic deep within the gem, begging to be released. Tentatively she reached out for it, wanting nothing more than to see what power lay beneath the surface.

"Shae, child, is something the matter?"

Realizing she was in a trance, Shae shook her head and withdrew her hand. "I can feel it calling to me. It *wants* me to pick it up. I don't understand." Greyania reached out, grabbed the ruined piece, and scrutinized it under the light.

"I felt it as well. There's power still here, thank the gods. Had it been fully destroyed, this whole endeavor would have been for naught. I believe I can extract the gem, but we'll need to refashion the setting to contain, strengthen, and re-attune the power to...*Coldfire*."

Grinning like a fool, Rhikter patted Greyania on the back. "I knew the name would grow on you!"

"Remove your hand. Now."

Still grinning, he quickly he pulled his hand back.

Closing her eyes, Greyania was silent for a few moments and then started to whisper something in an ancient tongue, so quietly that Shae could barely hear. Perhaps she was using a translocation spell? As Greyania's hands began to glow crimson, and then white, Shae knew it was no such thing. She was trying to *destroy* the metal around the gem!

"Greyania! It's too dangerous!"

"Yes...but the metal...fused with the gem...it is the only way," Greyania struggled as she spoke but managed to maintain her concentration.

Without being prompted, Shae immediately lent her strength to the spell, and was surprised to find Greyania resisting her.

"Let me help you at least!"

After a moment she nodded and Shae was able to add her power. Greyania was a much more powerful sorceress than she could ever hope to be, even with her elven heritage, but such a spell was one of the most taxing and required exact precision and concentration.

Placing her hands over Greyania's Shae could feel the heat radiating from within as Greyania continued to speak in a long-dead tongue. Nearing the completion of the spell was when Shae realized that Greyania was not trying to remove the metal but-

A burst of energy erupted from the amulet, throwing both women backwards. Thankfully, miraculously, neither was injured.

Something clanged to the floor and Rhikter knelt down to pick it up.

"By all that's holy..."

The gem and metal had not been separated, but joined into a new swirling opal of silver and deep midnight blue. It was magnificent, unlike anything Shae had seen in her life. No fires, magic or otherwise, could melt gemstone in such a way. She stared at Greyania.

Hunter was helping Greyania to her feet, and Shae realized they both seemed unfazed by the ordeal. She even felt somewhat refreshed. There was something far more going on here than Greyania was admitting.

"Once we refashion a setting for the gemstone, it will control forces you couldn't possibly imagine. However, I will need to figure out exactly how to do that," Greyania said

Shae's misgivings over what else was going on with Greyania faded as the thought of being one of those responsible for restoring a Behemoth Vessel back to its former glory came to the forefront. Completing such a task would make her entire clan proud.

"Here, give me the gem for safe keeping," Greyania took it from Rhikter and headed for the exit to the workshop. "We will leave at dawn. Prepare for a long journey."

"Where are we-" The door shut behind her, cutting Rhikter's sentence in half, "-going?"

"I do not like being blind in a plan," Hunter said in an annoyed tone.

He turned and headed deeper into the shop, grumbling to himself as Rhikter moved closer to Shae.

"So, we've got a whole day to ourselves. Shall we...get to know one another?"

Smirking like a fool at her, she couldn't help but laugh at his advance. While Rhikter certainly was attractive she had absolutely no interest in him in that way.

"I am Shae of the Elemental Winds. You are Rhikter Coldfire. That is *all* we need to know of one another."

Hunter's laughter roared behind her as she turned and left the shop.

THREE

GREYANIA STEPPED THROUGH the threshold of the portal she had conjured as it dissipated into a light green mist. One moment she was in the crown jewel of the dwarven empire, Aungermiest, and the next she was secluded in her safe hideaway. She usually felt drained after casting a teleportation portal, but instead she felt energized. It had to be the gem.

The room she was in right now was her bedroom, a smaller room with modest furnishings; just the bare essentials. She rarely slept there anyway, so it was more for convenience than necessity. The room was connected to her study, which was much larger and filled with all sorts of artifacts and tomes on the ancient and mystical. She always felt at peace here, surrounded by her collection of knowledge and the arcane.

Her familiar, a tabby cat named Thalyia, peeked out from under her bed, giving a quiet meow as she trotted up to her master. Greyania smiled and reached down to scratch behind her ears, before leaving the room.

Entering the study and placing the gem on a table, she went to find a tome that would explain how they could refashion the amulet into something functional. As soon as she opened the book everything went white, and she found her consciousness floating in a room without definition. She was not alone.

I see you've managed to find the amulet already. The voice filled her mind, but she could not see where it came from.

"In a manner of speaking. It was badly damaged and near worthless. Shae and I were able to save the gem."

Not just save, but enhance. You are welcome.

"I had a feeling you did something to the spell. I was originally going to destroy the metal to save the gem."

She could feel mirth surround her as more than one consciousness began to laugh in the expanse. She could not tell how many of them were there, but just the one continued to speak.

Without our intervention the gem would have died like an ember from a fire. We were also curious how the effects of combining the metal with the gemstone would turn out. It is far more powerful than any gem that has been imbued before.

"There is no doubt of that. If we can refashion a proper conduit for the setting, this vessel will be the most powerful ever constructed."

And capable of taking down the one who is free.

There was a mixture of sadness and anger, some of which was directed at her. It had been over a century and a half since the world had changed, so she did not fault them for the emotions directed towards her; if she couldn't forgive herself, how could they?

"Do you still not know where he is?"

He is a mockery of what we are.

An abomination. End his existence!

Our brother is a victim of his hubris.

Their voices all going at once was making her mind throb. It was hard enough to concentrate when just one was talking to her directly, but when they all began? It was too much and she started to withdraw into herself, attempting to leave the link.

Enough.

There, the one from before, the voice she knew so well.

"Gron'Tul...I don't even know where to begin to re-forge the amulet. What metal or alloy do we need to use? How will I set the gemstone to properly enhance the vessel? Who can craft such a thing?"

As the numerous questions flowed from her mind, the formless white expanse began to bend and contort, like a bubble popping, and suddenly she was in her study again. The original book she had taken down was gone and in her hands now was a completely different one, open to a particular page.

I have faith you will find the answers you seek.

"Please, do not be cryptic, I need to kno-" she looked down at the page and stopped mid-sentence. It was a book on the known races of the world, and it was open to the passages on the apocrita. The Children of Jek.

"This is a long dead race. Are you telling me that our only hope lies with them?"

Silence filled the room. When no answer seemed forthcoming, she demanded more.

"As the God's Eye you have seen all of this come to pass, have you not? Then you know what I must do next. Guide me!"

The continued lack of a reply in her mind was infuriating, but she tried to contain her anger and frustration. Justified as it may be, she was still in the presence of one whom she regarded as a god.

"For over one hundred and fifty years I've languished as your servant, waiting for the chance to redeem myself. Now that we have an opportunity, you give me no guidance and point me towards a race that no longer exists!"

I do not recall their death. Nor have I seen it yet to come.

"You don't mean..."

Seek them. They are easy enough to find once you understand where to look.

Then, true silence. The only presence left was that of her cat, gently purring on the table next to her. Just as well, she surmised, as it gave her more time to research. Dawn would come soon and she had to learn everything she could of the Apocrita. Especially where to start the search.

Gods how she hated insects.

*****

Yawning and scratching himself, Rhikter headed into the main area of the workshop, not surprised to find Hunter there, packing the last of the things they needed for the trip. Hunter was always an early riser. The only major thing he had to worry about was Coldfire, and he had no doubt the golem would perform spectacularly.

"Tell me, Rhik, do you think this is going to be worth it?"

"Well, we're getting paid, aren't we?"

"You know what I mean."

There was a grave tone to the orc's voice, and Rhikter couldn't help but be concerned. He reached into a cupboard and pulled out a piece of dried jerky, tearing off a chunk with his teeth.

"Yes, I know. The dreams again?"

Often Hunter would get visions, especially at times of possible turmoil or hardship. Not quite premonitions, but omens. Sometimes good, sometimes bad, but they always set him on edge. The orc confirmed his suspicions with a nod.

"This was the first time I was given no path. The spirits of my ancestors knelt before me when I implored them for guidance. Do you understand what that means for an orc?"

He honestly did not. Try as he might, he couldn't think of any time in the past that Hunter had described such a dream to him. Usually they were dark and foreboding or positive and hopeful.

"No, I don't."

Hunter slung his pack over his shoulder and attached his weapon to his belt.

"They did not turn their backs to abandon me, nor did they point me into the direction of a great hunt. They knelt and faced the ground because even *they* do not know what will happen. An orc with no destiny is a horkvash."

"A *what*?" Rhikter had never heard the term used before. They were brothers in all but blood, so he knew most of what Hunter meant when he described it. This term and the way Hunter spoke of it, however, had him stumped.

"Since neither I nor the spirits know the way my path will take, I am to forge it myself. The greatest known horkvash of my people was at the dawn of our race. He was the first chieftain of any clan. It is both an honor and a curse to have such a vision."

"Hey, things are gonna be fine, alright? We'll explore the world, rob a few graves, make some neat jewelry, and empower Coldfire. It'll be great!"

Shaking his head and chuckling softly, Hunter agreed. "True. We have been in worse scrapes...I just worry."

"Like any good mother hen."

"Wutkas."

Rhikter mocked being offended. "And you kiss your mother with that mouth!"

The orc smirked and walked over to Rhikter, grabbing a piece of the jerky for himself. As they both regarded Coldfire before them, Hunter spoke up again. "There is one aspect of all this that has been bothering me. *Why* are they doing this?"

"What do you mean?"

"Why restore the amulet? Why work towards empowering Coldfire? To what end? I only see one outcome."

Try as he might, Rhikter could think of no other possibility, and resigned himself to agreeing with the orc. "They want a weapon."

"The question that remains, Rhik, is do you want to become one?"

Nothing immediately sprang to his mind. No instant denial or acceptance of his possible role in the days and weeks to come. There was one memory that came to the forefront rather quickly, though. He was a boy, around twenty years ago, and it was before his father died.

It was his earliest memory, and he could still recall every detail vividly. His family ran one of the few above ground townships that existed, and he was standing in one of the watchtowers, looking out over the Dark Plains. It was the side of the world that was forever turned away from the sun. He could see a group of hawks nesting in one of the trees, and some elk grazing.

Something out of his sight had spooked the elk, and they ran further into the darkness. Watching them disappear from view unlocked a need deep inside of his soul. One day, he promised himself, he would explore what the world had to offer. He would not be shackled by the responsibilities of his birth, but go forth and have adventures in the great unknown. Nothing would keep him from this destiny.

"Rhik?"

Moments of quiet contemplation had stretched into an uncomfortable silence between the two. Hunter repeated his question pointedly, and Rhikter turned his gaze from the golem before them to regard his friend.

"I do not wish to become *their* weapon."

Hunter nodded and smiled, "A good answer, brother."

*****

The Yormsun had been shining brightly for nearly forty minutes and there was still no sign of Greyania. Shae wanted to have left shortly before it was activated, but it couldn't be helped. Despite the fact that Greyania could find her nearly anywhere and catch up, without her guidance to give them some semblance of where to go, there was no point in starting.

"She should be here any minute. I'm sure of it," she said, folding her arms. Shae was sworn to obey and protect Greyania, with her life, but that didn't stop her from being annoyed by her actions.

"If she doesn't show up in the next ten minutes, we're leaving without her," Rhikter stated.

"If you leave, you won't get paid."

"If we leave, you will have to find another Coldfire."

"If the two of you continue, *I* am going to leave!" Hunter exclaimed.

Shae couldn't help but laugh. He was more refined than she expected for an orc. In all her travels she had never spoken with one for more than a few sentences, but Hunter held himself rather respectfully. Completely contrary to the stories her clansmen had shared with her. Brutish warriors was the most common descriptor, but Hunter was anything but crass. Perhaps it was all the time he spent with Rhikter, among humans and dwarves.

"Fine. We'll wait. You began paying us at dawn anyway."

"I'm sure Greyania expected as much from one such as yourself."

He cocked an eyebrow at her, but then smirked. Gods, if he was going to be so incessant with his flirtations, she may end up murdering the fool before they got anywhere. As long as he didn't cross the line, she was content to let him follow after her like a lost puppy if it suited him. Were he to get more carnal ideas, however, she would be sure to remind him of his place with a swift knee to the groin.

Greyania walked in from one of the back rooms a few minutes later.

"How did you...?" Rhikter was flabbergasted.

"Teleportation. Surely you are familiar with such a simple concept?" Shae chided him, returning the same smirk he had given her before. When Greyania shot her a look, she composed herself as Hunter spoke.

"I take it there was good reason for the delay?"

"I apologize for taking as long as I did, but I had to be absolutely certain of our destination."

"I take it you found out how to refashion the amulet, m'lady?"

"Yes. We need to head deep into the Dry Oceans," Greyania confirmed.

Going out into the world was inevitable. Shae had understood that before she made the pact to accept the mission. Heading into one of its most dangerous and inhospitable regions was not exactly what she had anticipated, though. Hunter and Rhikter seemed to share her trepidation.

"We need to go *there*? What for? Can't we just get some dwarf or elven craftsmen to work with the gem now that it is free?" Rhikter's tone was full of doubt.

"If it were that simple, then we wouldn't need to go. However, the means of humans, dwarves, and even elves is limited when it comes to working with the materials we require," Greyania answered.

Nodding knowingly, Hunter spoke up. "Night silver. The setting needs to be made from night silver."

"Yes. Or, at least, something similar. Any magically imbued metal or alloy will do, really."

"Even the best jewelers can't use anything like that from scratch, m'lady. The most they can hope to do is alter or repair something already fashioned, and even then it is dodgy business at best. Who in all of Antembra can work with such metals?"

"The apocrita."

Shae knew she had heard that word before, but for the life of her could not place it. Another race? The only races she was familiar with were orc, human, elf, dwarf and sincit. Of those, sincit were the least likely, as their prowess lay primarily in feats of agility and strength. Still deep in thought, her concentration was interrupted by Rhikter's voice.

"You don't mean the insects, do you?"

That's it! Apocrita were the insectoid race! A race of humanoid, intelligent insects that had kept to themselves, even before their sudden and inexplicable disappearance. According to rumor, when their god disappeared, so did they. It was thought they could not exist without it.

"Yes," Greyania replied.

"They are extinct," Hunter pointed out. "Do we mean to find the ruins of their cities and try and learn how they worked the metal?"

"No, not exactly. I have information that they are not extinct, but still thrive in the heart of the Dry Oceans."

"Even a sincit would not head there, and you know how they love to sit and bake themselves in the sun."

Hunter had a point. Even the edges of the Dry Oceans were dangerous, but traveling right into the heart of the area? They would be fully exposing themselves to the onslaught of the sun. They weren't called the Dry Oceans because they were vast seas of sand. They were where the oceans on that side of the world had been before the change occurred. The sand was all that was left.

"If the sun does not kill us," Hunter continued, "the Eye of Gron'Tul will."

Shae shook her head slightly. The Eye of Gron'Tul was a massive hurricane-like dust storm that traveled around the expanse of the Dry Oceans. It had first appeared shortly after all the water had evaporated. Since the temperature was so hot the rain never fell for more than a few minutes before evaporating again back into the storm. Magic probably had a strong hand it in as well, as that area was hit the hardest by the unleashed elemental forces. Out of these factors, the never-ending storm was born.

"We needn't worry about the storm, Hunter. It should be no where near where we are going," Greyania reassured him.

"How can you be so sure? The same source that told you to seek out a long dead race?"

Hunter wasn't calling her out, Shae noted, but asking legitimate questions, the way anyone in his position might. He was smart and cautious; he wouldn't let himself or his friend be led to their deaths on a whim. It was an admirable trait, especially for an orc.

"To be blunt, yes. The same." Greyania looked Hunter in the eye. "You will need to trust me. I know that is asking much of you both, in such a short time, but, if we want to succeed we will need to take this risk. Now, are we ready to depart?"

Standing there, looking down at Greyania, the orc was unreadable; his expression was emotionless and stoic. After a moment he shook his head and answered her inquiry.

"No. Since we are headed to the Dry Oceans, we will need at least another few gallons of water. We can load up Coldfire and Rhik can carry it."

"Gods, why do I get stuck with the donkey work?"

Both Greyania and Hunter shot him a look, and then turned to look at one another, laughing as they realized what they had both done. Rhikter only rolled his eyes as he grumbled to himself about being a glorified pack mule, and Shae interjected her own thoughts.

"Make sure you bring sleep guards as well, for your eyes. The sun doesn't 'set' like the artificial one they use here in Aungermiest, and trying to sleep with the light beating down on you is enough to drive one mad."

"Ah, an excellent idea, Shae." Greyania nodded her approval.

"Well, we're leaving much later than I would have liked, and I'd say we're burning daylight, but where we're going?" Rhikter took in a deep breath and let it out slowly. "There's nothing but."

FOUR

TRAVELING TO THE surface had not taken as long as Hunter had thought it would. Whenever he and Rhikter managed to get up this far, it always took them at least two days. Now? Just a day and they were already entering the jungles that led towards the Dry Oceans. Perhaps it was just due to Greyania's drive. It was not often he found a woman, let alone a human woman, who intrigued him, but there was a quality to her he could not deny.

Unlike Rhikter, who seemed to have a new woman on his arm every chance he got, Hunter was far more selective in whom he chose to share his bed with. However atypical it may be for an orc. Most were encouraged to have several wives, to bring many young pups into the tribe. A practice that had became far more popular when their tribes were decimated after the world changed.

That pressure to marry was one of the numerous reasons he had decided to leave his tribe in the first place. It was not an unheard of practice, nor was it forbidden; he could return at any time he chose. He had also seen many tribeless orcs throughout his travels.

For an orc, to go tribeless was considered more a way of finding one's self, than it of turning their back on their people. Many great chieftains and spiritual leaders of the past had all been tribeless at one time or another, so it was even encouraged in some ways. There were trials to pass to receive the blessing of the chieftain, and those who failed were shunned as outcasts, impure of heart, devoid of honor, and without purpose.

He had passed the trials without effort, and he regretted nothing. Opportunities to learn and grow, as no other in his tribe had, were presented to him left and right, but he found what really drove him was his need to explore. It was what made he and Rhikter such good partners, and friends. They both had a love for the unknown, and a wish to learn all they could.

As much as he wondered what they had gotten themselves into, he found his thoughts kept straying to Greyania. She didn't look older than thirty or forty years, although he had never been good at guessing the age of humans. Her white hair, however, seemed to be caused by either age or trauma. Being a sorceress, he guessed the latter. Many times in the past he'd encountered powerful spell casters with hair as white as bleached bone. Strain on the body, one had told him.

Was it her power that attracted him? He preferred strong, independent women. Those who knew what they wanted, and took it without question. She was one of those types, and that was a good reason to feel attraction. There was something more, though. He could feel it every time he looked into her eyes. *A most unusual shade of violet.* It reminded him of a type of flower that grew near his tribe's homelands.

Since Coldfire had enough room for Rhikter and most of their supplies, it was relegated to being a 'beast of burden', and only a small amount of supplies were left to be carried by the other three. Shae walked up next to him, previously having been at the rear. Currently, Rhikter had taken point.

"I still think we should've packed more water."

"I agree, half-blood, but where would we have stored it? To bring more would mean we would need horses or a cart to carry the extra. And horses would be useless since Rhik could never keep up with them. We will have opportunity to refill our supply before we advance into the Dry Oceans. I trust Greyania's word on this."

"I trust her with my life." A brief pause before she spoke up again. "Hunter?"

He turned to look at her, wondering what she needed his attention for.

"Stop referring to me as half-blood. I find it bothersome to be referred to as *what* I am instead of whom. Either use my name, or if you must, my clan. But...never refer to me by just my blood again."

He was slightly surprised by this. Orcs had used this manner of identifying strangers or associates for generations. Looking at her face, though, he saw the conviction behind her words and gave a solemn nod in agreement.

"I will respect this request, Shae."

The features on her face softened as she smiled at him. "Thank you."

In a few hours they would be deep within the jungles, and crossing through dense territory that would greatly impede their progress. He was confident Coldfire's abilities would clear a path, and it was not the path that concerned him, so much as it was those who may also be upon it.

"Greyania! I would speak with you."

Leaving Shae to retake the rear of their convoy, he moved closer to Greyania. He couldn't be sure, but he detected the faint scent of blackberries as he got closer. Something he had never noticed before. *Keep your focus.*

"Yes?" Turning her head slightly to look at him, she continued to move forward, seemingly undaunted by the increasingly rough terrain they were traversing.

"We approach the heart of the jungles that border the Dry Oceans. I have only crossed them once and, while the jungle holds its own challenges and dangers, we should be mindful of the sincit."

"The lizard men? I hardly think they will be an issue. Are their tribes not peaceful?"

"Yes, in some ways. When others encroach on their lands without fair notice, they can view it as aggression. There are also those who would attack without any provocation, as well as bandits and thieves."

"I am aware of the dangers, but I believe we won't have anything to worry about. None of the sincit tribes have been seen within forty leagues of this place."

"Yes, but on the whole, sincit are nomadic. It is rare for a tribe to put roots in one place for long."

Furrowing her brow, she appeared to be deep in thought for a few seconds and then sighed and relaxed her facial features.

"There is nothing we can do about it now, aside from remaining vigilant. If they attack, we answer in kind."

"Preparation is the key to longevity."

"Orc saying?"

"Common sense."

*****

Night was a purely time-based concept, and while the jungle canopy offered a permanent shade, the sun shone eternally. Greyania pulled some sort of time device from within her satchel and nodded to herself before she announced they would make camp. Hunter was thankful. He could continue on if needed, but the rest would be highly welcome. They had been traveling non stop since yesterday, and they all needed the break.

Rhikter was the only one who did not seem pleased, which Hunter found odd. Usually his human partner was more than willing to take breaks on top of breaks. Perhaps riding in Coldfire offered him the ability to expend less energy.

"You can't go another two leagues? We'd be almost out of the jungle and right at the Dry Oceans!"

"True, but this will be the last opportunity we will have to sleep in some measure of comfort." Greyania motioned at their surroundings. "The foliage is dense here and provides a perfect shade. We won't rest long, just enough to recharge ourselves, and then we won't stop until exhaustion dictates."

As she took charge, Hunter could not help but admire her even more. *Even orc women would be hard pressed to match her tenacity.* He knew that he and Shae could manage the trek with minimal rest. Their races were better suited for journeys such as this, and they only required four or so hours of sleep to fully recharge.

Humans, on the other hand, required much more sleep, and their bodies weren't designed for such grueling expeditions. Had she endured simply because of her mastery of magic? Perhaps. Magic did not explain her character and leadership, though. Both were admirable and attractive traits.

He was not sure, but he could swear he caught her glance at him as he was beginning to set up the tents. Male pride getting the better of him, he put on a show, stripping off his shirt as he worked. If she was going to glance, he would give her something worthy of glancing at. A smile grew on his face and he began to hum a tune his mother had taught him as a child.

Just as he finished the last stake on one of the tents, as Rhikter finally exited Coldfire, Hunter heard a twig snap in the distance, to the north of the camp. Quickly glancing around, he cursed at himself for the clearing they had chosen for their rest. It was open on all sides and nearly impossible to defend properly.

A rustle in the brush, this time to the south; closer than the twig break. None of the others seemed to be reacting, so he took in a deep breath, closed his eyes, and listened. The rustle continued, as if someone were trying to slink out of the bushes, to avoid causing more noise. That confirmed it.

He dived for the sword lying near the freshly dug fire pit, bellowing, "AMBUSH!"

The others looked at him in shock as a dart whizzed past Greyania's face, the speed and closeness causing her bangs to flutter in its wake. War cries came from within the jungle as multiple sincit made themselves known.

"Rhik, Coldfire!" Hunter called over his shoulder, hoping the man was already scrambling back into the powerful device. They may not have to fight if they could muster a strong show of force. Sincit were crafty and vicious when they fought, but bands like this would often abandon their quarry if it seemed like too much work.

Looking to the other two, he saw Greyania's eyes turn white as she waved her hands in front of her, whispering some spell. Hopefully a ward to deal with any future darts. Shae had adopted a low stance, a small crossbow in one hand and a dagger in the other. Daring a look over his shoulder to see how Rhikter was doing, he gasped.

A form erupted from the jungle, a crude and rusty sword in its grasp as it lunged directly at the man. There was no way for Rhikter to dodge the attack nor for Hunter to reach him in time. Panic spread through him as he thought he was about to witness the death of his friend, but the space around the two warped and sent the sincit flying into a tree. Rhikter was thrown back and slid across the ground.

"I had no time to refine it!" Shae yelled.

"Better than nothing. There!" Rhikter pointed, scrambling to his feet.

Secrecy abandoned, the sincit that had been tracking them and waiting for the right moment to strike, now poured out from the jungle's confines. There had to be at least ten or twelve of them in all, easily surrounding the camp.

Each had a slash across their snouts, a deep scar that had long since healed, running from just below their left eye to their front right fang. Their tails were similarly scarred, but the number of scars was different for each of them. Each one also had a crudely fashioned prosthetic on the end of its tail; a small, sharp, scythe-like blade that Hunter knew was attached directly to the bone.

"I've never seen them so aggressive!" Shae cried out, as her crossbow bolt caught one in the chest. It slumped to the ground as another climbed over its body, hissing towards her.

They were dressed simply in leathers and loincloths, each armed with a weapon that had seen better days. They had painted their entire bodies to help them blend in more with the jungle, and their eyes were full of malice. Hunter immediately knew what tribe they were.

"They are Soul Harvesters! Leave none alive!"

Lunging with a guttural cry, he unsheathed his broadsword and brought it forth in a swinging arc to cleave the two closest to him. Blood flew in every direction, but he was more focused on the ones still alive.

Thrusting towards one foolish enough to get close, he ran it through and kept pushing, stabbing another just behind it as well, before getting his sword lodged in the trunk of a nearby tree. He pulled on it. Stuck. Uttering a curse he left it there; to try and free it might leave him open to attack. Today was *not* his day to die.

Rhikter was busy tussling with a sincit that had gotten between him and Coldfire. As much as Hunter would have preferred to go and help his friend, Greyania and Shae were getting outnumbered. Try as they might, neither the magic nor the crossbow bolts, were coming fast enough.

"Behind you!" Greyania yelled as she threw a torrent of flame right over his shoulder. There was no need to look back as his would be attacker cried in pain, and then was silent. Saving his life put hers into jeopardy though, as one of her attackers whipped its tail blade across her back, slicing deep. She went down.

"NO!"

Both he and Shae yelled as they rushed to her rescue. He felt darts pierce his skin as he tried to shield the other two as best he could, and was thankful for an orc's increased tolerance to poison. There seemed to be no end to their attackers and he turned to face them once more, ready to slay them with his bare fists if necessary.

"She'll live, but we need to end this. Now!" Shae leapt out of the way, narrowly missing another tail attack, and sliced the throat of her assailant. Hunter managed to grab the tail of one nearby, yanked him off his feet and swung him like a club. The crunch of bone and cartilage as it collided with another was satisfying.

Shae was right. If they did not end this soon, they would be overrun within minutes. Without magic to bolster their defense, they were helpless, and the sincit knew to keep them at arm's length as much as possible. They would whittle down their prey instead of a full out assault. How he hated Soul Harvesters.

"Get down!"

Rhikter's metal-tinged voice was like music, and both Hunter and Shae obeyed his command. A torrent of blue flame rushed over them, literally cooking the approaching sincit. Had the flames been any lower, Hunter was sure they would be just as dead. Six were dealt with immediately, with the remaining two shying away.

One turned to run, and Coldfire grabbed onto its tail and swung it with even greater ease than Hunter had done a moment before, smashing it against a tree. The final one decided there was no reason to die.

"We can't let it escape!" Hunter yelled as he jumped up and ran after it. It was fast, but terrified. It had been part of an ambush party that was decimated by a much smaller group of seemingly weaker prey. He reached for it as they ran through the thick bush and vines, but it was getting farther and farther ahead. *No! If it reaches the nest it coul-*

A crossbow bolt shot through the air, close enough to nick the side of his arm before it hit the back of the fleeing lizard's head. Momentum carried it forward a few more steps, and then it tumbled and skidded to a stop. Easing to a stop himself, Hunter looked behind him and saw Shae breathing out a sigh of relief as she lowered her crossbow.

Quickly making his way back to the group, Rhikter stayed within Coldfire for the time being, scanning their surroundings.

"How bad is it?" Kneeling beside Greyania, Hunter was careful not to move or jostle her unnecessarily.

"As I said, she'll live, but only if I can treat this now. The cut didn't hit anything vital, but it's deep and she's losing a good amount of blood."

"Do it. We are safe for now."

"How do you know they won't be back?"

"They're Soul Harvesters," Rhikter answered for him. "A tribe of sincit that only live for the hunt, and only survive off what they kill. When the animals are scarce, and travelers aren't coming into the jungle..." His voice trailed off.

"They wouldn't possibly resort to..." Shae's eyes went wide.

"Cannibalism," Hunter finished the thought. "However, when they hunt in this large of a pack, it is expected they will return. If none do, they are assumed dead and no rescue is mounted. However, if even one makes it back to the nest the entire tribe comes for vengeance."

Looking at the bodies strewn about the ruined campsite, he shook his head as Shae tended to Greyania.

"There have not been Harvesters even close to this area in years. Something has them on the move, and whatever that is, is not good. We are safe for the next few hours at least, but we need a location that is far more secure. Once she is safe to move we need to set up a new camp."

"Agreed."

Foolish. He chided himself for being careless. For showing off and being distracted when he should have been paying more attention. Had he been more alert, he would have known they were being tracked. Sincit were good hunters, but not infallible.

"I will find a suitable spot and make sure it is more easily fortified while we rest and heal," Hunter said as he pulled out several of the darts still stuck in his skin. He then headed off toward the west, where he spied a large rock jutting out of the ground. They could use it as a defensive point. He would not make the same mistakes again.

FIVE

GREYANIA OPENED HER eyes with a start and gasped at the scene before her. Gone were the jungles bordering the Dry Oceans; instead she was in a place that defied comprehension. The sky was the color of twilight, and a single star, orbited by debris like water circling a drain, pulsed like a beating heart in the distance.

All around her, ancient megalithic structures erupted from the ground, without rhyme or reason, making no sound or vibration. As soon as one had burst forth, it was receding again and another would take its place in a different shape. In the center of this chaotic landscape was a curious sight: a single table, made of onyx, with several humanoid figures seated.

She began to recall the events that led her to this moment. The attack came flooding back, along with the white-hot pain of the blade slicing into her back.

"Oh gods...is that why everything's different? Am I dead?!"

Hardly. We still have need of you, and would prevent such a thing from occurring. For now. Gron'Tul's soothing voice filled her mind.

Relief spread over her as the panic subsided. Alive, yes, but that didn't answer her question as to why she was here and why things felt so different. She looked to the table again. As she moved closer she could see the figures were members from each of the known races, as well as a few whose form she did not recognize.

What troubles you? Do you not recognize your Gods?

"But...I can see you! Is this how you truly appear?!"

In a way. Come, we have much to tell you.

Greyania was suddenly seated with no recollection of having actually sat. Up close, she could see eight distinct races. From the left to the right were orc, human, elf, dwarf, sincit, and what she assumed was apocrita. Of the next two, one looked like a crude humanoid statue with each large section of its body a different type of stone, while the other looked like an ogre. It was comical seeing such a brutish and large creature sitting at the table. Up close, she could also now see that there was an empty seat.

The orc was a male, but his skin was such an atypical color; dark orange, like a setting sun. He was wearing the fur of some dire beast. She couldn't be sure, but it looked like it was possibly a bear. His red eyes were piercing. The human was dressed all in golden threads, and wore ornate and immaculate spectacles. Her blonde hair was long, past the edge of the table, and there seemed to be a soft wind causing it to billow out behind her.

The elf was a male, and he was dressed in leathers so black, they seemed to absorb the light. By stark contrast, his skin was incredibly pale, and his yellow eyes never stopped watching her. The dwarven man looked plain in comparison with the others. Dressed in standard armor, the only thing worth noting was the massive battle axe leaning up against the back to his chair. It was made out of obsidian and gems.

The head of the sincit wouldn't stop darting from one direction to the next, unable to focus for more than a few moments. It resembled those that had attacked them, but only in form. Bright feathers were arranged in a beautiful headdress and well-tanned animal skins were draped over its torso. She had no idea if it was male or female. Greyania couldn't tell the gender of the apocrita, either, or even if it were wearing clothing. Its form was like a mantis; its front appendages were folded up and into themselves and its exoskeleton was the color of wheat, with differing shades all throughout.

The living statue, for lack of a better term, looked like a bunch of rocks and stones had been stacked together in a general approximation of a person. Every time it moved, even the slightest bit, the sound of stone rubbing against stone was loud and abrasive. Thankfully it moved rarely. Finally, the ogre. It had a broken tusk and rough patches of hair covering its forearms. One of its ears was pierced with a bone ornament, and great scars covered its bare torso. For such a savage creature, there was intelligence and wisdom in its dark eyes.

"You are unconscious, but your compatriot, the orc, keeps watch. You are safe." As the human spoke, Greyania recognized the voice immediately as Gron'Tul's.

"Though the passage of time, as you know it, will not press on." The ogre's cadence didn't remotely match his bulk and frame.

"Why am I here, then? Why do we not speak as we always have? And who is *who*?" She looked at each of those present.

Gron'Tul answered. "As I said, there is much we need to tell you. Communicating with us through thought alone is a taxing endeavor for you, especially if we all were to invade your thoughts at once. Currently you are in no condition for such stress. It has also been quite some time since we took the form of our children. As for who is who, I am Gron'Tul. You already know *me* quite well."

"I am Yorm. Father of honor and power," the orc said next.

Skipping Gron'Tul, the next in line to speak was the elf. "Progity, my dear child." His words flowed like silk; full of dread and promise.

"Ye can call me by mah given name, Karak," the dwarf said with a twinkle in his eye as he winked at her.

"Trinfrey. Mother of the ssscaled." The sincit's head darted to and fro, and she spit the words more than spoke them.

Mandibles closing and opening quickly, Greyania expected a language of clicks and chitters, but instead was greeted by a perfectly normal sounding male voice.

"We are Jek. Thought it prudent *yes we did* to greet you as one *not the two*."

"I'm not sure I understand."

The way the apocrita spoke was confusing. Like two, distinct personalities were sharing control of the single body.

"No. I suppose you would not. *She would not. No No. See our true form, then maybe.* Not here!"

Greyania looked to the others for an explanation as to why Jek spoke that way, but none seemed to be forthcoming.

Next was the being made of stone who did not face her directly, but instead turned its head from looking towards the left until it was fully turned to the right. A few more moments of silence passed, and then Gron'Tul sighed and started to speak.

"That is Abt-"

"I. Abtrue. This. Meeting. No. Purpose. Attendance. Courtesy." Abrupt and blunt.

She was starting to realize just how little she knew about those she served. At the forefront of her mind was why it had taken them *this long* to actually show themselves to her. She hoped they would answer all her questions before their talks came to an end.

"You will forgive him, yes? His words are direct and he holds his feelings naught."

Looking to the final member of the group, the ogre, Greyania was still surprised by the way he held himself; an air of nobility and dignity. She wondered why the creatures it represented were so slow-witted and brutishly violent.

"Deghat. Creator of monsters. It hath been my lot to bear the most foul of responsibilities. I bring to life creatures, both great and diminutive, for my siblings' children to test themselves against. In truth, I hath found the challenge most amusing. Though many of *my* children fall, those who survive doth grow strong."

There was sadness in its eyes, but a great pride as well. How many of its children had died over the years, simply for being what they were? Feeling a great pang of pity and sadness, she turned away from him to regard Gron'Tul again.

"And the empty seat?"

Gron'Tul shifted uncomfortably in her seat and looked to Yorm, who simply frowned at her. The others, except for Abtrue, all looked just as uncomfortable.

"That..." Gron'Tul's voice faded.

"She should know. *Yes, tell her. Tell tell!* It is the reason we're all gathered."

"Very well," she sighed and continued. "That is the seat of Res'Kel. Though now he calls himself-"

"The Withered King," Progity interrupted, sighing out the words with an air of regret. They were all visibly upset by the empty seat.

"Res'Kel was...unique," Gron'Tul went on. "He did not create children at the same time as the rest of us. When he finally decided to, there were...complications. It cost him his physical form."

"Bastard race, they were." Yorm did not try to hide his disgust. "An abomination like their *King*."

"Yorm! Enough!" Gron'Tul admonished him with a glare.

"His freedom cost us *dearly*," Yorm spat out.

"Wait, he wasn't imprisoned?"

Gron'Tul spoke. "Not fully, no. We are unsure why, but after we created the new races of the world, he was desperate to do the same, though without our help. He lost his physical form during the process. With his spirit separated from his body, he was able to wander the world freely. Then you performed the ritual and..."

"The Withered King was born. It was foolish of us to be so naive, to think that we could escape without paying a dire cost." Progity spoke each word gently, but the way he looked at her made Greyania feel uneasy. Like a predator regarding its prey.

"Our brother isss lossst. We have had no mental touch from him sssince the world broke," Trinfrey finally added to the conversation, "and we are ssstill prisonersss even though we are free. Maddening."

Greyania's face lit up in alarm. She looked right at the sincit and then the rest and accused them, "You all are free?!"

One hundred and fifty years she had spent seeking forgiveness for her failure. The things she had done, the pacts made and broken, and for what? There was nothing to absolve; they were already free.

"You have all *lied* to me. What possible reasons could you have for watching me suffer all these years?!"

"We are *not* free, Greyania. Not how you would think. You still remain our most valuable ally. Trinfrey spoke out of turn and without the full story." Gron'Tul glared at Trinfrey before continuing. "If we leave our prisons the spell of unbinding will be completed."

Taking in a breath, Greyania closed her eyes and let it out slowly. Anger and the feeling of being betrayed were hard things to swallow down, but she tried her best. There *had* to be a reason they had not given her the full story.

"Then explain to me why finishing the spell is a *bad* thing."

"There was something tied to the spell. *Hidden it was, yes yes. Even we could not see.* Like the Withered King's move to usurp us."

"We. Leave. World. Ends. Life. Ends."

"I would not kill my children for nothing. There is no glory to such an abrupt death," Yorm growled out, his voice steeped in a quiet anger.

"We knowest not if this was originally part of the spell of unbinding, that which was to free our corporeal bodies from their worldly shackles, or if it was a corruption caused by the most foul blood magic of the King," Deghat said.

They all started speaking at once, causing Greyania to become more and more frustrated until she blurted out, "By the Gods, which is all of you, someone give me a straight answer!"

Yorm smirked, and, for the first time, seemed pleased. "She still has fire and does not back down from us. Good. Here is your answer: if we leave our prisons, then *the spell continues.*"

"Gron'Tul just said that. Again I ask, how is that not the outcome we all seek?"

"The world as you remember it spun to face the sun and the moon each day, with neither question nor interruption. When the spell of unbinding began, we realized that it wasn't what we had thought; the world began to spin faster as magic, *our magic*, was released. This spinning would cause the ley lines to expunge all of their magic into the sun at once, as though through a funnel. We managed to stop it in its tracks before it could get worse, but barely. Otherwise, all life would have been destroyed, either by the sudden expulsion of magic, or certainly by what followed," Gron'Tul explained.

"Resulting. Explosion. Energy. Force. Feedback. Remake. Antembra."

"Remake?"

"We believe, now that we have had time to analyze the ssspell, that the sssun would rechannel the energy right back into the world, enhanced and amplified. It would remake the entire world in a way even we cannot fathom. Not just the sssurface, but entirely."

"Not only that, but we knowest not if Antembra couldst survive another cataclysmic event. Especially after suffering one naught but one hundred and fifty years prior. It is unthinkable," Deghat said..

"There is no way to reverse the spell. At least, that we are aware of," Yorm added.

"So this quest you have sent me on...to empower one of the vessels...it's to try and stop the Withered King, isn't it?"

"Yes. We believe he may try and find a way to continue the spell despite our interference. Stopping him will at least give us time to save Antembra and be truly free. But...his dormancy worries us." Gron'Tul looked down, folding her hands in front of her.

"Plans. Take. Time."

"And if it doesn't work?" Greyania asked.

"It must. *Yes yes, it must.*"

Crackles and pops from the nearby fire filled her ears as she suddenly woke. Gone were the Gods Who Walk, and she was surrounded by the jungle again. Rays of sunlight filtered through the canopy at any place where the leaves didn't overlap. Rhikter and Shae were asleep in their respective bedrolls, and Hunter was tending to the small fire as he sat beside her. *Has he been here the whole time?*

Her stirring must have alerted him to her being awake. Without looking at her, he reached over to his left and pulled out a chunk of cooked meat, skewered on a whittled-down stick.

"Here, eat. You need your strength."

It wasn't until the aroma of the meat hit her nose that she realized just how famished she was. Taking the piece from him, and wincing at how sore her back felt, she hungrily began to devour whatever it was. It tasted mostly of chicken, but with the faintest hint of fish.

"How long was I out for?"

"Honestly? I lost track of time. A few hours at most. Shae fixed you up, but your wound was graver than she first thought and it took much out of her. I volunteered to take the first watch so she could get some rest."

Finishing the meat, she tossed the stick into the fire and turned so she could lie on her back. Pain shot through her and she gasped. Rhikter snorted, but neither he nor Shae stirred from their slumber.

"That...was a mistake."

"According to Shae, since it was harder to heal, you need to take it easy so your body can do the rest. A few more hours and you will be well enough to travel. Where we are going, we all need to be in the best of health."

"Agreed. Though I am upset at letting my guard down, I am glad we have this time to recuperate."

"You let your guard down to save my life. I will not soon forget that."

Smiling up at him softly, she eased onto her belly and replied, "I did not relish the thought of traveling with just Rhikter and Shae. Their bickering would have driven me mad. It is nice to have someone to talk with."

"I will admit it has been nice to have a strong *woman's* perspective. Rhik can be very-" when he turned to look at her, she had already dozed back off to sleep, "-taxing."

He turned from her to look out into the jungle, his gaze scanning the surrounding areas for any signs of movement.

"Rest well. We will all need it for what comes."

SIX

TWO DAYS LATER they had left the jungle behind and were well into the Dry Oceans. Due to Greyania's recovery from her injuries, their pace had suffered greatly and they were now doing their best to make up for lost time.

Aside from the oppressive heat bearing down on them from the eternal sunlight, there was nothing but sand and pockets of long-dried mud stretching far into the horizon. The only thing giving any indication of where they were was the thinning edge of jungle along the horizon to their rear. Otherwise, there was no way to tell which direction was which.

Squinting against the harsh light, Shae looked up towards the sky. It was a clear day without a hint of clouds. At least the storm was nowhere nearby.

Complaints emerged from Coldfire as Rhikter voiced his concerns. "Gods. How the hells are we going to find our way out here? This is a death trap."

He has a point, you know. Shae sent her thoughts to Greyania.

He does, but while we are in their company, and when it is prudent, we should speak aloud.

Shae paused for a moment, before hesitantly agreeing. *Yes, m'lady.*

"The gods guide us, even now. Look, over there on the horizon." Pointing in the distance, to the left of their position, Greyania tried to get their attention.

Still squinting, Shae tried to see what she was pointing at. Her elven heritage afforded her better eyesight that most, but even she was having difficulty locating whatever Greyania was looking at, if anything was even there at all. "Are you sure there is something there, m'lady? The heat may be playing tricks on your vision already."

Ignoring Shae's doubts, Greyania took several steps towards where she had been pointing, her shoes sinking slightly as she struggled to move across the unstable ground. After a good ten paces she stopped and pointed again. "Can't you see it? The spire is just there, in the distance. That has to be where the apocrita are."

Moving to stand next to the other woman, Shae looked out across the horizon, using her palm to block the sun from her eyes. There was absolutely nothing, not even a trick of the light, to explain what Greyania was seeing. "It pains me to say this, but you are mistaken, Greyania. There is nothing out there, or in any direction, that is visible."

"Blast it all to the hells of Antembra...Use your *vision*, child."

"My..." Shae's voice tapered off as suddenly it all made sense. How do you keep an entire civilization hidden for hundreds of years? *Magic.*

Chastising herself for not thinking of it sooner, Shae closed her eyes, took in a deep breath, and exhaled slowly as she began to concentrate.

"What are you two doing?" Hunter's voice was thick with annoyance and confusion, but she blocked it out. Doing this was not an easy feat for her, and she had only done it successfully twice before. She murmured a small enchantment, hoping it was the right one, and opened her eyes.

Her mouth dropped as she saw, barely visible in the distance, a great spire where previously there had been nothing. Excitedly, she turned back to the two behind them. "She's right! There's a spire out in the middle of the sands that was hidden by magic!"

By now Rhikter had exited Coldfire to try and see better. Neither man moved from their spot; they just squinted their eyes and shielded them from the sun as they scanned the horizon.

"Don't bother. You won't see anything." Greyania said the words Shae was thinking and moved back to pick up her pack so they could continue. Shae followed suit.

"And we are just supposed to trust that the two of you see something out there in all this...desolation?"

"Rhikter, you can trust whatever you wish. The fact remains that we now have a definitive destination, and we will not stop until we see it through."

"Neither of us can see what you two claim to. Neither Rhik nor I are going to take another step until you show us."

"If you insist," Greyania replied.

What is she up to? Shae wondered as she watched the other woman remove her hood and grab onto Hunter's face with both hands.

"Gux jen'im vikon," Greyania's eyes glowed as she spoke the words.

"Greyania, no!"

Rushing over to them, Shae reached out but was knocked back the moment she made contact. Cursing to herself, she started to get up as Rhikter came up behind her.

"What the hells is she doing to him?"

"She...she's linking her mind with Hunter's."

"Why?!"

"*WHY?!* Because you two fools wouldn't trust us! You wanted proof." Shae jerked a hand towards the two. "*There* is your proof. I hope you're happy."

"Ok...so she's trying to show him by linking their minds. She's an accomplished sorceress. What's the worst that can happen?"

His utter ignorance at the seriousness of the situation angered her, but she knew, ultimately, that it wasn't his fault. Such a thing was hardly common knowledge, and it was forbidden for good reason. More often than not, those involved in such a link would become lost in the mind and memories of the other, and both would eventually waste away.

"If they don't find a way out, or if the link lasts too long, they will be stuck like this until one of them dies of starvation or dehydration."

"Will that free the other? No offense, but Hunter could outlive Greyania, easily."

"If one dies, they both die."

"Shit. This trip is getting better and better."

Sighing, Shae moved closer again. If she hadn't known better, she would swear they were just two in a close embrace. Unblinking eyes aside, there was no outward appearance of what was truly going on between them.

"Get into Coldfire. We have to make sure they are protected until the process is complete. I just hope they are both strong enough to break free."

"Why do I need to swelter in Coldfire needlessly?"

Shooting him an icy look, she spat on the ground in disgust. "I never said you had to stay in it. They'll need the shade. Or do you want them to die of heat stroke before it's done?"

Grumbling, he went to go move the vessel, muttering things under his breath even she, with her superior senses, could not hear.

Just as well. I don't need to get even more upset at him. Looking at the figures locked in their strange embrace, she felt a great pang of sadness wash over her. If anything happened to Greyania, Shae would be truly alone in the world; the other woman had become a surrogate mother to her when her own had died. She was family, and all she had left of her old life.

Come back. You have to, dammit.

*****

Night. A cool wind blew through her hair and she had never felt more alive. She was surrounded by her tribe, and this was to be her coming of age. Tonight she would choose a name.

No, wait...this isn't...

"Come, young one," a quiet voice spoke into her ear and a spear was thrust into her grip and she took it gladly, eagerly. To hunt a dire wolf on the plains was one of the most challenging, but rewarding, hunts for a young orc to attempt for their naming ceremony. She would come back a victor. She just knew it.

This isn't right! Suddenly, she was keenly aware of her surroundings but still had no control of the body she inhabited. Thoughts and feelings not her own kept bombarding her, and she tried her best to resist, to not become part of the memory.

There were five orcs in total, including herself. Two adults and two other teenage orcs, one male and one female. Somehow, instead of showing him the tower, she'd managed to become trapped in one of Hunter's memories.

I went too far, too deep. I just wanted to show you...

And now I will show you.

Hunter! Where are...never mind, it doesn't matter. We need to sever the link and return to our bodies. It was a mistake to try this.

I will show you, and you will be so impressed you will take me as your mate.

It was Hunter, but it wasn't in reply to her; the voice was coming from his thoughts in the memory. Cursing to herself, she tried to get him to snap out of it, but to no avail. At least he wasn't lost in her mind. There was no telling how she would untangle him from *that* mess.

The memory shifted suddenly, taking a still helpless Greyania along for the ride. A second later the three young orcs had been separated from their hunting party. The subtle fear and panic Hunter was feeling told her this was not a normal part of the ritual.

"Do not worry. I have a weapon and will protect us." The female orc smirked and spoke with confidence. Greyania could feel the admiration and attraction swell within Hunter.

"We are all armed, and we will take it down together."

Grinning at one another, they crept through the brush until they found their prey: the dire wolf slept at the base of a fallen tree, gently snoring as it breathed in and out. The beast was massive, and easily dwarfed Hunter as he was now. How in the world would three teenagers kill it?

I must draw first blood. Then she will see my strength. She felt Hunter think, and she tried to scream and yell for his attention. An ugly feeling settled into the pit of her stomach as she watched, helpless to do anything to affect events long since past.

Hunter leapt from the bushes too soon, and the wolf awoke faster than anticipated. It lunged at Hunter, who was helpless to alter his trajectory, and knocked him aside as it barreled past, into the bushes where the other two still hid.

Screams and a sickening snap of bone told her all she needed to hear. Try as hard as she could, she could not shut off her vision, or numb herself to the intense emotions that boiled over her.

Skittering out of the brush, the female had a broken half of a spear in one hand, and was clutching at her leg with the other. She was bleeding, but the wound wasn't bad. The other male never came out.

Instead, the wolf emerged, snout slick with blood and gore, and there was hatred in its eyes. Even though it was a wild beast, it *knew* the orcs had come to kill it, to hunt it for sport.

Hunter shed no tears. Greyania knew the dead male in the bush was more to him than a friend or tribe mate; they were brothers. She could feel the overwhelming shame that his need to impress the female had gotten his brother killed. Then pure rage, unlike any she had ever felt.

Taking his spear and breaking it in half, he ran full on at the beast, surprising it with such a direct attack. It opened its massive jaw and growled, trying to take him down with a single bite. As quick as a striking snake, he shoved his spear arm into the beast's maw, thrusting so hard that the sharp head of the spear protruded up through the snout. Yelping in anguish, the wolf tried to jerk away and Hunter used his forward momentum to slide under the wolf.

Hunter delivered a swift kick to the animal's soft underbelly, and Greyania heard something snap as the creature continued to howl in pain. No longer was the beast attacking, but trying to escape, which allowed Hunter get up and climb onto its back. Using all of his strength, he wrapped his arms around the throat and squeezed as hard as he could, choking the animal.

The movements of the wolf became frantic, then slowed as it started to die. The last thing she saw was one of its eyes, desperate, as the life within faded away. Then, every-thing faded and she was left with Hunter, on his knees, look-ing off into the distance.

"My brother died that night because I acted without honor. I tried to impress the female and it got him killed. She would have nothing to do with me after. My family knew it was my mistake that cost him his life, but they understood...it was the risk of the hunt."

"Hunter...you don't..." He held up a hand, interrupting her as he rose to his feet and continued, looking into her eyes. "He died on the hunt, and although he remained nameless, there was great joy in such a death. I was named by the tribe because my feats that night were legendary. Never before had any of my tribe taken on and killed a dire wolf, by themselves, on their first hunt. I became tribeless soon after, and tried to escape my own shortcomings. Even Rhik does not know of this."

He began to fade and they both now inhabited *her* body, but both were fully aware of what was happening.

What...what is going on?

Now, it seems we experience my *shame.*

It was the memory of when she had tried to free the Gods Who Walk from their prison. Since they were both fully aware, there was nothing to explain or to try and alter as they went through the motions. Looking at these memories again, with such clarity, was a harsh awakening. She had never fully realized how foolish she was, with her complete confidence that nothing could go wrong. Nor had she realized how strong her self-hatred was at the moment when she failed. Her doubt and self-pity were so bitter.

As the King faded away, so did the setting, and they were left alone again in the void.

"Now you know what I've done. How I ruined every-thing."

"You did as you were asked. *He* is the one who altered the spell."

She scoffed, wiping away tears she hadn't realized were falling as they looked at one another. "I am a fraud. I serve, but I serve poorly. I was so caught up in what I thought was my destiny that I never realized he could have done such a thing. If I had been more careful...more alert..." Letting her voice fade away, she shook her head. "We're getting distracted. We need to break the link so we can free ourselves before something more dangerous occurs, or a memory becomes so enticing we both become lost in it."

Nodding in agreement, he moved closer to her and looked around.

"How do we leave this place?"

"I'm honestly not sure. I wasn't even trying to *do* this kind of mental link. I just wanted you to see the damned spire. It's possible I misspoke the incantation...Magic of this type is touchy."

"You both are here because I have wished it."

The two of them whirled around and she was shocked to see Yorm standing before them, looking straight at Hunter Rage. He looked exactly as he had when she saw him sitting at the table, but somehow he seemed more imposing up close.

"Y...Yorm..." Hunter's tone was filled with reverence as he took a knee, humbling himself before the god.

"I demand no prayers. Stand and see me."

Hunter immediately rose and looked Yorm directly in the eye, but his admiration wasn't hard to see. Greyania hadn't thought any of the existing races held strongly to the beliefs of old, but it seemed that Hunter did.

"Yorm, why have you done this to us? I thought everything was already explained when we were all sitting at the same table."

"Greyania, you serve us, but I needed to see who *he* served. His loyalty is to his human partner, but much more than that...I see his true heart, now. I see what drives him. His purpose, and what his destiny will surely become."

Stepping back, Yorm folded his arms and called out, "Progity!"

A giant black wolf slunk out of the shadows and took its place just behind Yorm.

"You...were an elf before..."

"I am a great many things, woman." As he spoke, the words sent a shiver down her spine.

Hunter appeared unfazed by the sudden appearance of the wolf, but instead kept his gaze keenly on Yorm.

"The human male is Gron'Tul's problem, and the elf follows you as blindly as you first followed us. You, though..." Yorm gestured towards Hunter, and Progity moved forward until his snout was inches from the orc's face. Even Greyania could feel its hot breath from where she was. Hunter did not flinch.

"Am I judged then? To be sent to one of the hells for sins of my past?"

"You know your legends well, horkvash," Progity sat and spoke, tilting his head to one side as he focused on Hunter. As much as she thought she should distrust Progity, there was no denying the allure and sway his words held.

"Judge you, we do not. There is a great rage and fire burning within your heart. We do not wish it quenched, for you will need it. Yorm and I have decided."

"Decided what?" Greyania was completely ignored as Yorm stepped forward, produced a large knife, and, before she could react, plunged it right into Hunter's breast.

Hunter didn't utter a sound as a brilliant white light flashed and Greyania felt the sensation of falling, and then hitting the ground. Softer than she was expecting, her fingers groped for purchase. Sand. Everywhere she reached was sand. Blinking, she opened her eyes as Shae helped her up.

Looking over at Hunter, she saw he was groggily standing as well, then he doubled over and retched. Taking a few moments to compose himself, he shakily wiped his mouth. They had shared something very personal, and it created a bond between them. Yorm had seen to that, but to what end?

Before she could consider the possibilities of the encounter, her head began to spin and she turned and repeated what Hunter had just done, vomiting into the sand. Gasping for breath she collected herself and greedily drank the water Shae held to her lips.

"What happened to you two in there?" Rhikter asked.

Hunter stood, not answering the question, and turned on shaky legs to look out over the horizon. Gazing down at her, he smiled and nodded.

"I see the spire."

SEVEN

THE CONSTANT HEAT from the sun was oppressive, but it wasn't as bad inside of Coldfire as Rhikter had thought it would be. For some reason, even though its entire body was fashioned from metal, it repelled more heat than it absorbed, which suited him just fine. Had it not, he was certain it would have been impossible to travel as far as they had without being roasted alive.

The others were taking the brunt of the sun's heat, but were forging on at a steady pace. He was the only one who couldn't see the spire they were talking about, but he trusted Hunter.

In fact, Hunter and Greyania seemed to trust each other exponentially more than they had before their episode. He listened more attentively to her, and she seemed to take his advice more to heart. A tiny pang of jealousy hit Rhikter and he brushed it off, trying to ignore the petty emotion.

Hunter had been his partner in crime for years, and they had developed a strong, family-like bond; brothers in all but blood. Seeing him develop such a strong connection with this woman they hardly knew was troubling, but he did his best to ignore it. For as long as he could recall, Hunter had never really pursued a woman. If this was what he wanted, so be it.

Shae was another matter entirely. Physically she was gorgeous. It was her personality that left much to be desired. While he would love to have a more intimate relationship with her, he knew pursuing it would result in parts of his body being forcibly removed.

No means no. Besides, now that he knew there was no way in hells things could progress any further with her, he was free to entice any other women that they happened to come across. He found the roguish adventurer lifestyle conducive to ensuring his bed was rarely empty.

Finding someone to sweep off their feet in this place seems a bit of a stretch, though. They were on a slight decline now, and it was the only change in terrain since they started marching towards the hidden spire earlier that day. According to the others, it was growing larger with each passing step. At this pace they would reach it within two or three days' travel, more or less. The desert heat played tricks on one's eyes, magically hidden spire or not.

Once there, they would reforge the amulet, unlock the true potential of Coldfire, and he and Hunter could take their leave. There was just no reason to tell the women about his idea. He wondered if he should even let Hunter know he intended to leave immediately after. The way Hunter kept looking at Greyania gave him pause.

With or without Hunter, he was steadfast in his resolve to get the new amulet and leave. There was no way he was going to let himself be used as some sort of pawn in a battle - led by gods he knew nothing about - over a world that was in ruins - nor was he going to hand over the vessel. *With a su-*

per-charged Coldfire I would have my pick of jobs and payment. I could even reinstate the royal...

Rolling his eyes at himself, he dropped the thought. There was no reason to go down *that* path again and repeat the same words his father had drummed into his head all those years ago, before Rhikter left home for good. Looking out over the horizon to distract himself, he noticed something strange for the first time. As they moved, the horizon seemed to grow taller.

"Hey, guys, do you see that?" His metal finger pointed towards the change in the landscape, and the other three slowed. Greyania was the first to react, and she started running towards the horizon with renewed energy.

"Wait! Greyania! Why are you rushing? What do you see?"

They all picked up speed and the land continued to rise above them. After a few minutes Rhikter realized why: they were approaching a vast cliff. Looking to his right he saw no visible end. Looking to the left he noticed massive dark clouds in the distance.

"Gods...It's the Eye!"

Alarm spread as they realized that the eternal storm was advancing upon them, quickly. As unpredictable as it was dangerous, there hadn't been any warning of its approach until that instant. Moving ahead, he pushed the golem to the limit, trying to reach the cliff first. If he could somehow climb up it, create footholds for the rest, they could follow him up. *Maybe I can carry them?*

The land suddenly lurched upward as he got closer, some long ago effect of erosion, and he was about to leap over it when he ran into an invisible wall and fell back. Trying again, he hit the same barrier and fell back once more. He was about to use force to break through when the others caught up and stopped him.

"No!...Look over...the edge, you...fool." Shae pointed before she leaned over, hands on her knees and gasping for breath. The sun wasn't doing them any favors this day, that was for sure.

Moving slowly, the temporary barrier Shae had erected now gone, Rhikter approached the top of the hill and gasped. The land simply disappeared and a vast chasm spread out before them, going as far left and right as the cliff. They had nowhere to go, and the storm was bearing down on them far faster than anything he'd ever seen before.

"What do we do now? There's no way we can get across and there isn't enough time in the world to try and get around it," Rhikter hoped Greyania had some trick up her sleeve.

Desperation and fear were palpable in the air. Even if they tried to turn back, tried to run all the way back to the jungle, they would still be caught in the massive storm long before they made it to safety. If the legends were even partially true, it was stronger and more powerful than anything that ever occurred naturally. It was full of chaotic magic and raw, elemental force.

Their only option was to go forward, but even with a running start there was no way he could cross the gap to the other side. Especially if he was weighed down by even *one* passenger, let alone three. The worst part was, he could see the opening of a cavern just across the way, forever out of reach.

"Do we have anything that can help get us to that cave?" He pointed over at it, trying to get Greyania's attention. She shook her head hesitantly, and Rhikter had the feeling she was holding something back.

"Spit it out! If you know something, even something magical, that can help us, use it!"

The wind was beginning to increase and it blew her white hair every which way as she took a short breath and let it out quickly. "I can possibly open a portal to teleport us to the cavern."

"Teleport?!"

The implications of that sentence hit him like a slap to the face. *We could have simply teleported to the spire hours ago.* But with the storm bearing down on them, he realized this was not the time to have this argument. *But it is one we will have, mark my words.*

"If you can, do it!" Hunter yelled

"It isn't that simple! Opening even a small portal for one to pass through taxes me greatly. Opening one large enough for the vessel *and* the rest of us may very well kill me!"

"If you do nothing, Greyania, the storm will kill us *all!*" Hunter's tone was pleading, but still managed to maintain his dignity.

"Alright then. Throw me!" Greyania stated, looking at Rhikter with cold determination.

"What?!"

"You have to get me to that cavern! I can't open a portal to someplace I've never been before, and if I open it too close to the edge we may all fall to our deaths. You need to throw me up there!"

He had never tossed anyone he wasn't trying to kill before, and he was worried he might overthrow her and smash her right into the side of the cliff. It was a dodgy prospect, even without the strong wind from the storm.

After a moment, realizing there was no other alternative, he gave a curt nod. "Fine. Your funeral. Or ours, depending on how this ends."

Reaching over, he picked her up and positioned her in what he hoped was the best manner to toss her across the rift. As nervous as he was, he did his best to remain calm, waiting for her command.

"Now!"

Pulling his arm back and saying a prayer to whomever was listening that he wouldn't miss, he tossed Greyania. Watching her sail through the air, much faster than Rhikter had expected, sent a sharp twinge of panic down his spine. Thankfully, she flew through the opening unscathed.

"She's made it!" Shae exclaimed after a few tense seconds. "She is a little bruised, but nothing major. She will open the portal as soon as we're ready."

"We're ready now!" Rhikter had to scream to be heard over the howling wind, as it began to push hard against them. There was a bright flash of green to their right, and what seemed to be a wavy tear appeared in the air. On the other side of the portal was Greyania, motioning for them to step through.

Shae went through first because she was closest, and then Hunter. Just as Rhikter was about to step through the portal, the storm swirled around him. *How on earth could it move so quickly?* The wind, pushing harder and faster than he'd ever thought possible, started to move him away from the portal.

No! He strained, pushing forward against the force beating him back as much as he could. Heavy rain started to pelt the exterior of Coldfire as he reached a hand into the portal, feeling around for some form of purchase.

A second too slow. The wind ripped his arm out of the portal's threshold, straining it. Crying out in shock and pain, he was lifted up and into the storm. He tried to find a way to move back towards the portal, but the storm was too strong and the wind moved him too quickly. Stunned faces within the portal soon faded into nothing as he was carried off.

*****

"Do something!" Hunter's voice echoed in the cavern they had found themselves in. The portal started to close, with Coldfire and Rhikter quickly disappearing from sight.

"Hurry! Use your magic to pull him back before the portal closes!"

Even though Shae knew that Rhikter and Coldfire were crucial to whatever mission Greyania had them on, she also knew there was no way either of them had the strength or the ability to do what Hunter demanded. The vessel had moved away too far too quickly, before anyone could even react.

"There must...We have to save him!" Hunter continued to plead.

"If she tried," Shae responded, placing a hand on his shoulder, "it would kill her."

The portal began to quickly shrink in size. The three stood there in silence as it flickered and finally dissipated into nothingness.

"No. NO!" Hunter pulled away from her and slammed his fist against one of the walls of the cavern, causing Shae to wince as she heard a crack. Something had definitely broken in his hand. He either didn't care or didn't notice as he pulled back and did it again, harder this time. Blood seeped onto the wall where his fist was pressed against it and he pulled back a third time.

Greyania grabbed his wrist and spoke softly. "Stop. That solves nothing. Let me tend to your wound."

"We just let him die."

The words stung. They had *not* let him die, there was just nothing anyone could have done. Seconds were the difference between life and death and they simply didn't have enough time to save him from being carried off by the storm.

"There was nothing any of us could have done."

Silence settled into the cavern and it started to feel less like a sanctuary from the raging storm outside and more like a tomb.

"He...he could survive. Right?" Hunter's voice sounded hopeful.

Greyania was using a healing spell, speaking softly as she tended to the fractured hand. After a moment the glow faded and she turned to Shae and shrugged. In all the years they had known one another and traveled together, Shae had never seen her like this. Greyania looked so physically and emotionally exhausted, much more so than just the spell-casting would cause, and that worried Shae. *Was the vessel really that important?*

"The Eye is a magical storm, and the laws of nature don't necessarily apply. They could bend, or even break, dozens of times in but a few moments," Greyania explained.

"But the vessel...it is powerful enough to withstand the storm, right? It *could* protect him..." Hunter's tone was infectious, and Shae found herself believing Rhikter could survive against all odds as well.

"It would be highly unlikely," Greyania continued, "however, we simply don't know enough of the Behemoth Vessels. It could be shielding him from any wild magic, and protecting him like a shell. Or..."

Hunter finished her sentence, "Or, it could be making things worse. He'd be dead before he even hit the ground."

The wind outside was picking up, making its way into the cave and causing their clothing to billow about.

"Speculating about his fate isn't going to help us here and now. He may or may not be dead, but *we* certainly will be if we stay near the mouth of this cave." Shae pointed inwards, towards a tunnel that led deeper into the ground.

"Shae is right. We cannot do anyone any good if we all perish. We will make shelter until the end of the storm."

The three of them moved deeper into the cave system until they could no longer see the opening and could barely hear the howling wind. Setting down on the cold floor, Hunter looked at the two of them.

"What supplies do we have left?"

Using what light there was within the cave, she reached for her bag and sifted through it, the others doing the same. Among the three of them they had some medicinal items, enough food for two days, and only enough water for one. The bulk of their supplies were packed within Coldfire, but at least they had a fighting chance.

"We will need to ration to make it stretch, but if we are lucky and this cavern leads to the surface...at least we will be away from the sun for some time," Hunter said as he gathered up the supplies.

Shae was worried that Greyania might lose her motivation at the loss of the vessel, but if nothing else they could still restore the amulet. Who knew, maybe the apocrita could build another vessel. *They could be capable of anything, really.*

The thought gave her hope that this wouldn't be a complete failure. Part of her was bothered by her own lack of concern over Rhikter, but she had no time to mourn like Hunter, or to wallow like Greyania. She had to keep them moving forward, no matter what.

"You should get some rest, m'lady. Once you're fit to travel again we're going to get to the top of this cliff one way or another."

Greyania made no opposition to her plan, and she took that as approval. Nodding to herself, she uttered a spell and a small globe of cool blue light followed just behind her. There were only two ways out of the small place they had found shelter, and one lead right back to the mouth of the cave. Thinking it prudent to keep her worries between herself and Greyania, she reached out to her with her thoughts.

Make sure Hunter doesn't hurt himself again. I'm going to scout ahead and see if there is a way out of here.

He was overcome with grief...We both are.

I know. We'll get through this.

Greyania did not respond.

I'll let you know if I find anything. Otherwise get your strength up. We may have to levitate to the top of this cliff if we can't find a path to the surface.

Her demeanor was cold, but it was necessary. Perhaps this was why Greyania had insisted *she* be the one to accompany her. Not just the bond they had or their familiarity with one another, but Shae's ability to maintain poise under pressure and do what needed to be done, no matter what.

Either way, she was going to see this through with or without the vessel. Frowning at that thought she headed further into the tunnel, hoping it wouldn't just be a dead end.

*****

It was a wonder Rhikter hadn't vomited all over himself yet. As soon as he was lifted up into the air and carried off like a leaf, he pulled himself into a ball in an attempt to keep his arms and legs from being pulled from their sockets. Fully within the torso of Coldfire, he tried to will it to do the same with its own limbs, before he felt himself cut off from the vessel entirely. The storm was the likely culprit.

He was alive, but the feeling of utter helplessness was overwhelming. Even if he were able to take full control of Coldfire, it wasn't powerful enough to fight against the speed of these winds. Whenever he dared to look out the visor, it was enough to make him dizzy and lightheaded.

Strange...no wind or sounds are filtering in from outside.

He looked outside again, and realized that it was completely silent in the confines of the vessel. He stuck a finger out through one of the slits in the visor and could feel the cold, harsh wind bite at it.

"Are you doing this? Are you...protecting me somehow?" As he spoke out loud, he immediately felt ridiculous for talking to a machine.

He couldn't help but laugh at the absurdity of the situation until a voice came out of nowhere and startled him.

"The vessel isn't doing a damned thing. I am!"

"Who's there?!" Rhikter exclaimed, then let out an exasperated sigh at his own stupidity for blurting out the question. *How can there be anyone there when I can barely fit in here.*

The voice didn't speak up again, so he began to wonder if it was some sort of delirium brought on by his current predicament. It made a modicum of sense; he was likely going to die and his mind was trying to ease his apprehension and anxiety by hallucinating someone there with him.

"Well, there's only enough room in here for me, so unless you're a barmaid with a large mug of ale and a loose grip on decency, then I suggest you go haunt someone else."

Satisfied he'd scared off his psychosis, he moved to try and get more comfortable. Since realizing that he was relatively safe from the raging storm outside, the ride felt more bearable. He let his thoughts drift back to that idea of a barmaid and some good ale.

I'll probably be killed when I land, so maybe if I just...let myself doze off. He closed his eyes and tried to let himself drift away. If his death were in battle, he'd face it head on. This, however, was pointless, and he'd rather be dreaming of all the women he'd had the pleasure of getting to know instead of waiting around for death. Even though he was in the middle of a raging storm, he found the way Coldfire moved about oddly relaxing. He was just beginning to drift off to sleep when the voice returned.

"Communicating is problematic. They just *had* to have their damned storm. Such a waste of good magic, if you ask me."

This wasn't just some psychosis. Somehow, someone was speaking to him through Coldfire.

"Who in the hells are you?" he demanded.

"Ha! I'll tell you when you land. We have a lot to discuss, you and I." The voice sounded bemused.

"Is that so? What makes you think I'll be talkative? Assuming I survive the drop."

A few moments passed in silence and he wondered if the mysterious voice was going to come back. They'd mentioned that the storm was making things difficult, after all. As strange as it was, now that it was gone again, he found he missed it.

"Oh, you'll want to talk. I know that vessel inside and out."

"How do you know about Coldfire?"

"*Coldfire?!* Of all the...It's called *Nixturjekur!*"

"I'm not calling it that."

"Doesn't matter. I'll knock that ridiculous name out of your head once we get you down from there."

"And how in the hells do you intend to do that?"

"I'm working on it. The Eye is chaotic and messy, but it's also constructed and follows a...certain...order," each pause in the words was followed with the sound of something heavy being moved, and the voice seemed to be speaking under strain. *What in the hells are you doing?*

"Wait, did you say the storm is *constructed*?"

"Yes! It was made it to protect the colony. Bunch of self-indulgent xenophobes if you ask me. Spending hundreds of years hidden away certainly hasn't helped them any."

"By the gods, you're one of the apocrita!"

"Your kind always chewed out the term more than spoke it. Such a messy, often redundant, language. But no, I'm not a bug."

"But...what you said..."

"If you listened worth a damn, then you'd know what I said!"

Cryptic messages were the last thing he needed, and his annoyance was beginning to grow. The other voice could be the only way he survived this, but that didn't mean he had to play their games.

"Either help me get free of this storm and back to my friends, or shut the hells up and let me die in peace!"

"Alright, alright. Time to end this nonsense. Feel around Nixturjekur's breastplate for an indentation."

"Ok...Now what?"

"Take your amulet from around your neck and place it over the impression. Should give you the boost you need to free yourself from the storm."

"What if I don't have an amulet?"

When the voice replied, it sounded more distant, as if it weren't talking to him this time, but to itself.

"Doesn't...then how in all the hells is he even...Bah!" The voice came back to the forefront, loud as ever. "Since you're about as useful as a second ass, just sit tight. I'm gonna try something I haven't attempted in about a thousand years, but who knows, might work!"

A thousand? Before he could ponder the length of time any further, Coldfire suddenly sprang to life. Instead of the blue he was used to, it now glowed purple. Had the voice somehow put it into defensive mode remotely? Rhikter could feel it stretch its limbs out as far as they could go, until it was soaring spread eagle through the air. He imagined if anyone saw it flying right now, they'd think it a ludicrous sight.

The entire vessel lurched, and he felt like it was actually gaining altitude. He had to know for sure and chanced another look outside. As the storm swirled around him, he saw, sure enough, that he was rising above it.

When he had finally cleared the storm, Coldfire stayed motionless, hovering, before turning its entire body around in circles like the needle of a compass. He couldn't see the chasm *or* the cliff so he knew he was leagues from the others. Being alone left a bitter taste in his mouth. Just then, Coldfire jerked to the right, pulled in all its limbs so it was as straight as possible, and shot off like an arrow towards the east.

"It working?"

"What did you do?!"

"I'm just sending it back to where it came from!"

Why is nothing ever easy? Why couldn't they want Hunter and I to steal something from a nice, quiet tomb? Lamenting his current predicament did little to ease his troubled mind. The vessel was gaining speed, and, if he was seeing correctly, the ground was coming up incredibly fast.

"I'm seeing the ground coming up really fast here!"

"If you worship any of the Behemoths, now might be a good time to pray to 'em."

"You're crazy!"

"It got you outta that storm, didn't it?! Now brace your whining ass and let me know when you land."

Land was putting it mildly. At the speed he was going it would be a miracle if the vessel survived, let alone him. Speeding up more and more, he couldn't turn away from the fast-approaching sand dunes, wondering if they would soften the crash. Seconds before impact, he gave a small prayer. Not to any god in particular, just to any who would listen.

I swear, if I survive, I'll be your weapon. Just don't let me die in this metal coffin!

The landing was smoother than he thought it would be. Perhaps some part of Coldfire had been enchanted for just such a thing. He had survived being tossed around by the storm, after all. Skipping like a giant shiny stone, he could feel the impact as Coldfire immediately started to flip and tumble as soon as it connected with the ground.

After what seemed like an eternity, the vessel finally came to a complete stop. His heart pounding, breathing heavy, he risked looking out through the visor. *I...I made it!*

The voice sprang to life, "Are you dead? I told you to tell me when you landed."

"I'm...here. How did you know that would work?"

"To be honest, I'm surprised you made it. I didn't think the enchantments were going to be enough to soften the blow as it hit the sand. Was counting on getting the vessel back without a lot of extra weight."

There was humor in the voice's tone, but Rhikter didn't feel like laughing. He wanted answers, and he wanted to find the rest of the group so they could finish this damned quest before it killed him.

"How did you know it would work," he repeated his question, "and how in the world do you know so much about this thing?!"

"You stay put. I'll come to you...no telling how much damage the vessel took during all that. It's a wonder you haven't destroyed it before now."

Anger bubbled to the surface and Rhikter exploded, tired of his questions being ignored, *"How did you know?!"*

"Gods you are a persistent one, I'll give you that."

"Answer me!!"

"I *built* the damn thing!"

EIGHT

DEGHAT WASN'T ONE to spend much time with the others when they linked their minds. He was far more content to be within himself, letting days bleed into months, months into years, and years into decades. So when he felt something amiss with his physical body and excused himself, there was little suspicion.

"I grow weary of thy posturing, mine siblings. I shall go and retire, to regain strength for the trials yet to come."

"Jussst make sssure you do not ressst for too long. Lassst time you ssslumbered for three centuriesss!"

Smiling and nodding he left their presence and retreated back to his body. He was still surrounded on all sides by solid ice, which had also encroached over his limbs since his imprisonment began, locking them into place.

Deghat's true form was worthy of the nickname the mortal races had given him ages ago: the Hungering Pit. His body was a giant boar's, only instead of a normal snout, his was twice as long and filled with innumerable razor sharp teeth. His tusks were more like shovels, to funnel food directly into his ravenous maw. At the height of his power, he could level a whole forest in minutes, and still have room for more.

Taking a few moments to feel for the disturbance, his whole body shuddered as he touched upon an entity that was both familiar and foreign to him. It was there, with him, but had to be in some corner of his prison he could not turn to face. One of the few, rare times he cursed his bulk.

"With whom do I speak? Why dost thou linger just beyond mine sight?"

"Come now, brother. Surely you can tell who I am."

"Res'Kel?!"

Of all the siblings, Deghat had been closest with Res'Kel. Since Res'Kel originally had no children of his own, he helped to look after and support Deghat's. A welcome ally whenever the other mortal races were being overzealous in their hunting and killing.

Deghat understood and accepted why his children were treated the way they were, but he didn't relish it. There were times he wished they could stay hidden, away from the others, like Res'Kel's progeny.

"It is finally complete. You do remember, don't you?"

Deghat hesitated, unsure if he should admit that he did, or feign ignorance. How much could this being know? Was it really Res'Kel, or some trick of the mind?

"I'll take your hesitation as a yes. You also realize, then, that I remember just as well what *you* did. Admirable, if misguided, foolish, and ultimately futile. What would the others say?"

The way he spoke immediately dissolved any reservations Deghat had over this being's identity. There was no way this was not Res'Kel, and yet there was no way it could actually *be* Res'Kel. So perplexing.

"Thou...art thyself and yet thou hast the essence of another intertwined with thine own. Curious is this riddle of self thou hast presented before me. Whyfore hast thou come to this place?"

"Did I ever tell you how aggravating your manner of speech is? I may be a 'riddle of self' but your words are convoluted and over-spoken." Res'Kel ignored the question.

"Over-spoken, but under heard. Thy siblings and I have been worried, dear brother. Now, I see thou hast regained a new *physical* body. Such an interesting development."

He could feel the presence enter his mind, in the same way he and the others communicated. In his ogre body he looked down at the smaller man and finally was able to see him.

He looked desiccated, his dry skin full of wrinkles. His dark gray hair was tattered and messy, and the clothing he wore was simple. His beard was neatly trimmed, and he stood with his hands clasped behind his back. His eyes were a solid, sickly green. The air around him seemed alive, constantly shifting and distorting ever so slightly; perceivable, but hard to focus on.

"I thought it would be easier to speak to each other on a similar level."

"If thee sought a simpler task, why not take thine original form? Now thou hast new flesh and yet thou dost remain as a withered husk. Why?"

"Ahhh, yes. You don't understand, do you? May I?"

He held out his hand, which looked to be literally no more than skin and bone, and Deghat hesitated to take it. The power, the confidence, none of it were of his brother, and this gave him pause. In that moment he realized how much he missed the brother he used to know.

"Come, Deghat, and we shall delve into the past."

Seeing no alternative, Deghat took the hand. The size difference was comical, but the touch allowed their minds to fully communicate emotions and memories far more quickly than any speech would allow. For many centuries, it had been the only way he and his siblings communicated.

Images flashed into his mind that were so foreign, he had a hard time deciphering their meaning. After a few moments, he realized he was seeing the life and memories of the other presence within Res'Kel. There was a nagging feeling at the back of his mind that something was quite perverse about the way his brother and the presence intermingled.

A man of human royalty. Kidnapped. Kept barely alive, hands and feet removed after so many escape attempts. Tragic in a way, but necessary. Deghat had devised the spell of unbinding himself. Blood magic was chosen because it was the most powerful, but it had to be crafted with utmost care.

Res'Kel's memories now mixed with the human's. Deghat's eyes grew wide with shock and he immediately ripped his hand away, staring in horror at the thing before him, "Brother...tell me this is a falsehood. Tell me thou weaves a strange tale of fiction..."

"What you saw was truth. I changed your spell. We changed it. The human and I, we understood one another. At the time, I was the only one of us truly free. The loss of my body was an unfortunate result of my attempt to create my own race. Could any of you say you would have taken the same chances? Made the same sacrifices?"

Res'Kel, or whatever the thing before him really was, began to pace, placing his hands behind his back again.

"As you crafted your spell, steeped in blood, I crafted my own. His spell of possession was one I helped to influence and guide. I saw potential in the spell, and longed for a corporeal form again. At first the change was...tumultuous. After the initial joining he and I fought for dominance and control as our minds began to merge into one. It took decades for us *both* to realize that one could not exist without the other. Not anymore."

His smile was unnerving; something about how genuine and truly joyful it was made Deghat sick to his core, cementing the fact that his brother, as he knew him, was forever gone.

"The wonders we each felt! The empathy! The emotions! It all flowed through us like a flooding river and we took even more time to re-center ourselves into a single being. Do you have any idea how long it took before I stopped calling myself 'we'?" He laughed.

"Am I still to call thee Res'Kel, the Wandering Dream, mine brother? Or am I to use the moniker 'Withered King' as the others are so keen upon labeling thou with?"

"You, dear Deghat, most loved of all my siblings, may call me whatever you wish."

He moved closer, his form growing in height until he and Deghat were eye to eye. Reaching out he placed his hands gingerly on either side of Deghat's face. "I have always loved you, brother. I *had* to change your spell. It was...crude."

"Wh...what dost thou speak of? It was a spell of Unbinding, nothing more. Perhaps even less."

"*Exactly.* You lacked vision. I saw the potential there bubbling just beneath the surface. All that powerful, raw energy, begging to be utilized."

"I...I just longed..."

"...for freedom," Res'Kel finished his sentence. "I know, and I understand. I can't fault you for desiring such a thing. Which is why I've come with an offer."

"Offer?"

"We both know the spell can never be reversed, and we all know the effect that simply letting it finish would have on *everything.*"

"I admit, Res'Kel, it was a move most clever. As soon as I became aware of how completely the spell wouldst change Antembra, I did bid the others to stay and blamed I the spell's failure upon the human. Free though we were, the only way to keep the world from changing completely was to stay in our imprisonments."

Letting go of his face, Res'Kel, the Withered King, moved away, his size returning back to normal as he did. He looked over his shoulder at the ogre form of his brother. "Regardless of your reasons for stopping them, it gave me time. There are ways to alter the spell even further, since it is suspended."

"A means to reverse this purgatory you've damned us to?" Deghat made no means to hide the hope in his voice. How he longed to return to his true form and wander the forests of the world, feeling alive and free once more.

"In a way. I may have found the means to not only create my *true* race, but save yours as well. I want your help. I *need* it. Will you stand with me brother?"

When he was first devising the spell, it had been an easy enough deception to go behind the backs of the others. He had chosen blood magic not only for its power, but for its unpredictable nature; to more easily cover his tracks. Moving against them now, in a bolder fashion, felt distasteful. "I would never think to harm the others nor raise a hand against them."

"*Nor would I.* Even as they move to destroy what I have become, I love them more than anything. They will never come to harm. Their children, however, are of no matter. They can always make more. *If* we allow it."

"And what of the brinore?"

"They still serve a purpose. Though created by mistake, they are my children. I learn *much* from them."

Deghat looked at the form his brother had taken. It was that of a human, moments before death, a telling detail. He tried to feel for the mind of his brother, but the two presences were so mixed it was impossible to sort them out. *Can I trust the words of honey that flow from thy mouth?*

"I need to ponder this alliance. Such a move could spell the end of my children. Or mineself. Never before have we moved to conspire against the others in such blatant strokes."

"Oh? Am I no longer considered 'one of the others'?" There was hurt in his voice, mixed with a sarcastic and biting tone.

Deghat opened his mouth to explain, but Res'Kel held up a hand, interrupting him. "Take the time to decide, but don't take *too* long. I know what the others are planning, and I make my own moves to guard against it."

Their mental link was broken, and he was back in his prison again, in his true form. Shifting slightly in place, he tried to reach for the other presence but felt nothing. As soon as he had appeared, his brother had disappeared.

What foul treachery will I bring down upon us, my dear family?

The presence asserted itself back into his mind, as if it had never left. Never before had something been able to sneak up on him like this.

Is it truly treachery when they betrayed us first? Know this, Deghat: if you tell the others I visited with you, or why, my proposal is rescinded and your children will be wiped from the face of this world with the others. Only my own shall remain.

After the voice ceased, unease crept into his body and he felt wracked with an emotion that was oddly familiar yet strange. It was something he'd not felt in hundreds of years, not since the time of their imprisonment. It took him several moments to recognize exactly what it was.

Fear.

*****

There was no way to know exactly how much time had passed since the voice told Rhikter to stay put. Coldfire had apparently been damaged in the fall, to the point of being stationary, so the voice said he would come to fix the problem and get them both 'back home,' wherever that was. With the sun beating down, he dared not leave the relatively safe confines of the vessel. At least it continued to give some protection from the heat.

It was also a good thing the voice was coming to him. Almost all the supplies had been destroyed in the fall, and he only had a small amount of water left. How he had survived at all was nothing short of a miracle.

A loud bang on the side of Coldfire startled him and he called out, "Who's there?" No answer. Again, and then again, something hit the side of Coldfire. "Who is out there?!" It couldn't have been his benefactor. Surely he would announce himself.

Rhikter reached for a dagger at his side but it was no longer there. *Where is it?!* He glanced around the small area he occupied and finally saw it down by his feet. *How in the world did I not get stabbed in the fall?* No matter, he strained to reach for it just as the hatch burst open and bright light blinded him.

Grasping the hilt, he was about to defend himself when a smooth, metallic tube pressed against his temple.

"That any way to thank me?"

It was the voice. Breathing a sigh of relief, Rhikter lowered his arm. The tube remained pressed against his head. "If you were going to beat me to death with a pipe, you would have already," he joked.

"Beat you? Oh, by the heavens above."

The tube was pulled away and the figure aimed it at the ground. A second later a loud explosion sounded and a projectile hit the sand, spraying it every which way. Rhikter was surprised, and gaped at the silhouette standing before him. Between the position of Coldfire and the way the sun hung in the sky, he could only make out a male humanoid form, nothing more.

"What in the hells is that thing?!"

"Not sure yet. Only came up with the basic design about two years ago. Figured it'd be handy if you ended up being hostile."

A gloved hand was extended to help him up and out of Coldfire. *Guess he's really not an apocrita, after all.* Taking it, he was hoisted out so easily that he stumbled a bit as he hit the ground.

"Sorry, been awhile since I encountered anyone other than the bugs. Tend to forget how strong I can be."

Turning to look at the figure, Rhikter frowned. It wore a long hood drawn over its face, obscuring its features, and was dressed in rugged leathers from head to toe. The colors of its clothing were lighter browns and tans, closely matching the sands they were surrounded by.

"You have to be boiling under that."

"It keeps the sand out. Come on, let's get going." The figure brushed past him.

Ignoring the command and kneeling down, Rhikter began to move the sand and debris from around Coldfire. Even as he scooped up the first handful, he knew it was futile. "I can't just leave it here."

"It will be fine. Trust me."

"I barely know you."

"True. So, a gesture of good faith I suppose." Shrugging, he moved towards Coldfire, pushed Rhikter out of the way, and sank to his knees. "Such a doubtful race." Placing his hands on Coldfire's frame, he lowered his head and uttered words in a language Rhikter had never heard before, not even from Greyania. Still speaking, the figure rose, his hands high. He balled them into fists and brought them down onto the vessel's chassis. Immediately, it disappeared. The sand quickly moved to fill the sudden depression left behind.

"Wha...what did you do to it?!"

"Relax, kid. It's back home."

In all his years, he had never witnessed a teleportation spell quite like this one. Portals, any instant movement from one place to another, always left a sign, a noticeable change in the surrounding environment. Coldfire had simply disappeared without so much as a wisp of smoke.

"How did you do that?"

"Mirrors," the figure stated sarcastically as he stood and headed off towards the east. Rhikter had no way of knowing if it was the direction the spire was, but had no other choice than to follow.

"You spoke of the apocrita. Can you take me to them?"

"After we have a little chat. I saw Nixturjekur's leg. What in the *hells* did you use to replace it and what happened to it to begin with?"

"Steel," Rhikter replied.

Spitting on the ground, the figure cursed. "Godsdammit, steel?! By everything that's holy, you're as daft as you are pale. Still...the work was sound and you show a knack for it. This is good. I've got more to teach you before I'll let you use it again."

"*Use*? Coldfire belongs to me by right!"

Stopping in the sand, the figure spun around and jabbed a finger into Rhikter's chest, which hurt more than he expected it to. "By right? You *stole* it, kid. Plain and simple."

Rhikter was able to catch a glimpse of blue, scaly skin under the hood. He gasped. "You're a sincit, aren't you? You're just as much a scavenger as I am!"

Removing his hood, the figure took in a breath and his shoulders slumped as he let out a heavy sigh. Rhikter could now clearly see the face and features, and they were unlike anything he'd ever seen or heard of. Leathery skin and blue scales adorned a distinctly reptilian face, but a sincit would have had a snout, and pointed teeth, both of which this figure lacked, aside from a pair of pronounced fangs. Bright green eyes stared at Rhikter with annoyance, but not anger. A pony-tail of black hair sprouted from the back of his skull, cut short.

"Scavenger? I've been called-I've *been* worse. But sincit? That's like me calling you a cow because you've got the same color skin." Turning, he headed off again, this time walking faster. "Keep up, kid."

"Fine, you're not a sincit. You claim you built the vessel, a device from over two millennia ago, and you're as cryptic as a dwarven puzzle box. But you're wrong on one thing: Coldfire is mine, and not just by right of discovery, but right of birth and blood."

"Gods, I swear...Fine. Spit it out, if it makes you feel important. And if we stop one more time, I'm leaving you here."

"My full name is Rhikter-"

The figure interrupted him, "-Lehmann. The first royal family of humanity. I also know your family hasn't used that title since the world went tits up."

Rhikter was stunned. "How could you *know* such a thing?!"

"I told you: *I built the vessel*. Then I left it in the care of your family line...That's the *only* way to explain how you were able to pilot it so easily. You're obviously a direct descendant. Only way you *knew* you could was if your father told you, or you found some journal somewhere. Also, I may be out in the middle of the Dry Oceans, but thanks to the bugs, I keep current on 'topical' events."

"You seem to know everything about Coldfire, myself, and my family line, yet I know next to nothing about you. What do I even call you? What the hells *are* you??"

The figured remained silent as they continued walking, until they came to a small rock formation, with an opening to a cave on the side. Still not answering the question, the figure stepped into the cave, headed towards a wall, and uttered more words in that strange language. The wall disappeared and he motioned for Rhikter to follow.

"My name is Kovacik, and I'm last of the kin."

NINE

"THESE CAVERNS ARE a maze. There is no way we will ever reach the apocrita, let alone find our way out of here."

Hunter's voice was starting to get on her nerves. Whatever feelings she may be developing towards the orc were overshadowed by his constant reminder of the futility of their situation.

The vessel was gone, and even if they could find it again, there was no guarantee it would be in one piece. The storm was powerful, and, having been so close to it, she knew it was also completely artificial. Someone, or something, was controlling it. The Eye had appeared only when they were finally getting close to their goal, and she was certain it was no coincidence.

"We need to keep searching. There has to be a way out...the pattern of these tunnels is too precise, the walls too smooth. I don't think they're natural," Greyania reassured him.

"We should teleport back to the cliff and try and reach the summit," he countered.

"Hunter, enough. Even if I had the energy to open another portal, it would be pointless. The storm knew where we were and was acting like a watchdog. If we return to that spot, chances are, it will too." Anger colored her tone.

"Greyania is right, Hunter. At least in the caverns we're safe from the storm, as well as the sun," Shae finally spoke up.

He exhaled a snort, then remained silent. Greyania could tell from the look on his face, however, that he disagreed with them both. *At least he's not so stubborn as to go off on his own.*

Shae moved closer to her as they walked through the tunnels, the small orb of light following just close enough to light their immediate path. Her voice filled Greyania's mind.

We do need a plan of some sort, m'lady.

The path before us will be revealed when the time is right.

That's cryptic and meaningless. What happens if we discover the apocrita aren't as friendly and benevolent as we'd hoped? That storm they sent could have killed us all.

Continuing to move forward, Greyania sighed at the gravity of the situation. The thought that the apocrita could be hostile had never crossed her mind; at least not until their encounter with the storm and their subsequent loss of Rhikter.

"There's no need to continue to speak with our minds, Shae. Hunter has earned our trust and deserves to hear what we discuss related to this endeavor."

M'lady, that is completely unw-

"We all lost something back there, child. Keeping secrets now will only harbor resentment."

Shae looked like she was going to continue to argue, but instead she looked directly at Hunter. When he did not seem angered or offended at being excluded, Shae's features softened as she spoke directly to him.

"I was merely telling her we needed a plan, a solid one, in case the apocrita weren't as welcoming as we'd originally anticipated."

Hunter nodded. "Agreed. Although, we cannot hope to stand against an entire race. There is no telling how many live here in the sands of these dead seas."

Greyania was thankful he did not press the matter of their secret communication. Coming to another branch in the path, they all paused. There were three tunnels.

Greyania looked at each possible path. Finding a renewed vigor she stated, "If they are friendly, they may be able to rebuild a vessel for us. And if they are hostile, we will leave and I will try and commune with the Gods Who Walk again to find what their will is. I sincerely doubt they would send me on this mission to die."

"What makes you so sure?" Hunter questioned.

Picking a path at random, she pressed onward. "They haven't let me die yet."

As she took a step forward, a voice echoed through the caverns, seemingly coming from nowhere and everywhere at the same time. It was devoid of emotion and had a metallic tone.

"Stop," the voice commanded.

Hunter spun around, grabbing the hilt of his sword as he did.

"Who is there?!"

"You are in now passing. Please to be exit your enter, and us will be sure not allow you twice harm come."

"It isn't making sense, m'lady," Shae pointed out.

"No, it isn't."

Sounds of clicking filled the halls and then the clang of metal hitting metal. The voice resumed, its emotionless tone

unaffected, but Greyania noticed it was making far more understandable now.

"You are trespassing. You will please leave now, and
out the exit you entered. If you comply, no harm will come to
you."

Stepping forward and singling herself out from the
other two, Greyania responded in a pleading tone, hoping to
appeal to whomever she was speaking to. "Please listen...We
aren't here to harm you or anyone else. We simply seek
knowledge and help. We seek the apocrita."

"You seek that which does not wish to be found. Their
knowledge is not for you, so you will exit now."

"They are not listening to you, Greyania. If they are
those we are seeking, it would seem they do not welcome visitors," Hunter said.

"You have to help us! The storm may have killed our
friend and destroyed the Behemoth Vessel he was using! We
need your help to find it and fix it, if it is still functioning, or
help us build another!" Shae's plea echoed through the cave.
Looking at her, Greyania could see the fierce determination in
her eyes, and it made her feel proud.

Greyania added, "We were sent by the Gods Who
Walk to see out the apocrita, because they are the only ones
with the knowledge to help us rebuild the amulet and the vessel. Will you help us?"

A moment passed before the reply came.

"Circumstances have changed. You will take the next
tunnel leading left, and then the third tunnel on the right.
From there a guide will meet you to take you the rest of the
way. As for your friend..."

"Is he dead?" Hunter looked worried.

"He is with Kovacik. Along with the vessel. Both are
safe."

Visible relief spread across his face, and Greyania let out a deep sigh she wasn't aware she had been holding in. She had no idea if any of the gods had a hand in this, but she was thankful nonetheless. At least their mission would not be a failure.

"When can we see him?" Hunter demanded.

"Kovacik...is temperamental. Easily aggravated. Come. Meet with us and we will explain as much as we are able."

Moving more quickly through the tunnels now that they had directions, they soon found themselves in a perfectly circular room, with no visible exit aside from the tunnel they had just stepped out of. In the cool, blue light from Shae's orb, the walls appeared completely smooth with no signs of any other entrance.

As they inspected their surroundings, part of the far wall slid downward to reveal a doorway, and one of the apocrita entered, carrying a short sword and moving in a jerky, uneven fashion. It's mandibles were moving constantly, and its eyes were jerking from one person to the next. It had four arms, the smaller set folded across its chest, and appeared to be wearing no clothing or armor.

Clicking and hissing noises emitted from the apocrita, but Greyania couldn't understand a thing it was trying to say, unsure if it was even communicating. One of its smaller arms reached up and adjusted something by its throat. It then spoke with the same tone as the voice they had encountered earlier. "Forgive me. I am forgotten to turn on this. Language difficult. No words with long era."

Greyania smiled softly. "That's alright. Are we to understand that we're the first outsiders to find you?"

"No and yes. Kovacik is outsider, but always here. Three plus one are new."

It took some getting used to, but she could get the meaning of what it was trying to convey. Whatever device it was using translated its language into one they could understand, but poorly.

"We have many questions," Shae said.

"Yes. Understood you could. Questions will wait. Must go."

"How do we know this is not a trap?" Hunter's eyes narrowed as his hand rested on the hilt of his broadsword.

The apocrita looked right at him and cocked its head, much like an animal would when it was trying to figure out its reflection in a mirror.

"Storm only trap. You still live."

"We believe you," Greyania said, the look on her face urging Hunter to stand down, "but we're just being cautious. Now, you said you know where our friend is? And the vessel?"

"Yes. As was stated, both with Kovacik."

"Who is Kovacik? Your leader?" Shae asked.

"Us tell after Council. After the Library." It promptly turned and skittered through the door and down some unseen hallway without waiting for the rest of them. Greyania knew the apocrita would be an odd race, but communication with them was bothersome. Catching up with the insect she insisted, "We don't need to see a library, we need to get to your city and speak with your leaders."

"Library *is* city. Come. Ahead travel much."

*****

"Sit. I've got to inspect Nixturjekur...make sure you didn't permanently damage it somehow."

"*Me* damage it?! You're the one who sent it crashing into the dirt like a fallen star!"

Kovacik just shook his head and let out a long sigh. He looked like he were going to lay into Rhikter again when his amulet started to pulse with a dull green light. Touching it, his eyes shone with the same light for a few moments, and then they dimmed with the amulet.

"Hate when they get a hold of me like that. Much prefer simple scrying. Less of a damn headache." He rubbed his temples and closed his eyes. "Bugs found your friends. All seem to be unharmed and are being taken to the Council."

At least we'll all be reunited soon, I hope. Rhikter took the seat that had originally been offered to him, leaned back, looked at Kovacik, and wondered what was going to happen next. Questions kept popping into his mind, and it took everything in him not to blurt them out all at once.

Kovacik looked at him and then threw his hands up in exasperation. "Go ahead! Ask your damned questions. I'll look over Nixturjekur as you do."

"First question: what in the hells is a kin? Never even *heard* of anything like you before."

"You aren't one to mince words, kid. I can respect that. Kin were the first race of the world."

"I thought all the races were created at the same time?"

"All the *mortal* races, yes. We came first by a few thousand years."

Rhikter's curiosity got the better of him and he pressed further, asking, "What happened?"

Kovacik removed his cloak, tossing it onto an empty seat, and pulled his gloves off. On his right hand was some kind of mechanical prosthetic, replacing two of the fingers. Even from across the room Rhikter could see the craftsmanship was second to none. Kovacik answered as he removed the mechanism from his hand and rubbed the place it had been.

"As for what happened...it's what *always* seems to happen before a downfall. Hubris. Our civilization was massive and powerful. Over time, we ascended beyond petty infighting and civil wars and began to truly master this world. Then, we grew bored."

Moving across the room, he pushed a button on some sort of machine and put a cup under the spigot. It filled with a clear liquid, which he then offered to Rhikter.

"I'm good." He held his hands up, refusing the drink.

"It's water. Take it."

Pushing the cup into his hands, Kovacik then went and got himself a glass and resumed his story.

"Now, we were created by the Behemoths, or what your lot tends to call the Gods Who Walk. We were so full of ourselves that we wanted to actually *see* our creators. We used magic and technology in ways you haven't even dreamed of, and we managed to give them corporeal form."

"You...your kind *made* them the Gods Who Walk." Rhikter couldn't hide the astonishment in his voice.

"Always thought that was a stupid name, but that we did. And *hells* did we ever pay for it. We thought we were so advanced and brilliant, giving them form, but they went mad from the process. For hundreds of years they roamed the world as beasts. It's why we made the vessels."

"I was told the vessels were made by the Gods and had some of their essence imbued into each one."

"Oh, their essence is there, but not by choice. Once we saw what we had done, we knew we had to protect ourselves. So we took what we could, when we could, and used it to build the power for the vessels. Obviously, it wasn't enough."

He looked over at the vessel, and a sadness came over him. Rhikter couldn't help but feel it as well. An entire race of people wiped out because they made a mistake.

"Enough of the history lesson," Kovacik continued.

"But, I have mo-"

"I said enough, kid. Right now I need to fix Nix's leg and see if I can get a new amulet."

"The amulets are what hold the essence, aren't they?"

Kovacik smiled and nodded. "Gemstones always had mystical properties, and higher quality ones can hold limitless power. Even among the amulets, Nixturjekur's was special. Instead of the essence from a singular Behemoth to draw from, it drew from them *all*. When I built it, I made the most powerful and dangerous weapon any of us had ever seen. Shame we never got to use it."

Rhikter paused before asking, "How did it all end?"

Standing and moving over to the vessel, Kovacik began to hammer at the knee joint where the steel met the unknown metal. After just a few strikes it fell off like it had been held on by wet paper instead of heavy welds. When Kovacik disappeared from sight, leaving him alone, he knew he wasn't going to get an answer.

After a few moments by himself, a glass cube on the table in front of him started to glow. It then changed colors from white to green, much like Kovacik's amulet had earlier.

"Kovacik! Something's happening out here," he called out to the kin, hoping he hadn't moved out of earshot. Whatever the object was, Rhikter didn't know if he should be sitting so close to it or not. He got up and moved a few feet away as Kovacik came back into view.

"What's got you riled up, kid?" He looked and noticed the item glowing and let out a growl. "Damned bugs. *Now* they decide to use the device. They better have a good reason for contacting me again."

As soon as Kovacik touched it, the color went from green to blue. A voice came from it, slightly distorted. It reminded Rhikter of how everyone tended to sound when he was inside of Coldfire.

"Kovacik. Have need of you in the Library. Council requires you share wisdom."

"No." He took the cube and put it back onto the table.

"Three we found, needing amule-" Kovacik swiped his hand across the top of the cube. The voice cut off and the glow faded.

"That voice...it said they had three. Were they talking about my companions? We have to get to this Library and Council immediately!"

"Fine, contact them, then. *You* are free to do what you wish. *We*," he motioned between himself and Rhikter, "are going nowhere." Sitting down in a nearby chair and folding his arms, Kovacik kicked his feet up and leaned back.

I don't need you to get me back with the others anyway. Rhikter shrugged, unfazed by Kovacik's reluctance to help. He reached forward and touched the object. Nothing happened. "Is...is there some trick to this?"

"Yep. Gotta be kin or apocrita to use it." He motioned towards the vessel. "I really don't need to be distracted by whatever trouble your friends and the bugs are getting into. I need to fix the vessel."

"Fix it for what?"

"Because it needs it! The state it is in is deplorable."

"And then I can take it back?"

"Take it back?! It's not even yours to begin with, kid!"

"Then why did *my* family have it?"

Rhikter was sure he had him there. Even though he wasn't sure how he was able to operate it, there had to be some reason it had been left in his family's charge. Even if Kovacik was lying about building it, he had known his surname. There had to be more to all of this.

Kovacik furrowed his brow, frowning and turning away instead of answering the question. *Did I hit a nerve?* Anxious to get some sort of positive resolution for himself out of the situation, Rhikter continued to pry.

"Why did my family have the vessel?"

Turning back to him, Kovacik pointed a finger at him. "I'm only telling you to shut you up. I let your family line *hold* Nixturjekur for me. I never *gave* it to them."

"We were just glorified stewards for you, then?"

"In a way, yes. The instructions were to wait until I returned for the vessel. Some...things happened over the centuries and by the time I was able to see what its status was, there was no sign of it. I figured it was a lost cause and gave up. Call this *happy providence* that we found one another so you could return it to me."

Something in his tone made Rhikter believe there was still more to the story.

"Alright, prove it," Rhikter stated. "Climb inside Coldfire and use it."

"*Nixturjekur*. And no. I have no need to activate it now, nor will I in the immediate future."

"I'll make you a deal. Get inside, fire it up, and I'll stop calling it Coldfire."

"This is ridiculous, kid. Finish your water, get some rest, and *maybe* I'll take you to the Council after."

Rhikter was on the right track, he just knew it. A few minutes ago Kovacik was ignoring his plea to see the others. Now he was offering to take Rhikter to them as a distraction from the actual conversation.

"Are the apocrita hostile?"

"Ha! Hostile as bookworms," Kovacik snorted.

"Then there is no rush to see my friends. Activate the vessel."

"This stopped being funny about ten seconds before you opened your mouth, kid. Drop it."

"You can't, can you?"

"I mean it."

Rhikter continued to press. "Prove me wrong then! Get inside the vessel and show me that you can operate it!"

"I SAID ENOUGH!"

A gout of flame escaped Kovacik's mouth, and had Rhikter been standing any closer, it would have engulfed his face. Startled he backed up, tripped over his chair, and landed on his ass. Crying out, in both pain and surprise, he sat there on the floor for a moment, dazed.

"Gods...look, sorry about that, kid. Let's just get you to the bugs and forget about all this."

Rhikter looked up at him, not backing down. "Something happened when my family took the vessel, and I have a right to know what."

Looking like he might send out another burst of flame, Kovacik balled his fists as he stared down at Rhikter. A moment later his whole body relaxed in resignation and he moved to sit back down.

"You just won't quit, will you? Alright, you get the story. The *whole* story. And I swear to each one of those gods-damned Behemoths that if you interrupt me..."

Rhikter held his hands up, palms out as he took a seat across from Kovacik. "You have my word; I won't so much as sneeze."

Kovacik narrowed his eyes and shook his head as he let out a sigh. He then stood and poured them each a fresh glass of water, downing his quickly.

"Wouldn't this be easier with some wine or something a bit harder?" Rhikter asked.

"I want a clear head for this, kid."

Kovacik looked right at Rhikter, but his gaze was distant. After a moment of silence, he began to speak.

TEN

Kovacik's Story

KOVACIK WIPED THE grease and dirt from his hands, and marveled at his latest creation. "Holy hells, you're a stunner. Just need to name you."

The machine was powered down, but every part of it shone brilliantly; the amount of care put into its construction was apparent. Hands on his hips, he thought of a proper name for what would probably be the finest vessel he'd ever created.

"Nixturjekur. *Perfect.*"

A couple of minutes later, a kin with dark purple scales rushed into his work space, gasping for breath. He turned and looked at the sudden arrival with trepidation. Why had his brother, Nothias, burst in like that?

"Easy there. What's got you so worked up, brother?"

"It's the Behemoths. They've...*done* something. It happened quite a few years ago, but with things in the state they are, we only just now learned of it."

Glancing back at his latest creation, Kovacik clenched his jaw. "They've been doing several *somethings* since we started to fight back."

"This is different. They're showing signs of intelligence again."

"Impossible. The ones who originally cast the spell told us the effects were irreversible. That's the whole reason we've been trying to fight them!"

"Kovacik, listen to me...the Behemoths...they've *created new races!*"

"They-they what?!"

"Not just a singular people, like us, but *several*. The Gathering believes they're going to use them as armies to finally wipe us out."

Throwing his cloth down on the ground, Kovacik began to pace. When they had first attempted to bring their gods to corporeal form, they had no idea the spell would drive them mad. Now that they were showing signs of possibly reverting to their former intelligence, the first thing they did was create more means to eradicate his people. *Or perhaps not...*

"Is that why they sent you? To see the progress on the newest vessel?"

His brother was hesitant, and answered without looking him in the eye. "Yes."

"These were designed for defense, not offense, and especially not to be used against sentient beings that may not know their purpose in all of this!"

"Brother, why else would they have made so many of them? If not to fight us, then to what end?"

"I don't know! We haven't been able to tell what their intent has been since we cast the damned spell. Communicating directly with them was the whole point of it in the first place! Look what it got us, Nothias. What remains of our civilization is limping along, waiting for the inevitable."

"It is not our place to question, brother. You speak with a free tongue, but even your skill as a smith cannot save you from judgement if they decree it."

"I've had enough of ultimatums and decrees from those who think they know best." He met his brother's gaze. "These new creatures...are they like our race was at first, or..."

"In a more civilized state? Indeed," his brother replied, finishing his question. "They even have villages and cities."

"Hm. Makes sense. None of our kind live on that continent, due to the Behemoths, and news travels slow in times such as these." He became lost in thought, contemplating the possibilities these new beings could present, whether good or bad.

"Kovacik," his brother stepped forward and put a hand on his shoulder, "about the vessel. If it's ready, they want it activated and ready to fight by nightfall."

Shaking his head Kovacik turned to the vessel and folded his arms, not bothering to face his brother as he spoke. Nothias' willingness to bow to whomever held power sickened him. Family was still family, however.

"Know what I was going to name this one?"

The silence that answered him caused him to turn his head to see if his brother was still there. He was, but wringing his hands together with an aura of worry about him.

"No. I don't."

"Nixturjekur."

His brother did little to hide his discomfort. "It is in poor taste to name a machine of war after father, Kovacik."

"It's poor taste to simply use these vessels as weapons, when they are capable of so much more. Instead of using them as cannon fodder, we could have used them to protect what we had left. Now there aren't enough and we'll end up dying for our shortsightedness."

"The Gathering said-"

"The Gathering can go to the hells and burn for all I care!"

"Brother! Speaking such heresy..."

Spinning and pointing a finger at his brother, he spat out his next words. "Don't you *dare* speak to me of heresy, Nothias. What we, as a people, did to the Behemoths *was* heretical. The outcome was abhorrent, and now we stand at the brink of our extinction and all they want to do is hold meetings and continue to *judge* those who still remain. I'm done with it. All of it. I'll not see another of my vessels turned to scrap."

"Surely you can't mean to leave. Where would you go, brother?"

"You said the new beings have a civilization? Perhaps we *are* meant to speak with them."

"The Gathering has a plan to end this, and seal away the Behemoths. But we need the last of the remaining vessels and their gems to do it, especially the Viezal."

"And if I refuse?"

Nothias moved closer to his brother, his voice taking on a suddenly hushed tone that surprised Kovacik. He'd never seen his brother so nervous.

"They'll kill you and take it." Nothias held up a hand, causing Kovacik's argument to die in his throat. He'd hear his brother out.

"You're my brother, and blood is thicker than politics. I came here to warn you. I knew you'd never hand over another vessel, especially one such as this...it is *magnificent*. Nor would I entrust the Viezal to anyone but you." Reaching into his pouch, he produced a small object covered in cloth. He took it and pressed it into Kovacik's hands and clasped his around them. Even without uncovering it, Kovacik knew it was the amulet. Power radiated from it. "Go. Talk to these creatures.

Try and figure out what the Behemoths are up to before we have nothing left to save."

"Come with me, Nothias," Kovacik pleaded. "Surely there is nothing left here that would keep you?"

"There is not...not anymore at least. But if I leave with you they will know something is amiss and come after us both. I cannot allow anything to happen to my little brother," Nothias smiled.

Kovacik looked at the amulet in his hand and then to his brother. Placing it into his pocket, he pulled him in for a strong embrace and patted his back. "For all your faults, you always knew when to do the right thing when it counted, Nothias."

"You better get going. I can only lie to cover for you for so long. And by everything that is holy, bring good news back."

"Just tell me where to go."

*****

As Kovacik winked in and out of existence, teleporting himself to the location his brother had told him, he couldn't help but marvel at the accomplishments he and his people had achieved over the millennia. Despite the rigorous moral and societal standards impressed upon every kin since birth, the wonders they had discovered or created were that to rival the Behemoths themselves.

No wonder we let it go to our heads. Thinking they were *equal* to those gods is what brought about this mess in the first place. Most kin were satisfied with the way things were, but the Gathering, which his family had always had a seat on, had nearly unanimously decided to bring them to life.

The spell itself was a simple one: bring the essence of the Behemoths to a singular spot and give them a physical

body. Several kin had volunteered for the 'privilege' of sacri-
ficing themselves to such a divine purpose. Initially, when the
spell was cast, it seemed like it had worked, and all his worry
and protest had been for naught.

But the bodies of the kin weren't strong enough to
withstand the sheer power of the gods, and they soon began to
mutate into giant, monstrous creatures. Acting as nothing
more than beasts, they turned the city of Frenshalto into ash.
Only quick thinking on Kovacik's part had spared him and his
brother.

Unfortunately, the rest of the Gathering was spared as well.
The kin had been fighting the Behemoths ever since. *No, fighting was the wrong word. Keeping them at bay.* The kin kept to one
side of the world and, eventually, so did the Behemoths. Re-
ports on them were spotty, and over time had dried up completely. In seventy years they had finally begun to rebuild.

But reminiscing was getting him nowhere, and he refo-
cused his thoughts to the task at hand. Nothias had told him
of a large settlement of a new race about two leagues from
here. He dared not teleport any closer, just in case they *were* an
army amassing to finally wipe out the rest of his kind.

Inside Nixturjekur, he took the amulet out and marveled at it. A deep blue, it seemed to glow whenever it caught
even a tiny bit of light. The night silver was expertly forged
and crafted; even he couldn't have done a better job. His
brother had always been the better jeweler. Placing it into an
indentation in the chest plate in front of him, the vessel
thrummed to life.

"Let's see if we can't find some new friends."

Finding the settlement wasn't as hard as he expected it
to be. What his brother had described sounded to be barely
more than a village. What he found, though, was far more advanced. There were homes, shops, stonework, a gated entrance; all the hallmarks of a flourishing civilization, not just a

pocket of brand new beings eking out an existence. *How long have we let things go without* really *taking a long hard look at the world?*

Isolation had helped keep them alive, but he felt suddenly dwarfed. Nothias had said there were multiple races, and he had no idea if they were all this advanced. Were some even further along?

One odd thing that stuck out to him was the street lighting. It looked so familiar, and yet he couldn't place it. Exiting Nixturjekur, he made sure to hide it within a thick cropping of trees to avoid detection. He placed the amulet into his pocket for safekeeping. No sense wearing it and putting it on display.

"Here we go," he muttered under his breath. As much as he hoped they would be friendly, and perhaps offer some insight as to what the Behemoths had been up to all this time, he knew he was taking a huge risk. He drew up his hood to help conceal his features without being too alarming. There was no doubt in his mind that he was the first kin to cross their doorstep.

Walking toward the main gate, as much as he tried, there was no shaking the knot in the pit of his stomach. In a matter of moments he'd either be on the other side of the barred door, or on the other end of a spear.

"Halt!" A guardsman approached from the side. "State your business, stranger. Friend or foe?"

Friend or foe? Do you really expect me to admit if I were a threat? Wait a moment...How can I understand them? He had expected to cast a small incantation to use their language once they had spoken to him. There was no time to speculate about the reasons behind his ability to understand them, though; the guard was waiting for an answer. He just hoped they'd be able to understand him as well. Keeping his head lowered to help obscure his face, he spoke in a low, even tone.

"I come in peace. I would hope to have a word with whomever is in charge of this settlement."

The man looked at him with scrutinizing eyes. These things had no scales, and the hue of this one's skin was pale. Looking at the other one, Kovacik saw his skin was dark as pitch. *So they have different colors, but nothing near the vibrancy of the kin. Guess the Behemoths ran out of pigment after us.* They also had hair or fur in odd places all over their heads. Just looking at it made Kovacik itch.

"Let me see your face, stranger."

Well, at least they could understand one another. Hoping for the best outcome, he took in a breath and held it as he lowered his hood and stood straight, looking the man in the eye. The guard's eyes went wide with surprise.

Here we go...

"I apologize, sir! We had no idea a kin would be coming tonight." Turning to the other guardsman, he barked out an order. "Open the blasted door!"

What in all the hells of Antembra is going on here? Curiosity gnawed at his mind. Other kin had visited this settlement? Maybe the scouting party that had discovered it also made some form of contact? It made some sense; protocol for such an event had yet to be invented, simply because introductions with a new race had never been necessary or anticipated. If that were true, however, why was more information not shared with the rest of the Gathering? With his brother?

Grunting and the sound of wood sliding on wood came from the other side of the door, and a moment later it swung open. An imposing figure wearing polished armor and a flowing green cape stood with his hand resting on the hilt of the sword at his side. The craftsmanship of his gear was average, at kin standards, but again, leaps and bounds ahead of what he was expecting. The man nodded at him, looking poised to leap into combat, if need be.

"I am Captain Gherald Lehmann. I will be escorting you to the Lord Regent Adalgar Lehmann. We were not expecting your visit until tomorrow. Where is the kin we normally receive?"

Such pompous sounding titles...apparently ego is not a trait inherent to only kin. None of this was expected. The only choice was to play along. If he admitted to not being who they thought he was, they could turn hostile and think him a spy, or worse. The die had been cast and he needed to see this through.

"I was sent at the last moment. I'm not even sure who I've replaced, to be honest. It is why I come a day early and at such a late hour. I need to speak with the Lord Regent immediately to get things back up to speed."

Lying was an art form. The trick was to believe in the lie as much as you wanted others to believe in it. The captain scrutinized him for a moment, and then nodded, seemingly satisfied with the explanation.

"Right this way. We'll wake him at once."

Present Day

"Two things I need to know," Rhikter interjected.

"What in the hells did I say about interrupting me?"

Rhikter folded his arms and frowned. He wanted the story to continue, especially after Kovacik dropped the name of the Lord Regent, but there were two glaring things that just seemed too big to ignore without some better explanation.

"First of all, did you ever figure out how you understood one another? You're speaking common tongue to me now."

"I'm getting there. You just need to be more *patient.*"

"Fair enough. The bigger question I have right now is, how on earth did humanity advance to the state they were in in just *seventy years*?!"

Kovacik grinned, but it didn't seem to be an amused one.

"The Behemoths gave the kin meager beginnings. We used to live in caves like animals before we started to evolve intellect and reason. No one knows exactly why, aside from the Behemoths, but with the new races they...sped up the process."

Rhikter was confused. "Ever since I was a child I was told all the races of the world came from those meager beginnings as well, and grew into what they are today."

Kovacik shook his head. "The Behemoths borrowed a lot of what they had learned from making the kin and implemented it on an accelerated pace. They gave you intellect and reason right from the start, and even gave you some kin technology and abilities, such as the aptitude for magic. Best I could gather, from speaking with each of the races, some kind of communal memory was implanted deep within your minds to hide this fast-paced growth."

The information was a lot to swallow and Rhikter wasn't even sure he understood it all. Apparently the origin of his race, and the others, was some lie they had been spoon fed.

"How do you know all this?"

"Honestly? *Let me tell my story*! Even then, it was never fully clear why things happened as they did. A lot of what I just said is educated guesswork, really."

Pouring himself a fresh glass of water, he drank it and looked at Rhikter with an annoyed gaze. "Now, are you going to let me finish or do we just stop here?"

Nodding his agreement, Rhikter took his cup and poured himself a fresh glass of water as well, suddenly noticing how thirsty he still was. Abrasive attitude aside, Kovacik spun a great story, and he honestly couldn't wait to find out the next part.

The Past

The home of the Lord Regent wasn't as immense as expected. It was a modest dwelling with several rooms he couldn't see into, a set of stairs leading to a second story, what he presumed was a kitchen towards the back, and a den just to the left of the foyer. Nothing like the homes of the members of the Gathering. Opulent didn't even *begin* to describe their tastes in decoration and furnishings. This was actually functional, and he found it refreshing. Captain Gherald led the way towards the den, which doubled as a small library.

"The Lord Regent will be with you shortly..." The captain looked at him expectantly. Kovacik realized he hadn't introduced himself.

"My name is Kovacik."

"Kovacik." The captain gave a curt nod, and then disappeared down one of the hallways.

How in the hells do they have so many books? Inquisitive nature getting the better of him, Kovacik perused the titles as he waited. Most of the books were written in the language of this new race, but there were several that were of kin origin. Some were considered dangerous due to their heretical nature, and were forbidden. *Gods, they even have some of our spell books.* Seeing all that kin literature among the rest of the other books confirmed his biggest fear.

It wasn't a scouting party, but someone in a position of power, who had reached out to these creatures. Someone working in tandem with them. *But to what end? Why would a kin be giving these things spell books?*

"Your predecessor did the same thing, you know," a voice behind him spoke up. "Looked at the books with amazement the first time she was here. She never told me *why*, though."

Ignoring the implied question, Kovacik turned to face the man. His features were incredibly similar to the captain's, but appeared much older. If he had to guess, he would say the Lord Regent was Gherald's father, or much older brother.

"Lord Regent." Kovacik gave a curt nod, the same one the captain had given him, assuming it was their way of greeting others. Lehmann walked over and extended his hand. Rising, Kovacik looked at it, unsure of what it meant. Taking a guess, he extended his hand in the same way and the other man took it and shook it vigorously.

"Please, call me Adalgar. Had I known one of the kin was coming tonight, I would have prepared a feast! Please, take a seat." Gesturing towards one of the chairs in the den, he moved to pour two glasses of a dark red liquid. He handed one to Kovacik and then took a sip from his own glass.

Kovacik had never encountered a drink quite like this before. He could tell it was some form of alcohol, but the scent seemed much sweeter than kin spirits. Tasting it, he found he rather liked it, and downed the whole glass.

The man just smiled, and chuckled softly to himself. Kovacik wondered if he was supposed to have drunk the liquid so quickly. *Focus.* He was spending too much time getting hung up on minor details instead of learning what he needed to know.

"Tell me, my predecessor, who was she?"

The man's features hardened, as he placed his own glass down and folded his arms. His tone became accusatory. "Shouldn't you know that? *You* replaced her."

"Yes, true, but this was all poorly planned and I'm as confused as you are by my visit. I didn't have enough time to properly prepare myself, and if I could just know her name, I'll know exactly what to do." Long-winded, but exact. He hoped the man would buy the lie and give him something to go on when he returned to Nothias.

"Ah, well, that is troubling. It was a kin by the name of Festocina."

It was difficult to hide the on his face shock at that revelation. Festocina was not only a member of the Gathering, but sat as the ruling head. She was also one of the most powerful spell casters to ever have lived; she was the one who originally developed the plan and the spell to bring the Behemoths to Antembra in corporeal form.

To say he distrusted and despised her was an understatement. Corrupt and hungry for power, though none dared to confront her on it, she had plotted and schemed her way to her position. Apparently ruling over the kin was not enough; she had designs on controlling whatever these creatures were as well.

Having nothing to lose, and needing solid proof to take to the Gathering, he decided to be truthful with Adalgar. Assessing his exit strategy, should the encounter take a turn for the worse, he was about to speak when the man beat him to it.

"You're not her replacement, are you?"

"No...How could you tell?"

"Just mentioning her name caused your entire demeanor to change. Your eyes went a bit wider and you instantly clenched your jaw. Also, she spoke as if she were the ruler of your people. Hardly someone you *replace*."

Fight my way out it is, then. Balling his fist, Kovacik began to stand but the man raised a hand to stop him.

"Believe it or not, I am not your enemy. Seeing your reaction, however, proves to me we share a common one. I'm thankful not all kin are like her. Humanity would not have lasted much longer if that were true."

Humanity. Interesting name for a race.

He continued. "You must have questions, and reasons, for coming here. I will answer them all to the best of my ability."

"You originally seemed rather pleased I had come, with talk of feasts."

"Ha! I'm a politician. I know how to court disaster and keep it from bringing down its full wrath. I'd make for a terrible leader if I ended up inadvertently damming our settlement after a few hundred years of growth."

"Few...*hundred*?"

"Yes. We originally came from the mountain regions to the north, and settled here a few hundred years ago. We've built a thriving community and have trade with several other settlements in the nearby regions. Dwarf, orc, elf, other humans...we trade with them all."

"That is impossible. You and your people *can't* have been here that long."

"I can assure you, we've been here for far longer than that. In fact-"

Captain Gherald burst into the room, interrupting Adalgar. "Father! The monarox is back!"

"Damn it all to hells!" Adalgar exclaimed.

Kovacik was confused. "What is a monarox?"

Both men looked at him as if he'd suddenly sprouted a second head. Not waiting to explain it to him, they ran out of the room. Still needing answers, Kovacik followed after.

"Are there no monstrous beasts where you're from?" the captain asked him.

"Nothing by that name," he responded, hurrying to catch up with the men.

Arriving back at the main gate, the two guards from earlier were now on the inside and the one he had first spoken with ran up to the captain. Giving a salute, the guard quickly brought them all up to speed.

"Sir! The creature was spotted about ten minutes ago. At first we thought it was simply going to continue back into the forest, but it suddenly changed its direction and came straight for the gate. We barely made it back inside before it began to-"

Something massive hit the gate with enough force to cause the ground to tremble. Kovacik cursed himself for leaving Nixturjekur hidden on the other side. No doubt the vessel could make short work of whatever was trying to break in.

"-do that," the guard finished his sentence. "We've never seen it so agitated before."

Adalgar cursed. "Will that damned thing hold?"

"It should. It did the last time the monarox decided to attack."

"That was over five years ago, soldier! And that time, it didn't give up until we drove it back, losing good men in the process!"

The door and ground shook again as the creature rammed it once more. A guttural, deep cry echoed through the night as it continued its assault, causing the blood to freeze in Kovacik's veins. *Surely this was created by the Behemoths, but to what end?*

The next two hits caused the massive beam locking the gate shut to crack.

"Brace that! Now!" Captain Gherald ran forward, helping others place support beams against the gate to try and secure it in place. Again, the creature cried out, and then everything stopped. For a few tense moments, the night became eerily silent. That was when Kovacik noticed the clawed hand grasping the outer wall, pulling something massive behind it.

"Over there!" He pointed and shouted.

"By the Gods! It's scaling the wall!"

"Impossible!" Someone shouted. "It's twenty sheer feet!"

"Defend the town at all costs!" Another cried.

Kovacik watched as a dark bulk hoisted itself over the wall, sailed through the air with unnatural grace and ease, and landed with a thunderous slam. His mind could barely comprehend what he saw before him.

The skin was dark purple, with patches of thick, dirty hair sparsely scattered across its hide. Kovacik could tell the creature was normally covered in fur, but it seemed to be suffering from an extreme case of mange. Short stubby legs held up the massive bulk of the torso with assistance from the arms. Comically long, they ended in clawed hands that were curled inward, with the knuckles resting on the ground.

Most terrifying was the thing's face. Folds of skin and fat seemed to be pulling the features downward, surrounding a nasty looking serrated beak. A single, black eye dominated the forehead. This was no creation of a kind or benevolent god. This was an abomination straight from the hells. When it screamed in rage, Kovacik felt like his soul was under siege.

Not waiting for a call to attack, several of the nearby soldiers rushed it, weapons drawn. Those looking for glory or a swift victory, and not paying attention, were cast aside with a single swipe, with one man crushed against the wall like an over-ripe berry. The smarter attackers used spears to bait and prod, trying to distract the creature from attacking those with swords as the second wave approached.

"Can you fight?" Adalgar turned to him as he drew his sword.

"Yes, I can hold my own." Kovacik nodded, hand going for the hilt of his sword.

"Then prove I can trust you, and help us kill this thing!"

Not waiting for a reply, Adalgar rushed forward with his son, as the monarox was trying to bat away the spearmen. It had managed to grab one of the spears and shove it back against the soldier, piercing him with the blunt end. It then lifted both spear and man and tossed him at the others, knocking several back. It turned just in time for Adalgar to stab it in its side.

It cried out in pain, swiping at the trio, its focus on them now. Kovacik barely managed to keep a claw from lopping off his head. He couldn't tell if they were sharp or dulled, but he didn't care to find out. Instinct taking over as much as his training, he swiped at it and managed to cut off the claw and part of the finger as well. Howling, it pulled back the hand just as Adalgar went in for another strike.

Kovacik saw it coming and tried to cry out, but a clawed hand scooped up the human quickly, using him as a shield against Gherald's attacks. If they didn't act quickly, Adalgar would surely die.

Uttering a few words of magic, Kovacik touched the blade with his finger, drawing a small bit of blood. Immediately the sword burst into green fire, which caught the creature's attention and mesmerized it for a moment. The distraction was enough for Gherald to strike, slicing the tendons of the elbow, and nearly cutting off the arm that held his father.

Impossibly, the arm did not falter, nor did the creature utter a cry. Surprised that his blow had not landed as true as he'd thought, Gherald was caught off guard when the creature leapt over to Kovacik. It tossed Adalgar like a bored child would discard a toy, and his body sailed through the night sky, landing behind a nearby building. Kovacik wasted no time communicating with Gherald.

Go help your father!

Wha...how are you–

GO!

Gherald turned and ran, a few of the men following. Kovacik readied his blade, adopting the stance his father had taught him to use when fighting an opponent of greater strength. Although he had a feeling his father never intended for that opponent to be at least double his size.

"Kooooovvvaaaaacccciiiik."

It *spoke* his name. How in all creation could it know his name? Trying to not let that unnerve him, he ran forward to strike, eyes watching the arms, body ready to dodge out of their way.

The creature did nothing to defend itself as he jumped and buried the blade deep into its belly, his weight causing the sword to tear down through its body, gutting the creature in the process. Viscous, foul-smelling, black blood and offal poured forth, covering him, as he dealt the mortal blow. Gagging at the stench, he nearly vomited as he freed himself.

Even with such a strike, the creature did not falter. Instead, its single eye started to glow brightly, and Kovacik could see a form within it. Anger overtook him as he saw it was Festocina.

"Kovacik. I never thought you a *fool*. No matter. I had hoped to find you here with the vessel. Pity. Nothias was mistaken it seems. This will affect the ritual..."

"What ritual? What are you talking about?"

"The humans were to help us, far more than they imagined, and your newest vessel was to be the linchpin in all of this. With it, I could have started the Binding tonight."

"What have you done with Nothias?!" His mind raced, panic and fear gripping him, as he worried for his brother's safety.

Ignoring his plea, she continued. "In the end, I suppose it matters not. I've struck a deal and once we find a way to complete the Binding, all kin will *revel* in our birthright once again."

"Where is my brother?!" he screamed, throwing his sword at the eye, piercing it and causing it to explode in a burst of magical energy. As the spell was broken, the creature suddenly regained itself and screamed as it fell over, limbs contracting and jerking as death quickly overtook it. He felt a pang of sympathy for the beast; as dangerous as it was, it was just a pawn in all this.

Pulling his sword from the eye socket, he turned over to where Adalgar had been thrown, hoping for the best. It took him a few moments to catch up with the group. Gherald was kneeling at his father's side, comforting him. Even without knowing much about these humans, Kovacik could tell his injuries would prove fatal. When Adalgar saw Kovacik, he waved the kin over.

"The...monarox? We heard a scream..."

"Dead. It was sent by Festocina to find me. I am the reason for what happened here tonight."

Shame overtook him. Had he been more careful, perhaps brought the vessel with him, so much death could have been avoided.

"Nonsense." Adalgar started to cough violently, spatters of blood escaping his mouth, hitting his chin and chest.

"Whether or not it came for you...*you* stopped it. For that we are...thankful. There is so much...to tell you, but you need to know what...Festocina planned." The more he spoke, the more pained his breathing became.

"Father, please...you need your strength." Gherald turned and yelled at the gathered men. "Where in the hells is that damned healer?!"

"He needs to know the...deal we struck."

"Deal?" Both Kovacik and Gherald asked the same thing.

"We...we were to be spared...as long as we swore fealty..."

"Spared from what? My people are hardly in any position to wage conquest. We're still recovering from our war with the Behemoths."

"Her end game. We were to be spared...from..."

His eyelids fluttered, he exhaled suddenly, and his head lolled back.

"Father? Father!!"

His son shook the body, but it was too late; the man had passed. Captain Gherald held the body close, and he began to weep. Aside from his occasional sobs, they were enveloped in silence. Kovacik was the first to break it, placing his hand on Gherald's shoulder.

"He's gone. We need to talk."

Composing himself, Gherald closed his father's eyelids, gingerly placed him down onto the ground, and rose. He turned to one of the soldiers.

"Take him home and send for the priests to perform the funeral rites."

"At once, Lord Regent."

He paused at the new title, and frowned. It was obviously not the way he'd wished to inherit the position. Kovacik waited until they were alone before he spoke, hoping his plan would work.

"I'm sorry for your father and your loss, but you need to do something for me."

"I'm not in the mood to do *you* any favors. Your kind brought this destruction to us, and while my father may have trusted you in such a short time, I do not."

"I don't give a flying damn if you trust me or not. You weren't there when Festocina spoke to me through that...thing."

Gherald stared hard at Kovacik before asking, "What did she say?"

Kovacik repeated everything that happened, growing more and more furious as he thought of his brother. It was nigh impossible that he would still be alive, so his true focus now was vengeance. He hoped Gherald shared the sentiment.

"Alright, so what is this favor, then?"

"You need to take Nixturjekur, the vessel. I can ward it from her, tune it so only your bloodline can operate it, but it needs to remain hidden. Without the vessel it's possible that whatever she's planning can't happen."

"Do you really think it will work?"

"Nixturjekur is the most powerful thing I've ever created, and that's even *without* the amulet empowering it. With it out of the equation I don't think her plans, whatever they are, can come to fruition."

"And if she comes to look for it? If she can control a creature like the monarox from such a distance, what hope would we have against her?"

"She may, she may not. Either way it's the only solution I can think of right now to our mutual problem. If she does come, you can at least try and use Nixturjekur against her."

Frowning, Gherald shook his head slowly. "It seems I have no choice."

"Glad you understand."

Present Day

"So, I retrieved Nixturjekur, warded it from detection, and attuned the amulet and vessel to your family's bloodline. Over the years they rose to become the first *true* royal family. That, however, you should already know."

Rhikter was enraptured with the story, but he still had one burning question

"You said you would tell me what also happened to your people. So what *did* happen?"

Kovacik hesitated, before sighing and answering.

"I don't know, exactly. Two days later, since it took that long to simply get everything sorted, I blacked out. According to Gherald, I turned as white as a ghost, uttered something in my native tongue that they couldn't understand, and just collapsed. When I came to, I knew something was wrong. *Very* wrong. I instantly teleported back home and found the Spire deserted. My brother, and then Festocina's mocking message through the beast, were the last interactions I've had with any kin since."

"Gods...and you've been alone this entire time?"

"I tried to acclimate. But the wounds of losing your entire people run deep and I eventually gave up on it. The apocrita had adopted the ruins of the Spire as their home, and I hadn't the will or the resources to evict them. They tend to respect my privacy because of who and what I am, so we have an understanding."

"That was some story."

"I'm sure I embellished. My memory is not what it used to be, kid."

Rising, he moved over to the object on the table, tapped it twice and waited for it to glow green.

"I would have audience with the Council, now."

"Ah, Kovacik. We will expect you."

The glow faded again as Rhikter rose out of his seat. Stretching and yawning despite himself, he laughed as Kovacik frowned.

"Gods, it wasn't that bad of a story, was it?" Kovacik got up. "Come on, we've got some bugs to talk to."

Slapping Rhikter on the back, he uttered a few words and they were both immediately teleported into the Library.

ELEVEN

"I DO NOT understand why they are keeping us here. They have already told us Rhik is alive, and that he still has Coldfire. Why can they not take us to him, or bring him to us?"

"I don't know why either, Hunter. We should still be thankful that they weren't hostile." Greyania rubbed her temples as she looked around the room. They had been waiting for what seemed like hours before they received the full story about Rhikter. The relief Hunter felt was palpable, and it put them all into much better spirits. She was especially pleased to know the Behemoth Vessel was unharmed.

When the apocrita they had met in the caverns escorted them out, they didn't fully understand that the entire city was indeed something of a library. Books, scrolls, lost tomes of all manner and type were everywhere they looked. According to their guide, however, where they were going housed the most important and precious volumes.

The foyer they had been instructed to wait in was still a grand and impressive area, with the walls lined with books of various sizes. Part of her desperately wanted to peruse them, but they had been instructed to touch nothing until they had met with the Council. Respecting their wishes and customs was easy enough, but after several hours she couldn't help but wonder if they would ever *actually* meet this Council.

Looking over at Hunter and Shae, she could tell they were also getting restless. The good news about Rhikter and the vessel had given them all a boost, but it soon wore off as they were left to do nothing but wait. They couldn't even occupy their minds by cleaning their weapons, as they had all been confiscated. While she didn't normally carry much, and relied mostly on her magical ability, being without her dagger made her feel vulnerable. A feeling she did not relish.

"Excuse me, can you please tell us when we will meet with the Council? We grow tired of this endless waiting."

Shae was badgering the guards that had been assigned to them again. It wasn't the first time she had asked them how much longer, and every time she did, she managed to word it differently.

The guard held a small device up to its throat and spoke. "Council meet with you when it is decreed. No sooner. Friend on way with Kovacik."

"Who's Kovacik? Is he part of the Council?" Shae asked.

"Kovacik is part of none. Kovacik is kin."

"Useless!" Throwing her hands up, Shae walked over towards Greyania. "M'lady, you should talk to them. Perhaps they will listen to you and stop being so cryptic."

"I don't think it's intentional. It's a miracle we can even communicate with them at all. Whatever that device is, it translates their words immediately into something intelligible for our ears. I wonder if they would let us have one..."

"Is now really the time for interest in trinkets? What if this 'kin' of theirs is dangerous and has done something to the vessel or Rhik? What then?" Hunter inserted himself into the conversation.

"Hunter," Shae sighed out, "I highly doubt they would tell us he was safe only to harm him. Greyania?"

"I agree. Rhikter's safety is important, and they know that. We just need to trust that our hosts are being honest with us, and hope that he arrives soon so we can continue onward."

Having focus kept Greyania's mind sharp. When they had thought the mission lost, she had felt so devoid of purpose that she wondered if she could even go on. The stark realization that this mission, and the end result, were all that were motivating her was a harrowing one. The unfortunate reality of it was made even more acute by her improved mood once they learned that Rhikter and the vessel were fine.

What happens when we are successful? What will I do with myself then? She thought to herself, doubt creeping into her mind. When the doors to the foyer flew open, she welcomed the distraction.

Three apocrita, Rhikter, and a humanoid she'd never seen before all entered. Hunter bounded over to his friend and embraced him, lifting him off the ground. Greyania swore she heard a slight crack as he hugged the smaller man.

"Gah! Easy there, big guy, or this will be a short-lived reunion!"

Her main focus, however, was the one who came in with them. He was incredibly similar to a sincit, but without the protruding snout. His gaze met hers and he immediately came over.

"I take it you're Greyania? Rhikter told me you're the one I should speak with about the vessel."

Just what in the world was he? She had never even heard of a race close to what he was, aside from the sincit. Also, the way he carried himself and the way he was dressed proved that he was as far from their ilk as she was. So many questions flooded her mind, and she pondered the best way to interrogate this new being without coming across as invasive.

"You think any harder, you're going to break something."

His words broke her out of the stupor she had found herself in and she shook it off, giving a friendly smile and attempting to play it off.

"I was just distracted by seeing Rhikter alive and well. When we last saw him, it seemed doubtful we'd ever see him or Coldfire again."

He frowned slightly, speaking in a louder voice so everyone nearby could hear, "I'm only gonna say this once: It's *not* called Coldfire. The vessel's name is *Nixturjekur*." Shaking his head he muttered to himself, barely audible, "Coldfire. A *youngling* could've named it better."

He not only knew about the vessel, but also presumed to rename it? Opening her mouth to protest, she was stopped by Rhikter.

"It's a long story, Greyania, but he's right. The vessel *is* named Nixturjekur, and if he'll tell his story again, you'll see why he's so adamant about it."

Rolling his eyes, Kovacik let out a long, drawn out sigh. "Holy hells. I should've just kept my damned mouth shut. Alright. Since you saw fit to put it out there, kid, may as well get the rest of you up to speed, or I'll be answering questions until I lose my mind."

*****

Shock. Being in shock was the best way to describe how Greyania felt the moment Kovacik ended his story. Not only had she learned that the races of the world were not the first created by the Gods Who Walk, but also that they had *not* created the vessels. Her mind rebelled against the notion, telling her Kovacik was a liar and knew nothing of what she knew.

Had he communed with the Gods themselves? Been in direct contact with one for most of his life? The more her mind fought against the ideas he brought forth, the more the rational side of her put forth the fact that he had no reason to lie. What could he possibly gain from this? His knowledge of certain things was hard to deny as well.

If his words were indeed true, then it meant the entire timeline of history was wrong, and the Gods had lied to her. There was so much more here than simply trying to atone for a failed spell.

"What now?" Shae was looking at her, her eyes filled with doubt. The woman was seeking answers Greyania could hardly provide. Only Rhikter and Hunter appeared unfazed by these revelations. If they only knew the true ramifications of Kovacik's story.

"How do we know you speak the truth? How can we possibly believe this isn't some elaborate lie you've concocted to further your own ends, whatever they may be?" Greyania did nothing to hide her accusatory tone.

"Frankly, you don't. I don't give a damn one way or the other if you believe me or not. However, my goal here is not to appease your smug sense of self-righteousness in your *divine mission*, but to figure out why the Behemoths want my vessel at full power again so badly, and why they've sent you four to do it."

"That is none of your concern," Greyania stated.

"Since I built it, I think that makes it *expressly* my concern. The last time this vessel was in high demand, the kin were wiped out. If you don't, *or won't*, question this whole thing, you're a damned fool."

"How dare you speak to her that way!" Shae jumped to her feet, shouting at Kovacik. "She is acting under direct orders from both the Gods Who Walk and the elders of my clan. Who are *you* to question such authority?"

If he was upset or insulted by Shae's words, he gave no indication Greyania could detect. He simply folded his arms, leaned back in his chair, and smirked. The sheer audacity of his demeanor only infuriated Shae further.

"Do you think this is some game?!" she yelled at him.

"I had heard the elves had changed. More volatile, passionate...This is a good thing. I thought your race was rather droll and bland before. But you? You have fire."

"You stinking piece of-"

"Shae. That is enough. We are not here to trade barbs and insults." Biting her own tongue to keep from doing just that, Greyania turned to Kovacik and frowned. "I expect the same from you. We are not mere children for you to bully or belittle."

"Alright, fair enough. I suppose I was being unkind, and I'll admit to that. But you're not getting a new amulet *or* the vessel back until you tell me exactly what it is you want with it."

"That is not for me to say. As for the amulet, I'm sure the apocrita will aid us once I plead our case."

He shook his head, his body language changing. His shoulders slumped slightly and he narrowed his eyes. The way he looked at her made her feel that even if the apocrita were to listen to their case, they wouldn't help.

"The bugs won't do it," Kovacik said.

"I'm sure that if they just underst-"

"They *can't* do it," he further insisted.

"Meaning what, exactly?" Rhikter seemed genuinely interested, but Greyania had a feeling she already knew the answer to the question.

"Meaning," Kovacik explained, "they have all the information on how to do it, sure. But they don't have the skill of the ability to *actually* carry it out. Only one being in all of Antembra does, and you're looking at him."

"And you will not do it unless we tell you what you wish to know."

"The orc pays attention. You all could stand to learn from him."

Greyania let out a short, curt sigh. "Enough with the passive insults. Being the last of an ancient race, you could show more decorum."

He sat up at that, unfolding his arms, and leaned forward. He rested his elbows on the table and interlinked his fingers together, then leaned his face against his hands as he looked at her. His gaze was unnerving, but not invasive. It felt like he was pondering something about her she wasn't yet aware of.

"The Behemoths picked you for a reason. You tell me why, and why they want the vessel, and I'll make Nixturjekur as powerful as I am able."

Tell him.

The voice in her mind caught her off guard, and Greyania could only stammer as she processed the command. It had been nearly two hundred years since the Gods Who Walk made themselves known to her, and she had been so sure they would not wish this kin privy to the reasons why she was chosen, nor their ultimate plans for the vessel. Yet, Gron'Tul was in her mind, urging her to do just that.

Do you understand what he's asking of me? Of you?

Of course. You dare to question my will in this? If this is the only way to get the vessel fully functional then so be it.

Gone just as soon as it had arrived, the voice left her in silence and she hesitated. Not even Shae knew the full story of how she came to serve them, or why they needed the vessel.

She spoke softly, meeting Kovacik's eyes with her own. "Very well. Do I have your word?"

"That you do. A kin never breaks an agreement."

A sudden wave of shame washed over her as she remembered her hand in things. Swallowing it down, she took in a ragged breath and let it out slowly, calming herself.

"I am the reason the world is broken, and the vessel is the only thing that can help fix it."

Kovacik showed far more interest and emotion in the next few seconds than he had in the entire time since they had met him. He slapped both hands onto the table and leaned forward.

"You're the damned fool that nearly killed us all?!"

"Greyania...*you* performed the Unbinding?"

All eyes, save Hunter's, were on her, and their combined gazes burned into her skin like coals from a roaring fire. Looking down to avoid their judgmental looks, she continued.

"I mean exactly what I just said. I performed the ritual, the Unbinding, and something went wrong."

"Something went *wrong*? The something nearly destroyed Antembra!" Kovacik exclaimed.

She looked up, feeling sick to her stomach and feeling her eyes begin to grow wet from emotion. The only face that was not shocked or repulsed was Hunter's, and she was eternally grateful for that.

"I only tell you all this because Gron'Tul has told me to do so. Otherwise, as the Gods decreed when this all began, none of you would know any of this."

She started from the beginning with the visions she had received as a child, which lasted into her adulthood and shaped and molded her into the sorceress she was now. When the Gods Who Walk came to her with a task, she was more than eager to repay their tutelage in magic with anything they required.

"Several of the gods worked to fashion a new spell that would undo their imprisonment. Unfortunately, since they were sealed with blood magic, only blood magic could be used to free them. A spell that powerful required...a sacrifice. A *living* sacrifice."

"You *sacrificed* someone?" Shae sounded like she was becoming ill, and Greyania couldn't bear to look at her. She hoped that after she was done telling her story the elf wouldn't think less of her for too long, and that she would eventually, somehow, forgive her for these transgressions.

"They demanded it. Blood magic could only be undone by blood magic, so I had to follow their instructions to the letter. To empower the spell I..."

"You had to torture whomever you used as the catalyst." Kovacik's correct interruption surprised her, but she nodded in agreement.

He continued, explaining it for the others. "Blood magic is volatile, but potentially the most powerful type of magic. Despite its name, it feeds on and uses life force more than actual blood. So the more you torture a life beyond what would normally break it, the more you enhance the spell. How long did you keep them?"

Greyania hesitated. "Forty years. We kept him at the threshold of death for nearly forty years."

Despite the others and their reactions, the look on Kovacik's face, of sheer horror and revulsion at what she had done, struck her as particularly devastating. Even though Shae was an accomplished spell caster in her own right, she'd had minimal experience in this type of magic. The kin knew far more than she had anticipated.

"However, he somehow took control of the spell by killing himself before I could complete it, and possessed one of the Gods Who Walk. It also caused the world to shift and become what it is now. The Gods remain in their prisons to keep the spell in a kind of hiatus, keeping it from fully destroying the world."

"Tell me everything you did and said. Now!" Kovacik demanded as he stood and moved towards her.

"I...They told me to prepare him for the ritual," she stated. "I was to take a piece of bone from their long dead brother, Res'Kel, and grind it down to dust. Then I was to combine it with blood they supplied, from every race that they had created."

"What were the words? Tell me the incantation."

She tried to recall exactly what she had said, but it was hazy. Why was Kovacik pushing so hard for the exact details of what she did? What could he possibly gain?

"Kovacik, is that really necessary? She is suffering enough by reliving it," Hunter pleaded with the kin, and again she felt appreciative of his support.

"You don't understand. *None of you do.* Blood magic is powerful but the spells are rarely multi-faceted. If this one was, it means damn well *anything* could have been added. You need to try and remember the words, exactly. They have no power, not without the catalyst."

His tone had softened, but the fire and urgency in his eyes remained. It had been decades since she had felt so powerless, and she hated it. She hated him for making her feel this way, but deep down she knew it was her own actions that led her to this.

Closing her eyes, she focused. Using every bit of her will, she forced herself to face that night again, working backwards from when she crawled out from the catacombs to when she had begun the ritual. The words felt close enough to touch, and she reached for them with everything she had. Why were they so difficult to recall? Just as it seemed they would slip away from her mind again, a burst of clarity hit her and her eyes shot open.

"Et donga ut et Entranthas, yar les ay nok'lot. Ay nok'lot fet hux'ka fyr'gr'. Slo'fyr tue yershalwa hux'ka ve!

Komplux et zer'fy' Husticar ru et Ent'Tra wu fet ke vishe hu drosh dubl."

"Are you *absolutely positive* those are the words you used?"

"There is no doubt in my mind."

"Do you know what they mean? Did the Behemoths ever tell you?"

"The Gods never told me. I was instructed to recite the spell as it was written. Do you know what it means?"

"It's Kintare. *My* language. Roughly it goes: the bone of the dead god serves as a key. A key that must be reformed. Blood and conviction must be one! Sacrifice the withered husk to the dead god so that he alone may walk again." Sitting heavily, he continued. "You never realized what happened, did you? The Withered King never stole the spell out from under you. What happened is *exactly* what was supposed to."

Greyania was shocked. "That's impossible! The Gods would have never-"

Kovacik interrupted her. "The mixture was to enhance his body for possession. It was a key to allow Res'Kel to inhabit the body and take over the spell! Did the Behemoths know what spell you used? You said more than one concocted it."

"Yes, but only one came to me with the actual spell..."

We need to speak.

Gron'Tul's voice surged into her mind and was full of urgency and rage.

But the others, I can't just leave them.

Then you will all speak with us. Now!

In the blink of an eye, Greyania and the other four were in the same surreal mindscape she had visited before. Seated at the onyx table were the Gods Who Walk, all in a heated debate, minus two.

Deghat and Jek were nowhere to be seen.

TWEL VE

"THE OTHERS HAVE sent for us."

"Yes, but they can wait. We always rush to their side when they command it. Always rush rush rushing."

"What if it is important?"

"Then they will force us. Yes yes, and we will have no choice. Until then? We rest. Yes, rest rest rest."

Jek felt fortunate. Both of its minds did, actually. Of all the Behemoths they were the only ones imprisoned where they could continue to interact with their children in their corporeal form. The cell itself was housed within a massive cavern near the Spire.

Their body was the size of a large house, but when they stretched out fully they could be three times as long. Its general shape was that of a mantis, with dozens of additional spindly legs, and two heads instead of one. While they got along most of the time, when one head felt particularly bold, it would eat the other. It always grew back quickly, and the argument would resume.

When they were originally summoned, they could sense the panic in the voices of the others. Always panicking. If only the others knew how to properly cope with their emotion.

"We know how to cope."

"Depends on your mood. Last time you ate my head and felt smug about it for days."

"I was right, and had to prove it. Yes yes."

Their squabble was interrupted by a single apocrita who came up to them, bowing low to the ground and thrumming its wings as a sign of fealty and respect.

"Oh, yes yes yes. You bring news, little one?"

"Please, do tell!"

A series of clicks and buzzes filled the air as it spoke in a hurried manner in its native tongue. *"The ones from outside have gone into some kind of trance."*

"Oh...oh dear."

"We should have gone when we were summoned. It's just that Gron'Tul can be so so so dramatic."

"Indeed." Both heads turned to the bug on the ground before them, waving it off with a massive claw. "You may leave us, little one."

The only explanation for all of the visitors to go into a trance at once was that they had been summoned as well. Gron'Tul and Yorm must have worked the others into a frenzy. When those two worked in tandem, they were busy as bees. Both of Jek's heads chittered at the joke as they closed their eyes to join the others.

They projected their unique dual consciousness to the same location as always, taking the form of a single apocrita. Upon opening their eyes they found themselves in a cold, dark place. An oppressive force held them there, and concern grew in their mind.

"This is not what I had intended. *No no no...this is quite alarming. What happened?* I have no idea. We need to try and leave this place."

"I'd prefer if you stayed for a while. It's been so long since we had a discussion, just the two of us. Well, *three*."

The Withered King moved into view, hovering above the ground with his hands behind his back. Jek blinked at him several times, cocking their head to one side as they regarded their brother.

"Ah, yes, Res'Kel...but not. The others are not pleased with you. *No no brother-deceiver, they are not!* Why have you brought us here?"

"I felt we needed to talk. I've already spoken with Deghat and he seems amiable enough for what is to come, but the spell I want to fashion takes more than just the two of us."

"Why not speak with us before? *In our cell yes yes.*"

"Of all the prisons, yours is the most...public. I thought it prudent to not show myself just yet. No telling who might be watching from the shadows."

"Ahh, you speak of Progity. Always watching. *Yes yes yes. Always peeking where he should not.*"

"Would you expect no less from Yorm's lapdog?"

"Seems you still have no love for your brother, Res'Kel-but-not. *None no none.*"

"You are so right, brother. However, I *am* trying to fix that, which is why I've come to you like this. This world needs to be reborn. You all can leave your self-imposed prisons at any time and be free once more, yet you remain. Why?"

"You know exactly why, brother. *We leave, the world dies. Dead dead dead.* We do not wish to see it end in such a manner."

"The failed experiments of the others are over. First the failure that was the kin, and now all these other races making a mess of Antembra. There is no other choice but to remove yourselves and let the spell finish. Join us, and with the help of Deghat and myself, the apocrita shall be spared. It would be a shame for them to die with all that knowledge."

"And we assume your...creations will be spared as well? *Abominations of the deep. Clicking clacking amalgamations.*"

He frowned, crossing his arms as he floated over in front of Jek. Leaning in he spoke in a low tone, brimming with held-back fury.

"The brinore are none of your concern. You all had your fun and now it is *my* turn."

"Speaking of children, you sound more human than Res'Kel. Petulant. *Arrogant.* Unwise. Such a far way to fall brother. *Hit the ground you have, yes yes.*"

Jek tilted their head at him, tittering with their mandibles to mimic laughter. They had no feelings one way or the other about Res'Kel before the imprisonment, nor when he attempted to make his own race without the help of the others. Now, however, they felt pity for what he had become.

Bellowing in rage at the taunt, the Withered King shoved his arms outward, floating up into the air so that Jek was forced to look up at him. His aura started to glow a bright purple, with tendrils of black and green energy licking at his flesh.

The amount of power Jek could feel right now was far more than they'd ever experienced before from him. How was this possible? Just a moment prior there had been nothing. Now, there was so much it was overwhelming.

"Brother...*what have you done?*"

"No. Not brother. Not any more. I came to you with honest intentions, Jek. But *you* had to throw them aside like so much chaff." He spoke with a sneer on his face and waved his arm. Jek was suddenly tossed across the room and thrown against a wall.

Their head darted about, looking for some means of escape. Desperately they tried to will themselves out of that area, to get away from the rage exuded by their sibling.

"What are you doing? *Brother stop this. Stop stop!*"

"I grow tired of your endless prattling."

Dread filled their core as they found they were unable to speak, either of them. Trying to reach out with their thoughts they were met with such strong resistance that even trying sapped at their strength.

We need to get out of here. Warn the others.

On a warpath he is. No longer idle threat, no no, now he is making his moves. Stop him! Stop stop stop!!

"I can...*still*...hear you!"

Flying over quickly, he grabbed onto the sides of Jek's head, and screamed at them as he pulled. Agony shot through their body and they cried out in pain for the first time in thousands of years. Pain, panic, sadness, confusion, and terror flooded their minds as they tried to fight against whatever he was doing to them.

As quickly as it had begun, Jek fell to the ground in a heap, gasping for breath and his body shaking with the after effects. Looking up at Res'Kel, he suddenly noticed his mind was silent.

"Wh-did you...?"

In Res'Kel's hand was a ball of pure energy. Jek felt so empty inside that he immediately knew what that energy represented: his other half.

"I didn't think I was going to do *this*...I intended to kill you!" The joy in his voice made Jek feel ill as he tried to stand up. Losing his equilibrium, he fell back onto the floor. The silence in his head was overwhelming.

"Now isn't this better? So...*quiet*."

"P...please..."

"You should have taken my offer when I presented it, *brother*. You would still be whole."

"No...don't take..."

Coming down to land on his feet, and then crouching on his haunches before Jek, Res'Kel held the ball of energy just out of reach as he spoke, his words filled with nothing but scorn and disdain. "This is what happened because you made a joke I found displeasing. Imagine what will happen when I extract my true vengeance on the ones who *actually* wronged me."

Jek lunged for the ball of light, but found only air as the Withered King dissipated, leaving him there in that cold dark space. Immediately he rushed back to his body, hoping that this was all some kind of trickery.

He turned to look at his other head, and wailed in horror as he saw it was desiccated; nothing more than a dried out husk filled with nothing. One of the sobs that wracked his body caused it to break loose, fall to the ground, and shatter into thousands of pieces.

"No...NO! I *need* him!!"

Before he completely lost himself to grief, he willed himself to join the others. He had to warn them. Res'Kel, whatever he had become now, was far more powerful than any of them realized. There was nothing they could do to stop the rising tide of his vengeance.

*****

The shouting was deafening. Shae tried to understand what was going on, but it only served to confuse her further. Giving up on following whatever argument was going on, her thoughts kept going towards Greyania and her revelation. So many years she had trusted her, mentored under her, even loved her as family. Would it be enough to forgive the truth?

Kovacik was the first to try and speak over the arguments. "What in the hells is going on here?!"

One that looked like a sincit snapped back at him. "You will ssspeak when ssspoken to, Kin!"

Shae could see the tension of his jaw as he clenched it, biting back whatever retort he burned to spit back at the sincit, but he must have realized that it would fall on deaf ears or he would suffer strong consequences for talking back to a god.

Everything went eerily still and quiet as the shouting and arguing died down. The human-looking one was glancing frantically all around the room, like she expected something to happen. Something incredibly bad.

A moment later, an apocrita appeared out of nowhere and slammed onto the table, nearly sliding right off. The orc caught it just in time, and helped to prop it up. The apocrita was shaking violently as it tried to speak. The voice caught Shae off guard with not only how normal it sounded, but how much sadness and fear was in its tone.

"Res'Kel...He...took..."

"What is it, Jek, what did he take?"

"Me."

Curling into himself, the others exchanged worried glances and tried to prod him for more information as the scene descended back into a chaotic mess. Shae looked up just in time to see a brutish ogre-looking thing lumbering towards the group.

"Ogre!!"

Instinctively reaching for her bow, she cursed at her own stupidity. They were in some sort of mindspace, and only here in spirit. Her weapons were still on her body and completely useless here. Everyone looked up as she shouted, but Greyania and the other gods visibly relaxed.

"Deghat," the human-looking one spoke again, "it is about time. What took you so long? Jek was attacked by Res'Kel but he isn't making sense."

"Whatever dost thou mean, mine sibling?"

The voice and mannerisms Deghat exhibited were jarring to say the least. Shae had a hard time wrapping her head around an ogre acting prim and proper, even if it *was* one of the Gods Who Walk.

Jek meekly tried to speak again. "Deghat...is..."

They ushered over the ogre, and he leaned towards Jek. "Curious. It would seem thou hast met with a fate most foul, and lost a goodly portion of thyself. A malady most dire." Deghat looked over Jek, inspecting him.

The more Shae watched Jek, the more she realized his movements weren't caused by his condition, but by his actively *fearing* the ogre. The others were far too busy trying to soothe and calm him to notice. Before Shae could say a word, her gaze and Jek's met, and everything froze as Jek's voice entered her mind.

So...little time.

What is going on?

No time! I can...feel myself slipping away. I may never recover, so you will take my essence. Use it to expose the deceiver. I implore you!

Essence? What are you-

Searing pain shot through the core of her being. Her soul felt like it was being boiled right within her body and she screamed out in horror as she doubled over, clutching her sides. Rhikter, being closest, was the first to come to her aid.

He tried to help her up. "Shae! What happened?!"

Struggling to speak, Shae stuttered, "S-so m-much..."

Power. It flowed through her; coursing across her mind and over every inch of her body. Rhikter backed away, raising an arm to shield himself, as arcs of lightning bounced off her skin. Shae stood up slowly, the pain and torment dulling until they were no more than a throb at the back of her head.

Looking at Jek again, she saw his body go slack, and he fell into the orc's arms. She was unsure if he were alive or dead, but she could *feel* his elation. In fact, she could feel the emotion from everyone nearby: Greyania's lingering shame, Rhikter's immature inclinations, Hunter's desire, and even Kovacik's...loneliness.

"G-Greyania! What's happening to me?!"

Shae looked to her for help, but the look on Greyania's face showed that the other woman had no idea what was happening either. Looking to the gods, they were all staring at her with wonder. Their emotions were far more complex, but if she concentrated, she found she could read them nearly as easily as the others.

It was when she focused on Deghat that she understood the request Jek made of her. Without even thinking, she moved forward quickly and grabbed onto his arm. He cried out in shock, and everything changed. A place she'd never seen before entered her mind, and she found herself a spectator of memories that were not her own.

A female kin was standing in a large room, speaking to Deghat.

"We have just started to rebuild our empire, and your lot is content with new races to occupy yourselves. Why should we even bother with this plan of yours?"

"*My* children art a source of scorn; they art tormented and killed by the children of the others. Hast thou any notion what pain I have thusly felt? The spell I will give to thee shall seal away my brethren. I cannot bring myself to destroy their children, but they must be brought to task for their transgressions against them."

"And what of the kin? We have surely transgressed against your children as well."

"Do this, and thou shalt tap into our life force unto the end of time. Thou shalt be as we are now. A *god*..."

Fading into the ether, the memory was replaced with another. This time Deghat was in the form of a giant, mutated boar with a huge mouth, trapped in his prison. She could not see whom he was speaking with, but could sense an immense power.

"Tho not as intended, thou still hast children to call thine own, dear brother. While the accident destroyed thy body, thou enjoyest a degree of freedom we shan't know again. What more wouldst thou have of me? We art doomed to fester in these cells forevermore."

"Perhaps. You *owe* me, Deghat. You helped fashion the spell to imprison the others, but it cost me my body."

"I owe thee nothing. The spell imprisoned myself as well."

"There is no telling what the others would do if they knew your involvement in all this. So, you will fashion the spell I require. We will free all of them at once, with a caveat."

Deghat responded hesitantly. "Such as?"

"I feel I deserve a *new* body."

"A new body? Dost thou think thee can find one worthy of thine countenance?"

"With proper conditioning. I've been formulating spells myself, brother, but you weave them together as a maestro. Can you do what I ask?"

"Yes. But what thee asks wilt take time. Hiding it from the others will be most difficult."

"Leave that to me. Once you fashion the core mechanics, I can help craft the details."

Collapsing to the ground, Shae's head pounded, her heart thundered in her chest, and her breathing came in quick, ragged breaths. Glancing up, she saw Deghat's jaw set squarely and his gaze burning into her. Unsure if she was the only one to bear witness, a burst of fear filled her gut and she wondered if he would do whatever it took to keep her quiet.

As he turned towards her, the human-looking woman spoke in a low tone, her words full of hurt.

"You *turned* on us, Deghat? Your own family?"

Shae realized, as she looked at the faces of everyone there, that she had not only tapped into his memories, but projected them to the others as clearly as she had seen them. *Just what in the hells did Jek do to me?*

Deghat continued to stare at Shae. It was then she realized she was still grabbing his arm. Letting go she stared right back, but didn't sense any hatred, or even anger towards her. Most of what she sensed was shame and resentment towards himself. Breaking the stare, he turned and addressed all the gods.

"I have no regrets for that which I hath wrought. I did what I felt prudent to protect mine progeny. I wished for no ill to befall my family, but some occurrences were unavoidable." He looked at Jek, his limp body nothing more than an empty shell now.

"You have betrayed usss," the sincit spat out, "like that ssslime Resss'kel! We ssshould have wiped him from exissstence when we had the chance. Now you ssshall have hisss fate."

One by one, each of the gods, with both hatred and sadness in their eyes turned their backs to Deghat.

"Brothers, sisters! I implore thee to hear my side of these events which have transpired! Not all is as it would seem!"

"We have seen enough, or are your memories fabricated, dear brother?" The elf tilted his head at Deghat. He was the only one, Shae noticed, that exhibited no outward emotion towards Deghat, nor gave off any emotional reading she could sense. It was like staring into a void when she glanced at him. It made her gut clench.

"Nay, Progity, but there were situations and events that were not shown! I can explain these actions readily if given but a chance!"

"No. We gave such chances to Res'Kel. Now we see his poison seeps into your mind and essence as well. So we shall give you no further opportunities for betrayal. Begone from this place at once. You are-"

Progity's decree was interrupted by another voice. One Shae had never heard before, but it caused the gods to turn, their emotions changing abruptly. A man with a crooked crown and tattered clothing floated before them. Glancing over at Greyania, the other woman looked as if she had seen a ghost. This had to be the Withered King, Res'Kel.

"I don't think they want to give you the benefit of the doubt, Deghat."

"Betrayer!!" Yorm's bellow startled Shae and she watched as the orc sailed through the air, suddenly equipped with a giant spear, ready to run the interloper through. Holding up a single hand, Res'Kel managed to stop his assailant a hair's breadth away from striking him. Yorm's face contorted with rage and disbelief.

"I have not come to fight, Yorm. If you can't put away your silly sticks and speak in civil tones, then I'll take Deghat and leave with what is left of Jek."

"You are not worthy of staining my weapon with your blood." Yorm spat on the ground, and whatever force held him in midair let go. He landed on his feet, looking back up with scorn. All watched as Res'Kel lowered himself to the same level.

"Not quite the welcome I expected, but I suppose it shall have to suffice. Gron'Tul," he nodded towards her, "you're looking as pensive as ever. I've been wondering why I haven't been invited to these little meetings of yours. I'm beginning to feel left out."

"You have no place here," Gron'Tul responded. "Not anymore. Not after what you did back then, and certainly not after what you've done now!"

He narrowed his eyes as he spoke. His words were like ice and made Shae shy away, wishing she could block them from her mind. Every time she tried to look at his emotions as she had with the others, it was difficult to feel anything beyond a cold, endless hatred. Trying to read further made her head ache.

"And what have I done that you deem so offensive, hm? Attempted to create progeny? Left you all here with a *choice* to move forward or languish in your own self pity? I am not the villain here, Gron'Tul. You all have grown fat on your complacency over the centuries. It was only when Deghat tried to make a deal with the kin that I found our salvation."

"Ya freed us but continued ta force us ta be prisoners! Ye really think that's gonna endear us to yer cause?" Karak's tone was pleading, trying his best to reason with his brother.

"My methods may have been a bit crude, but I've never intended harm to come to any of you." He pointedly looked over at Jek. "What happened was unfortunate. I...I am not even sure how I did what I did. But I wish to make it right. To make Jek whole again."

"We are to believe you've only come to give back what you've taken from him? Generosity was never your strong trait, brother. How are we to trust you?" The others nodded in agreement with Progity's assessment.

"You are right, dear, *distrustful* Progity. A show of good faith, then? I brought back the other half of Jek."

Holding his hand out, a great ball of light suddenly phased into existence. It was brilliant, and Shae could see the fear and panic it felt, much like the emotions of the others. Whatever it was, it had a consciousness.

"Just let me give it back, and then we can talk," he glanced at Greyania and the others, "without prying eyes."

Gron'Tul's face was stoic and and emotionless, but Shae could see her feelings and knew what the god would decide. Giving a curt nod, Gron'Tul conceded to the terms. Smiling broadly, Res'Kel closed his hand, causing the ball of light to disappear, as he slowly approached Jek. Yorm's muscles tensed, ready to strike at a moment's notice.

Leaning down over Jek, Res'Kel placed an empty hand on his brother's brow, gently stroking it. "Jek, I am so sorry for what I've done. Let me fix this." The hand then moved from the brow to just over Jek's chest and Res'Kel uttered a single inaudible word, and braced himself. When nothing happened, Shae could see the confusion radiate from his aura. "What is..." he tried again, this time using more force and power. The word he was uttering was still inaudible to her, but Kovacik's face lit up in recognition.

"He's saying romvas! It's-"

"Extraction! Stop him!!" Gron'Tul's voice was powerful and commanding, and each of the gods, except for Deghat, sprang to action. The King used the same trick he had used on Yorm before, and suspended them all in the air. Helpless, they could only watch as he attempted it again.

"ROMVAS!!" He stood and gave up trying when the third attempt failed. "Why isn't it working?!"

Eyes wild, he looked around the room until his gaze settled on Shae. She was frozen in fear as she could feel the emotions that were coming from him; dark, full of dismay, and deep sadness. Gods, a sadness so deep she felt she could drown in it.

"I don't know how he did it, but *you* are coming with me. Deghat, we're done here."

"Art thou certain that is a prudent course of action?"

"You dare question me?!"

The way he yelled at Deghat was frightening, but Shae could see he was full of doubt and confusion. Things were not going the way he wanted and he was becoming more chaotic and reckless because of it. Before Shae could react, Hunter and Kovacik appeared in her peripheral vision and attacked.

What they thought they could accomplish against Res'Kel she didn't know, but they managed to catch him off guard enough to tackle him to the ground and thus free the others from his grip.

"DEGHAT! NOW!" Res'Kel thundered. Using his power he brushed both Hunter and Kovacik aside as easily as one would a fly. As Shae watched him stand, she saw more and more of his true self. This wasn't just his emotional aura and energy she was detecting, but the full vision of what Res'Kel truly was. Dark tendrils, moving like tentacles, flowed out from his body, and she started to see barnacles appear on his skin.

"Res. Kel."

Hearing Abtrue's voice, he turned to face the rock creature, a look of surprise on his face. "I'm busy, brother."

"Perhaps. *Should.* Chat. From. Prying. Eyes."

"NO!"

The last thing Shae saw, before waking with the others, was one of the tendrils strike out to wrap around her. They all glanced at one another, then all eyes focused on her. Tears streamed down her face but she barely registered them.

"What did he do to me?" Shae asked no one, and everyone, as she sat there, looking down to avoid being overwhelmed by their emotions.

"I...I think he gave you what was left of his essence, if that makes sense. There's no telling what you are capable of now." Kovacik's spoke with an air of wonder.

"We need to help you find a way to control it, before it overwhelms you." Greyania put a hand on her shoulder. Shae shied away from it at first, but whatever lies and deceptions Greyania had committed, were dwarfed by Shae's need for comfort. She felt herself collapse into the embrace, quietly sob- bing into Greyania's shoulder.

"Shhhh...It's alright," Greyania soothed her. "We'll get through this. He won't take you, I promise."

"It...It isn't that." Shae shook her head and looked up at Greyania.

"What troubles you then?" Greyania asked.

"What I saw when I looked at the King. At first his emotions were so guarded it was impossible to tell what he felt. But as he got angrier and more desperate, his mental bar- riers went down." Shae looked and saw all eyes were on her, full of concern.

"At first it was just deep sadness. Longing like I've never experienced. The kind of desire that is all consuming. Anger and rage soon followed, but what bothers me the most..." Shae let her words trail off.

"What did you see?" Kovacik prodded as Shae re- mained silent.

"Confidence. When he looked at me he felt confident and unstoppable."

THIRTEEN

THE GROUP HAD accepted the hospitality of the apocrita to stay within the Spire until they could figure out what to do, or until they received word of what was to happen next. The mood of the entire population was somber and mournful; their God was dead. As for the group, the past few days had left them with their own burdens of grief and stress.

They were all gathered in a den off one of the main corridors leading to the massive library. Surprisingly, Greyania noted, there were no books in this room. Every room they'd seen so far had had several scrolls and tomes of forgotten knowledge squirreled away within it, except this one. The sound of Hunter's voice brought her out of her daydream and crashing back into the reality of their situation.

"It has been two days," Hunter's tone was filled with annoyance, "and we still have not heard from Gron'Tul or any of the other gods. In that time we have repaired the vessel and refashioned a new amulet. What more is there to wait on?"

"Your impatience is understandable, Hunter, but without a clear idea of what the gods had planned for the vessel, and without knowing how Shae's condition changes things, we need to continue to wait." Greyania tried her best to sound hopeful.

Since she wasn't privy to the full scope of the gods' plans, she didn't even know where to *begin* should they decide to strike out on their own. Being cut off from them was maddening. There had been times when they had ignored her prayers and pleas, but nothing like this; it felt like her ties to the gods had been completely severed.

"We can't just sit around and do nothing! It's only a matter of time before the Withered King figures out where Shae is, if he hasn't already. We need to get her to safety, and figure out a way of fighting him head on."

Rhikter was being brash, and foolish, to think they should attempt to directly confront the King, but he was right about Shae. The longer they stayed, the more danger she was in. But where could they take her that would be safe? If the King was gaining power at a rate that frightened the other gods then what hope could they, mere mortals, have?

All eyes looked to her for guidance and for some idea of where to go or what to do, and she let her shoulders slump as she sighed, "I'll repeat it again: until we have guidance, our best strategy is to stay put."

"You can sit here and wait to die if you want to. I, however, am going home." Kovacik stood and made his way to the exit.

"Where do you think you're going? We need you!" Rhikter exclaimed.

"No, you don't, kid. I've helped you reforge the gem, and even given you some pointers on how to operate the vessel. *This is not my fight*, and to be honest I'm not sure it's a fight that any of you should lay claim to either."

"You should not just leave, Kovacik. We may still need your counsel and wisdom in the coming days. If nothing else, your knowledge of magic and fighting would be invaluable."

"For an orc, you're rather cunning, Hunter," Kovacik smiled, "but this is not where I belong. I've remained as long as I wish. Since the gods have seemingly ignored every attempt at contact, and you seem unable to move as a group, I'd rather not languish."

"What are you hiding?" Shae stepped right in front of Kovacik. He started to shift in his spot uncomfortably, clearing his throat as she continued, "I can sense it...you're apprehensive, even worried, about something. So I ask again: What aren't you telling us?"

He paused before speaking. "If we stay any longer, *any* of us, we will *all* die. The Behemoths know I still live. May have known the entire time. Which means the King knows. What if he manages to put two and two together? The Spire was my *home*, and like a fool I've stayed close. Continuing to stay here, especially now, is suicide. I'm being pragmatic and looking out for myself. I could try to convince the rest of you, but it would fall on deaf ears because of her."

It was then Greyania realized Kovacik was pointing directly at her. Frowning, she got defensive. "I am doing what I think best. What would *you* have us do? Run away from all our problems and responsibilities?"

"No. I would have you face them, head on, and do something about it."

A dismissive snort left Greyania's lips. "You saw what he was doing before we were spirited away. He held the gods at bay with a *whim*. What possible chance would we have?"

"Maybe none. But we have something they don't," Kovacik persisted.

"The Vessel isn't as powerful as you seem to make it out to be, Kovacik. It's a fine piece of work, to be sure, but it pales in comparison to what we're up against!" Greyania stated.

"I'm talking about her!" Kovacik pointed at Shae.

When all eyes fell on her, Shae shied away, avoiding eye contact. Greyania's heart went out to her. The amount of power coursing through her body was so incomprehensible to the rest of them, that they couldn't help but treat her differently now. Her new ability to read emotions as though they were words on a page was the cause of unintentional ostracization.

"I never asked for this, for any of it. I don't know what you think I represent, but I'll have no part of it." Shae made a point to stare right at Greyania. "Not anymore."

Greyania could only feel shame, and made no effort to hide it from the elf. Taking a step towards her, she spoke softly. "You may not have asked for it, but the King is sure as hells making you a part of it. Jek gave you his *essence*, and that essence is what the King wants and needs."

"Assuming he did not extract it from another. Things looked grim when we left," Hunter pointed out.

"And if he didn't?" Shae's voice cracked slightly.

"Conjecture and wondering 'what if' aren't going to get us anywhere. Regardless of if we have their blessing or not, we need to do *something*." Rhikter turned away from the rest and kicked a chair. He ran his fingers through his hair as he exhaled a deep sigh. "Godsdamned if we do, godsdamned if we don't."

Kovacik folded his arms, and spoke in a softer tone. "Speaking as someone who has lost it all, I'd give every last piece of my soul to be able do something, *anything*, to stop what happened to my people."

When he looked up to meet Greyania's gaze, she didn't see his usual 'damn it all' demeanor or attitude. She saw someone who had suffered as no other.

Kovacik continued, "I will ask this just once before I leave: will you act?"

An awkward silence descended upon the room, each person looking to the others. Rhikter was the first to break it.

"Unless you plan to reattune Nixturjekur, you'll need someone to operate it. I'll follow where you lead. Hunter?"

Kovacik's lips curled into a smirk as Rhikter used the name he had christened the vessel with. Greyania could tell he was more pleased than he was showing.

"I follow where you lead, Rhik." Hunter nodded.

When Hunter looked over at her, she knew there was no resisting the changes to come. Part of her felt relieved to no longer shoulder the burden of this choice, but another part of her knew there were dark times ahead. They would all need strength to survive; a strength that few possessed.

"I leave the decision of my fate, and her own, in Shae's hands," Greyania looked at Shae and continued, "because I have much to answer for. I will always regret not being forthcoming with the truth, and cannot ask for forgiveness, merely understanding. But this journey...what Kovacik proposes...it is not something I will thrust upon you."

She moved over to Shae, and placed a hand on her knee as she knelt beside her. Greyania gave a light squeeze. "Since I damaged your trust and faith in me, the only way I know to repair it is to put all *my* trust and faith into you, right now."

Again, the air of silence settled over the group. No one dared even breathe, for fear of affecting Shae's decision. Finally, after taking in a breath and squaring her shoulders, she looked at Greyania and smiled ever so softly. Moving her hand, she placed it over Greyania's.

"It will take time. But your sins are not yours alone to bear. I never asked for this burden, so I'm going to be damned if I have to die because of it. I say we go with the others."

They embraced, and Kovacik seemed to return to his normal, gruff self.

"Perfect, but can we save the emotions for after we've departed? We can regroup at my home, and I can fill you all in on my idea."

"What idea is that?" Greyania inquired.

Smirking as he turned and walked out, he spoke over his shoulder. "To get some damned food."

Stunned by his response for a moment, not sure what she expected, but certain it was not that, she could only laugh at the absurdity. She looked at Shae, who shrugged. Greyania got up and followed after him, wondering if this eccentric was the best person to follow after all.

*****

Not wanting to draw attention by any large expenditure of magical energy, they opted to travel on foot to Kovacik's home in the caves. The trek took almost a full day, and everyone was tired and ready to collapse once they arrived.

The few cots and blankets thrown into the main storage area seemed like luxury after the lodgings they had endured over the past few days. While the apocrita had let them stay, their dwellings were not well suited for non-insectoids. They were cramped, uncomfortable, and had an odd odor. Here, the worst smelling thing was their own bodies and the subtle tang of machinery oil.

Someone was speaking to Greyania, but the moment she saw a place she could stretch out, with actual blankets and a pillow, she ignored everything that wasn't that bed. Within moments of putting her head down, she was fast asleep.

Dreams never came readily to her, not since she had given herself in service to the Gods Who Walk. Even the visions they gave her usually occurred during times she was fully awake and alert. So when she found herself in a vast dream-scape on some distant world, looking up at a strange sky, she immediately felt uneasy.

"It was smart, you know, not using magic to move about. I had guessed the Spire, but you're no longer there."

The voice startled her and she spun around. The air around her felt thick, like syrup, and she could barely move. However, she felt no panic or fear, just annoyance at her body's resistance to her commands. When her torso finally turned in the direction she wished, she came face to face with the Withered King. Only, not as he was now, but as he had been when she first met him. His name slipped from her tongue before she even knew she was speaking.

"Eldric."

"I'm impressed. Over a century and a half, and you still remember."

He put his hands behind his back and started to amble about the area her mind had created, marveling at the colors.

"You know, I never would have expected you to be the fanciful type."

"What do you want, Eldric? Or is it Res'Kel?"

Ignoring her, he looked up at the sky, his gaze focused on a distant nebula bursting with colors, and the stars covering the canvas of the night like spilled paint. Without turning to face her, he spoke. "I always thought you to be single-mind-ed and boring. But *this*? Tell me, do you desire to visit other worlds? Different planes of existence? Or is it all no more than a passing dream to you?"

Folding her arms, she blinked, the vision before her blurring then slowly coming back into focus. She was unsure if that was his influence or the dream as she replied. "That is none of your concern. Why are you here? *How* are you here?"

"Your link to the others. I was able to utilize it much like they do. It really *is* quite lovely in here. If I wasn't so busy these days, I could easily find myself getting lost in this beauty and splendor."

"So...they are dead."

He laughed and shook his head. "Dead? Hardly. We're in a stalemate of sorts. My power has grown, and Deghat, while hesitant, is proving useful for now. It is still five against two, and neither side is gaining ground. Frustrating, really."

"I really don't care about your stalemates, Eldric. What is it that you want? Do you mean to somehow track me this way?"

He shook his head as he waved his hand. The setting they were in melted away into one more domestic; a grand hall, ornately decorated with the finest furniture and tapestry. An amazing feast was spread out on the table, filling it to the point it seemed it would break in half. Saliva filled her mouth despite her best efforts to resist it, knowing it wasn't real.

"I'm merely here to talk, and see if we can't reach an agreement."

"This is a dream. Nothing more than figments. If you mean to bribe me with with such lavish accommodations, you will have to do better."

"Don't think me so crude, Greyania. Despite what you did to my former body and mind, I hold no ill will against you, nor anyone else. But things have run their course as far as they can, and the next stage of this world begins with my *true* children."

"*Your* children? Are you two so mixed together that there is no Eldric nor Res'Kel? Just this new being that adopts the look of the former?"

"Does it matter? There is no 'we' anymore. Just myself. I promise you, and those you travel with, will be spared if you just tell me where the elf is. I can extract Jek's essence without harming so much as a strand of hair on her head."

Laughing, Greyania picked up a bright red apple from the banquet and bit into it. She could feel the sweet juice dribble down her chin as she pulled away a hunk of the firm flesh with her teeth. Gods, how she wished that apple were real. Continuing to eat, she grabbed a piece of cloth from the table and wiped her mouth, turning to him.

"There is no way in hells I would agree to help you in any way. I know you intend to erase all life on this world to make way for these...abominations you call children."

The soft, friendly expression on his face melted away to an angry and cold one. She looked down at her apple, about to take another bite, and found she was holding a hunk of rotting meat, maggots and slime covering it. She gagged, tossing it away and frantically wiping her hand on her robe.

The banquet was gone, and they were back in her original dreamscape. Only, this time, the sky was turning crimson as the stars blinked out one by one.

"Hopes. Dreams. Aspirations. I can obliterate every last one you have. I'm in your mind, you filthy animal. You *mistake*. And you dare to call my children abominations?!"

His size grew until he towered over Greyania and he slammed his fists into the ground. Fissures ruptured around her, cutting her off from any means of escape. She could feel her body move more and more sluggishly and she screamed for it to listen to her, to obey her commands, to run away, to leave, to wake up, *anything*.

"You are as insignificant to me as a gnat to the storm. I came to you to offer a compromise. I see now you will learn only in fire and blood."

His form was massive now as he reached out to grab her. She tried to avoid him, but her body still refused to move and she was scooped up and brought right up to his face, which began to dry and shrivel into to the form she remembered most; the way he looked just before he died.

Snarling, he opened his mouth, but stopped before he could say anything. His features suddenly softened and his mouth took on a crooked grin.

"I know where you are."

Her dreamscape immediately returned to its former glory, and she was dropped. As she fell through the air, she could only watch as he turned away. His body began to fade.

"Should have accepted my gracious offer, mage."

She awoke with a start, breathing heavily, her brow covered in sweat. Rhikter was snoring loudly in his cot, and the rest were nowhere to be found. It didn't matter.

The King knew where they were, and they were all going to die.

FOURTEEN

HUNTER COULDN'T SLEEP. He knew it was late in the evening, but as he moved towards the exit of the cavern housing Kovacik's home, the bright sunlight caused him to squint. Part of him missed the dwarven city with its artificial sun, simulating day and night. He had not had a single period of restful sleep since they had taken this job.

Then there was the matter of Greyania. Again his thoughts drifted to romance, but human and orc relationships were difficult enough without considering everything that had happened recently. Such an endeavor would be stressful, at best.

In orc culture, keeping prisoners, even for serious crimes, was considered taboo; if a criminal could not pay back their debt to the tribe or otherwise atone for what they had done, they were either killed or exiled, as decreed by the victim or the victim's family.

Not only had Greyania kept an innocent man prisoner for decades, but she willingly and actively tortured him as well. He had known she was responsible for the Unbinding and what had happened to the world, but he had not known what extent she had gone to trying to accomplish it. For what? A spell that plunged the world into chaos.

He wondered what the world had been like before things changed. Nomadic bands of orc tribes, their numbers in the thousands, hunting and living off the land, instead of ek-ing out existence as refugees. The more he thought about it, the more he wondered if he could truly forgive her for such a transgression against his people, even if it was unintentional.

Hunter continued to approach the exit to the desert, just beginning to feel the warmth of the sun on his face, when a cry came from behind him. Concerned, he ran back to find Rhikter and Shae on either side of Greyania, who was hurried-ly packing her things.

"What happened?"

Greyania didn't pause as she answered Hunter's ques-tion. "The Withered King visited me in my dreams. He knows exactly where we are, and isn't going to stop until Shae is in his grasp. We need to leave immediately!"

"There is no way," Kovacik stated as he entered the room just behind Hunter, "he could know where we are. I've placed wards against even the Behemoths themselves to pre-vent anyone from ever finding me."

"He knew we were in the Spire. Now there's a space nearby that he can't see into? Your wards may as well be bea-cons, now."

She continued to throw things into her pack. Once she was done, she slung it over her shoulder and waited a mo-ment for the rest of them to do the same. When they only re-mained standing, staring at her, she barked out her order again. "Grab your things, *we need to leave!*"

Hunter was the first to approach her, and he placed a hand on her shoulder. "Are you sure he knew where we were? What if it was some trick to force us to expose ourselves?"

It was clearly the first time she had considered the possibility, and she stopped looking quite so frantic. Her gaze fell slightly and she didn't seem to be as tense. At least now he knew she was considering his words carefully.

"You...you didn't see or feel what I did. They are still fighting with the others, he and Deghat, but he seemed so self-assured that the stalemate would end. If he even *thinks* he knows where we are, then we're in grave danger. The only place I know of that is truly safe is my hideaway. Shae, we need to open a portal immediately."

"Like hells we are!" Kovacik yelled. "The whole reason we didn't do that to begin with is that such a large amount of magical energy will be easily detected if the damned King is looking for it! We're warded here. Nothing can happen!"

Rumbling came from deep within the earth, to challenge Kovacik's words. Greyania's eyes went wide with fright. "He's here. It's too late!"

Kovacik cursed as he ran out of the room, heading deeper into the cave. Rhikter was hot on his heels, and Shae looked about with no idea which way to go. Greyania grabbed her hand.

"Shae, I cannot open a portal and keep it open long enough for all of us to get through. Not without help."

"What? M'lady, we-"

Kovacik ran back into the room, panting and out of breath. Rhikter was close behind, inside Nixturjekur.

"Everyone out! She's right...We'll die if we stay here, wards or not!"

Following Kovacik's command, they all ran outside as quickly as they were able. The blinding light of the sun forced Hunter to shield his eyes. The rumbling continued, but there was no indication as to its source. Only one thing was apparent: it was growing more intense.

"Where is he?!" Rhikter's metallic voice came from within Nixturjekur, as they all spun around to see if they could detect anything. The sound was becoming deafening, and just as he was about to say something more, the ground underneath Rhikter erupted, sand and dirt flying everywhere.

It took a moment for Hunter to comprehend what he was seeing. A giant worm had broken through the sand and swallowed Rhikter and the vessel whole. It continued to shoot straight up into the air, and he could see its body arc back down to the world below. They all ran out of the way, too deeply shocked to worry about Rhikter's fate.

"What the hells is that thing?!" Shae screamed, as she ran away with Kovacik.

"It...it's a damned orthoxson! They're supposed to be extinct!" Filled with disbelief, Kovacik's voice trembled.

"Then why the hells is it here?!" Hunter's question was never answered, as the thundering crash of the beast burrowing back into the ground drowned it out. A moment later it was gone and all that remained was two craters and fading rumbles.

"We need to get to solid ground! They can't burrow through rock!" Kovacik yelled.

"Back to the caves!" Greyania cried, and started to head towards the entrance again, but Kovacik reached out and grabbed her arm, yanking her back.

"No! It may not be able burrow through them, but it could trigger a collapse and turn the whole damned thing into a tomb. We need to get to the rocks on top of it!"

Hunter could see no exposed part of the cave that was very large; the entrance immediately descended into the sandy dunes leaving only a small outcropping of rocks and boulders. As risky as it was, it was their best chance.

"Come on!"

Running towards the entrance, Hunter made his way around it and up to the top, glancing about, ready to react if the rumbling got more intense. Once everyone was as safe as they could be, he finally began to wonder about Rhikter.

"It...it just swallowed him whole. Like he was nothing..." His voice sounded muted and strange; he must have been deafened slightly from the sound of the initial attack. The quality of the words in his head made him feel as if they were not his own.

"If he remains in the vessel, he should be fine...I think."

Kovacik's words did nothing to comfort him, and, looking at Shae and Greyania, they obviously weren't feeling particularly comforted either. Their concern for Rhikter mattered little, though, as the orthoxson came back then for another attack.

Instead of bursting straight up again, as it had when it first appeared, the sand surrounding the rock they were standing on started to move and push up as the bulk of its body began to surface.

"This isn't good," Kovacik murmured.

The long body was still slithering from the hole as it coiled around their rocky ledge, doubling up on itself as it lifted its head. The bifurcated mouth opened and Hunter expected it to roar. Instead, the sound that emitted from its maw was more of a groan, followed by a gurgle.

A moment later, the creature fell, hitting the ground hard enough to cause them all to lose their balance and fall. It uttered another pitiful noise and then was silent. As they righted themselves, Hunter saw movement near its middle.

"Look!" Pointing, Hunter quickly slid down the side of the rocks they were using for protection and ran over to where he saw the movement. Taking his sword out, he slashed at the thick hide, trying to cut into it. "It is Rhik! It has to be! Help me cut him out!" Kovacik yelled something that he couldn't hear as he plunged the blade deeply into the side of the beast and started to saw through the skin. Thick, yellow blood gushed from the wound. Something started to push out, and he smiled. "Rhik! We thought you-"

The words died in his throat as a smaller version of the orthoxson emerged from the hole, hissing at him before lunging. He barely managed to swat it away before more of them poured from the gaping wound. The creature had been pregnant.

Stumbling back, he noticed Rhikter climbing out of the beast's mouth, and Kovacik yelling for him to return to the rocks.

"If they get into the ground there's no telling where they'll come from!" The kin yelled at him.

Not needing to be told twice, Hunter left his sword stuck in the leathery hide and ran back. Daring to glance over his shoulder at what was going on behind him, he saw so many of the things wriggling their way free that he lost count. Most were squirming and thrashing on the ground, not yet viable. The ones that looked more mature were beginning to burrow into the sand.

Getting to the rocks just in time, he hoisted himself back up as Rhikter rejoined the group.

"Didn't you hear what I was trying to tell you?" Reaching out, Kovacik gave Hunter a hand.

"No, I was too concerned with saving Rhik. I thought he was still inside."

"I got stuck on the way down, and clawed my way out." He turned towards the creature. "Seems I didn't agree with it."

"That's what I was trying to tell you Hunter; that I saw Rhikter climbing out of it's mouth."

"We need to fashion a teleportation spell that won't be easily tracked and get out of here while we're still able. Shae, I need your strength," Greyania said.

"Wait, Kovacik can teleport in a way I've never seen before. Can't he get us out of here?" Rhikter questioned, and all eyes fell to the kin.

"It's not possible. The spell you saw me use is far too limited and takes exponential amounts of energy the more I try to move at once. Too much, and the strain would kill me."

"Fine. At least we're safe from those things on this rock while we fashion the spell."

"Yes and no," Kovacik stated, looking at their surroundings pensively. "While the adult was limited in how it could attack us, the smaller ones can climb up the rocks like snakes. We'd never know where they were until they attacked. Believe it or not, an infant orthoxson is far deadlier than an adult."

"We'll start the spell regardless. We need to get out of here before the King shows up." Greyania turned to Shae, and both women joined hands and began speaking in a hushed tone.

Before Kovacik could agree or disagree, four of the smaller orthoxson appeared on their left, one leaping, its mouth open wide, right at Shae. No one was close enough to stop it from attacking her, and both women were too wrapped up in their incantation to notice. Hunter felt a knot grow in the pit of his stomach as the blow was about to land.

Shae's arm shot out with unnatural speed and she managed to grab the beast just under the mouth, causing it to writhe frantically as it tried to free itself. The other three were being more cautious, waiting to see what happened. She held it there, before her, and opened her eyes. A moment later it gave off a wretched, pained screech and went limp in her

hand. She dropped it and turned towards the other three creatures.

"These I can handle, but seven more come from the
left." The way Shae spoke sent a chill down Hunter's spine.

Not waiting for an explanation of these new abilities,
the rest of the group turned in that direction as the creatures
appeared. Hunter swung his fist and struck one down as it
leapt at Kovacik.

"I'll be fine! Make sure they don't interrupt the
damned spell!"

One managed to latch onto Nixturjekur's faceplate,
and Hunter could hear the sound of teeth scratching against
metal. It caused his skin to scrawl and distracted him for a moment. One of the orthoxson slithered around his right leg and
squeezed, trying to throw him off balance. They displayed a
cunning pack intelligence that unnerved him.

"Something isn't right." Kovacik seemed to mirror his
sentiment as he sliced one in half. "Normally they are smart
enough to flee a superior foe...they should be retreating. These
are literally throwing themselves at us to die."

It was true; for every one they seemed to kill, another
appeared. Hunter swore not nearly this many had escaped
when he cut into the mother. He managed to kill the one con-
stricting his leg, but another bit into the meat of his shoulder.
Ripping it off was painful, but the wound was mostly superficial. It was then they heard the voice.

"This really would've been much easier if you had
agreed to give me what I wanted."

Up in the sky, with the sun at his back, was a figure.
Hunter could not see who it was from where he stood, but
there was no doubt from the voice that it was the Withered
King.

"Face us, you monster!" Hunter cried up at him.

"Oh, I have plenty of 'monsters' to do that for me. No need to dirty my hands when they are more than willing." Lowering himself, he stayed a few dozen yards out from their position. More of the orthoxson came up to attack, but Hunter could see their numbers were finally thinning.

"Seems you are running out of monsters, *King*. Ready to dirty your hands now?" Hunter spoke the title with a tone of mockery.

"What are you doing?!" Kovacik's voice hissed behind him. In truth, he did not know why he was drawn to taunting this being that was like a god. *Was* a god. Something in his soul yearned for it. For the conflict. His blood began to boil as he stepped forward.

"I am buying us some time," he said to Kovacik over his shoulder. Regarding the King again, Hunter shouted, "Or are you going to find some other beast from the depths to annoy us?"

"Bold words for the dead."

Hunter felt as though his whole body was being squeezed, and he was lifted up off the ground. Looking back, he could see Shae turn towards him, about to act.

"No! Stay back! Finish the spell!"

The Withered King pulled Hunter up to face him, smirking, his eyes as deep and cold as an endless sea. He licked his lips slowly, cleared his throat, and spoke so only Hunter could hear.

"Orcs. I knew you were a *savage* race...but to rush so headlong into your death? You shouldn't have told the elf to back down. She, of all of you, might have had a chance to slow me. You? You are unfit even to crush beneath my boot."

The rage and fury in his soul overtook him, and Hunter grinned back. "You do not know me, *King*."

Frowning slightly, the Withered King spoke with disdain. "If that is what you wish your final words to be, then tell me: who are you?"

"Hunter Rage."

Hunter's eyes lit up with a wild fire and his grin widened as he suddenly found he could move his arms. Grabbing hold of the King, Hunter saw fear in the god's eyes before his face twisted in anger.

"Unhand me!" Throwing out his arms and pushing, he managed to break free of Hunter's grasp, but they remained on equal standing, in the air, levitating face to face.

"What *is* this?" the King questioned.

Hunter answered with his fist, slamming it into the King's face as the rage took over. Throwing blow after blow, he could feel the facial bones crack under the pressure, and blood poured from the King's nose and mouth. Feeling even more emboldened, he continued to strike until an eerie laughter filled the air. It was coming from the King.

"I did not expect this. Perhaps orcs are more resilient than I gave you credit for. Good show. But it is over."

A force threw Hunter towards the ground with incredible speed. He thought he could hear someone yell his name, but as he looked up all he could focus on were the quickly approaching boulders the King had thrown after him.

The impact shuddered the land, throwing up dust and debris. Rhikter cried out, and turned to face the King, whose face was already mended as he mocked all of them.

"I probably would have spared him, had he any manners. Next time, teach your pets to heel."

"I'll kill you!!" Rhikter screamed.

"I highly doubt that, but I'll be more than glad to-"

A powerful explosion went off near where Hunter had landed, alarming everyone, including the King. There was a bright flash, and Hunter flew out from under the boulders, striking the King and knocking him out of the sky. The King roared in shock and pain as the two hit the ground.

Rising with an aura of flame surrounding him, Hunter looked down at his foe and smirked as he understood what he had become. The stories he had heard as a child told that when Yorm had need one would become his Avatar, his divine instrument of justice in the mortal plane. When Yorm and Progity had visited he and Greyania in their mental link, they had bestowed upon him a rare and precious gift.

"You worthless mongrel!"

Dark tendrils erupted from the King's back and arms, shooting out towards him. As quick as he was with his new power, he was not fast enough to avoid all of them, and what few connected sent bolts of pain into his body. It felt like being touched by death itself. They yanked him down, and he saw an opportunity.

Moving with their speed, he overtook them and felt their grip go slack as he crashed into the King. Both forms tumbled through the sand and finally came to a stop. The fire surrounding Hunter glowed brighter and hotter as he went in for another attack.

More tendrils came at him, but as they wrapped around him he could feel the flames covering his body burn them away, causing the King to cry out. Growling his defiance, he rushed right at Hunter, slamming him back and away.

Rhikter ran up then, giving Hunter a sideways glance. "We need to wrap this up."

"He is mine!"

"You can have him! But Greyania is almost done. Like I said: we need to wrap this up. Now!"

"I agree!" The King's voice boomed as Rhikter was lifted by an unseen force and the front of the chestplate was ripped off the vessel, exposing the man inside. He threw up one of Nixturjekur's arms just in time to deflect one of the tendrils that was trying to grab at him.

Bellowing in rage, Hunter jumped in between the King and Rhikter and grabbed onto the tendril, ripping it from the King. It writhed in his grip, then dissolved into nothing. Before he could react, the King threw everything he had at Hunter, immobilizing him. He tried to find a way for the rage to fuel him even more, to escape, but found he was still stationary.

"*Finally*. You've grown past a curiosity for me and have turned into an annoyance."

Indescribable pain bloomed behind his eyes as both his mind and body were assaulted by the King. Hunter thought he was screaming, and he felt like he was drifting away from reality. No matter what he did, he couldn't make it stop.

"No...NO!" White hot anger burned inside Hunter. The power he was trying to focus to use against the King was building up much too quickly.

"What are you...Stop it!" the King yelled, trying to let go of Hunter. "You're going to destroy us all!"

Hunter tried, but found he could not stop the build up within his body. He began to glow white hot, and shake; it felt like every part of his body was going to explode. The King tried to pull away from him, but he was just as stuck as Hunter was. Hunter could see the panic in his eyes, and in that moment he felt at peace with what was going to happen. If this was to be his death, at least he would take that thing with him.

Before that could happen, Rhikter slammed into him, covering his body as best he could with the vessel, attempting to sever the connection between Hunter and the King.

"No! Get back! I can kill him!"

"And you'll kill everyone else in the process!"

For a brief moment they shared a look.

"Talk about a shit da-" Rhikter was cut off as Hunter felt all the energy leave his body in a giant rush. A scream was all he could hear as the world went white.

Silence fell over the battlefield as his vision returned. Nixturjekur was a good twenty feet away, overturned. The King looked dumbfounded and heavily wounded. Anywhere a tendril had been was now nothing more than a charred stump. The King just stared at the vessel, and Hunter could swear he saw...sadness in his eyes? Without saying a word, the King disappeared.

Hunter felt exhausted and the King had escaped, but it didn't matter. He immediately moved to the vessel to try and turn it over. Yelping, he quickly pulled his hand back; it was hot enough to singe his flesh. Shae, Greyania, and Kovacik all came running up next to him, and Shae used magic to turn over Nixturjekur. They all gasped.

Rhikter, what was left of him, was inside. His body was horribly burned, still smoldering, and he was making a horrid gasping noise. Any part of his flesh that had been touching the vessel had fused with it, and the newly reforged amulet had melted into his chest. His eyes had been burned out completely, causing him to look more like a husk than a man.

Hunter fell to his knees and howled out a deep, mournful dirge.

FIFTEEN

CHAOS AND CONFUSION erupted instantly. Kovacik and Shae were yelling as Hunter stayed on his knees, fists pounding the sand beneath him. Greyania, however, couldn't take her eyes off of Rhikter. She was amazed at the amount of damage his body had sustained and she wondered how he was still alive.

The stench of burning flesh filled the air, and yet he was struggling for breath. Nothing any of them could do would save him at this point, and she slowly moved forward. None of the others seemed to notice her as she stood before Rhikter, looking down at the pitiful, ruined thing he'd become.

"Forgive me," she said, and she reached forward to place her hand on his forehead, to end his suffering in the gentlest way she knew how. But the moment she touched him she found herself in another mindscape, next to Rhikter, who was whole again.

"What...what happened?" Rhikter's eyes darted about, trying to comprehend what was going on.

This was not her intention. She turned to Rhikter and answered his question with one of her own. "What is the last thing you remember?"

"Tackling Hunter to the ground to try and shield everyone..." He paused, meeting her gaze. "Shit. I'm dead, aren't I? But...if you're here...then that means...Oh gods, I failed, didn't I?! Is anyone else dead?"

"Calm down. We're not dead, at least not yet. You took the entire blast by yourself and somehow managed to survive. Though, the state you're in, I think you will agree it is hardly survival. I...was about to end your suffering when," she motioned to the space around them, "*this* happened."

"Oh thank gods. I was afraid it would be bad news."

"You *do* understand what I meant when I said I was going to end your suffering, right? There is no saving you, Rhikter."

"Yes, I know what you meant."

"You seem oddly at peace with it."

Shrugging, he walked in a wide circle, examining the blank space they found themselves in. "Am I happy about the outcome? No. I *am* happy it worked, and that no one else was hurt, but I would rather my journey not end here."

Seemingly content that there was nothing of interest in this space they found themselves in, Rhikter turned back to face Greyania, his face taking on a serious expression. She had never seen him so resolute.

"There is one thing I would ask of you," he stated, "when we're finally freed from this conversation. My 'last wish' as it were."

"Anything," she agreed. Perhaps this was the reason for their surprise meeting. Maybe it was a result of his being fused with the vessel and amulet; a magical byproduct that allowed their minds to connect in his last moments.

"Make sure Hunter knows this was not his fault. He'll take responsibility for this, but a burden that terrible could destroy him."

"Of course. I'll do my best."

"That's all I can ask." Looking around one last time, he folded his arms, closed his eyes, and readied himself for whatever came next. "Ok. Do it."

"Are you ssso eager to sssee your life end?"

Both of them looked for the odd, yet familiar voice. Trinfrey appeared, standing next to Rhikter as if she had been there the entire time.

His demeanor changed completely, and he squared his shoulders as he glared at her. "So you are responsible for this."

"Resssponsssible for coming here, yesss. However, thisss isss all on you, Greyania."

"I don't understand. All I wanted to do was end his suffering."

"In a way, you are. But there are other reasssonsss for why we are here."

"I don't want to die, but I knew what I was doing when I made my choice, and I'm ready for the outcome." His voice did not waiver, something Greyania respected about him.

"And if an alternative were presssented?"

Rhikter's face hardened. "I don't trust any of you. Hells, I never trusted your lot *before* we met! You treat us as pawns in your grand games, send us out against your wayward sibling, and then act aloof when we need you the most. If you presented an alternative, I'd wonder what the caveat was."

Trinfrey let her tongue slide across her teeth, and Greyania could swear she saw a smile. She had never seen a sincit smile, but she imagined that it would be close to what she had just seen.

"A lot of passsion in you, there isss. Perhapsss that isss why I've come. Perhapsss not. You are correct, though: there will be a price." Turning, she pointed to Greyania. "A price *you* mussst pay."

"The choice, and its payment, are hers alone, Trinfrey." Gron'Tul appeared right next to Greyania just as suddenly as Trinfrey had originally appeared, a look of concern on her face.

"I don't understand. What is going on here? What choice is mine?"

"And if this is all about her, then why am I here?" All eyes fell to Rhikter, who had an annoyed look on his face and had folded his arms. "Either let me die or let me have a say in this argument you three are getting into."

Trinfrey moved until she was standing right before him. Greyania hadn't realized how large she was; a good two feet taller than Rhikter. Unfazed, he looked up at her, arms still defiantly crossed.

"Well?" he asked indignantly.

"You are here becaussse we need you for the moment. Nothing more. You ssshall remain quiet while we ssspeak and ssshe decidesss both your fatesss."

"No. Not this time."

Trinfrey looked over her shoulder as Greyania spoke, her emotions unreadable as she responded. "*What?*"

"I said no." Taking in a deep breath and steeling herself, she shook her head slowly from side to side and then looked Trinfrey in the eye. "I've been waiting for days for something, *anything* from the gods. Some sign you were alive, or what path to take. When we finally have a *true* need of you, this is how you decide to show yourselves?" Gesturing towards Rhikter, she continued, "He was nearly destroyed saving our lives. Whatever Yorm did to Hunter was too powerful and he couldn't fully control it. Or was that his plan all along?

Turn him into a living weapon to kill the King? Either way, Rhikter saved us, and now you act as if he's no more than window dressing. Our part in your games stops here."

"Greyania, child, please. You don't-"

"No, Gron'Tul. You don't get to tell me when I can or cannot speak. Not any longer." She narrowed her eyes as she turned to look at the other god, frowning as all the anger and frustration she had been experiencing bubbled to the surface. "Where were you? Where were *any* of you?! Either of you could have done *something* to help us, but you waited until he was an instant from death before giving me an ultimatum? What, my life for his?"

The way the two exchanged glances was all the answer she needed.

"Well, my answer to this *choice*," Greyania continued, "is that you will restore him to his full health, without so much as a single hair singed on his head. You will release us from this limbo you've brought us into, and you will either give me a direction to go for our next move, or you will stay out of our way as we clean up the mess you've made by allowing Res'Kel to run rampant!"

By the end of her tirade, she was breathing heavily and her brow was furrowed. This was where she drew her line in the sand. All her doubts, all the self pity, it was because of how she had been treated. True, her aptitude to magic had been gifted to her by these same beings, but that was where her appreciation ended. They had been cannon fodder long enough.

"We...we were going to try and bring you to us, to empower you like no other," Gron'Tul tried to explain. "We felt it would be best to do so in such a way that you gave up your humanity, your ties to the others, in a selfless act. The opportunity presented itself when he gave his life. In a way, it was our gift to you, and our way of making you strong enough for the trials ahead. Strong enough to face him."

Greyania would have none of it. "You have the *gall* to think I would *wish* to be like you are? That I lack the strength to fight because of a few missteps? I have served, and continue to serve you. I have *worshiped* you as the gods you are. However, I had *no* designs to ever become one of you. Nor will I. The way you squabble like children when faced with a crisis...How you devolve into helplessness when faced with a stronger foe...You came to us for help, and assistance. And now you expect me to willingly give up my life, as long as it has been, because you think I will leap at the chance to become a god? Strip me of my power, then. I'll have no part of this."

There was silence, and even Rhikter looked stunned. Trinfrey then moved until she was standing right in front of Greyania.

"I've made my peace, and my *choice*. You, all of you, will just have to make your own peace with it." Greyania folded her arms just as Rhikter had and looked up at the imposing figure.

She couldn't be sure, but she thought she saw that same smile on Trinfrey's snout. Licking her teeth in the same manner she had before, the god spoke softly, and reassuringly, towards her.

"I have alwaysss been doubtful of you, Greyania Terrell. Originally, ssso were the othersss, believing putting our faith in you wasss a missstake. Gron'Tul convinced them otherwissse very quickly, but I never relented. Missstake after missstake happened, and I blamed you. Yet, when faced with what Gron'Tul told you, even with the promissse of becoming a god yoursssself, you did not back down from your conviction. Thisss was the tessst, and thisss isss what I wissshed to sssee. We have indeed treated you all asss game piecesss on our board. However, sssome piecesss are more valuable than the ressst."

"To hells with your tests! We-"

Blinded suddenly, Greyania had to shield her eyes from the harsh light that surrounded them. She was back in the Dry Oceans standing over the vessel, looking down at Rhikter, as if no time had passed. Kovacik, Shae, and Hunter were all still too absorbed to notice anything had changed. *Had it?* She wondered.

Rhikter extended his hand and she took it, helping to lift him out of the vessel. Most of his clothing was brittle ash, breaking and falling from his body as he rose, leaving him nearly naked before her. His skin and body, however, were fully healed. His eyes had returned, and he looked as healthy and strong as he had the day they'd met.

"What...what does this mean?" he asked.

She shrugged slightly, smiling at him. "I don't know. Whether or not they continue to assist us, at least I know who I am and where we're going."

"Where *we* stand. What you said took courage, and I won't forget it."

The others noticed that Rhikter was up and healed, and rushed to his side. A flurry of questions bombarded the both of them.

"Look, everyone, we'll explain it all to you as soon as we are safe. We need to get out of here. Maybe then we can come up with a decent idea for what to do next."

All agreeing in unison, they managed to find the chest piece for the vessel as Greyania and Shae finished the incanta-tion to open a portal to the hidden sanctum. As the others filed forward through the swirling opening, Greyania took a mo-ment to turn back and look at the Dry Oceans one last time. She spit on the ground, and looked up towards the sun.

"May I never return."

Stepping through the threshold into her study, a cold feeling filled her body. That was one part of transportation spells she would never get used to; the remarkable chill that overwhelmed the senses.

The others were all staring at something but their bodies obscured her vision, so she wasn't able to see what they were looking at. Closing the portal behind her and stepping forward, she wondered aloud what had caught their attention.

"What are you all staring...at..." The breath caught in her throat as she saw what they were all transfixed on.

Sitting in one of the chairs near the hearth, one hand holding a glass of wine, the other idly stroking Thalyia as she lay across his lap, was Progity. His words were quiet as he addressed them.

"Good, you're all here. I've such terribly wonderful things to tell you."

SIXTEEN

"WHAT THE HELLS do you want?!"

It was impossible for Kovacik to hide his rage at seeing Progity, sitting there with a smug look on his face. After everything they had all suffered through, Kovacik wanted answers.

"Perhaps you should calm dow-"

"No!" He interrupted Greyania and continued. "We deserve to know why they're toying with us!"

He was ready to stand his ground, but Greyania conceded with a nod. "We do."

Mildly surprised, Kovacik turned back to Progity and repeated his question. "What do you *want*?"

Taking a sip of the wine and then licking his lips, Progity set down the glass. Shooing the cat away from his lap, he reached for a nearby book, and opened it about halfway. He began to read silently to himself.

A second passed. Then another. When it became obvious that no answer was forthcoming, Kovacik reached out and ripped the book from Progity's hands.

"ENOUGH!" he bellowed. "We've been through the hells and back, and you remain silent. Your lot obviously restored Rhikter, which we *are* thankful for, but this damned convoluted, cryptic treatment ends now. Give us something solid, or so help me..."

Progity smirked and straightened in his seat. "I was worried that all those centuries of near-isolation had made you complacent and soft, Kin. Or, at the very least, a far cry from the petulant children who sought to kill their parents and take their place. You wish to know my *real* reason for being here? I have a simple question that only you can answer, Kin. In doing so you will be tested, and judged."

"What do you mean?" Shae had stepped forward, next to Kovacik. There wasn't a hint of fear or anger in her voice, just curiosity. Kovacik admired how resilient she was, particularly in the face of everything she had endured.

"Yourself, for instance," Progity replied. "Jek gave you his essence. A feat no mortal should have been able to endure. Yet here you stand before me: cognizant of the world around you and *not* some gibbering mess or mutated monstrosity. Rhikter threw himself into harm's way without a thought for his own life. Hunter proved his worth and was chosen as Yorm's Avatar. Greyania has proven herself loyal and resourceful time and time again."

"No...I meant what question could possibly be a trial for Kovacik?"

Progity smirked. "I know what you meant, Shae. I thought it prudent to remind you that you've all faced trial and hardship, but have come out of it far stronger."

"If you think we are going to lavish praise and adoration upon you, then you're mistaken. I'll have no part in this and refuse to answer any damned question. You have no *right* to push us any further!" A tiny gout of flame erupted from Kovacik's mouth as he admonished Progity.

"I may have no right, but it must be done." Progity's face took on a stoic expression as he regarded Kovacik. Standing before the kin, he folded his arms and licked his lips again. Kovacik felt that every movement, every action the god made, was all part of some puzzle only Progity could see or comprehend. He looked at the others, then back to Kovacik, and continued. "Would you prefer if we had our discussion in private?"

"Whatever you're going to do or say, out with it. I've no time for games. We've got *your* battles to fight." Kovacik words were laced with venom. Even when his race was young and vibrant, before everything that had happened, he had felt nothing but disdain and contempt for the Behemoths. Emotions that had only grown and festered over time.

"Wait! Before you begin," Greyania stepped forward, a curious look on her face, "how is it that you're here? From what Gron'Tul had told me, you were all trapped in your prisons, and could only manifest physically *within* those cells. Any of you leaving could have disastrous results."

"Who said I am outside my prison? There are a great many things we are able to accomplish that Gron'Tul has...neglected to mention."

Kovacik could tell Progity's answer was less than satisfactory to Greyania, but she took it at face value. Her brow furrowed slightly and she stepped back. Kovacik felt that the god was too dismissive of her; she had been their loyal servant for years, yet Progity was treating her as a child speaking out of turn. He balled his fists, drawing Progity's attention. The god glanced down at his hands, frowned slightly, and then met Kovacik's gaze once more.

"My question for you, Kin, is-"

"If you are going to speak to me, then you damned well better call me by my name."

A smirk played across Progity's lips and he gave a slight nod. "Kovacik, what would you do if I told you that you were the last of your race, but *not* the last of the kin?"

Confusion was the first emotion he felt, followed quickly by a bark of indignant laughter. "The kin are long dead, and I am a forgotten relic of an age long past. Your riddle has no merit."

"Yes...and *no*. As I stated, you are the last of your race, but not the last kin *alive*."

Before anyone could react, Progity waved his hand and they were surrounded by darkness so black that Kovacik couldn't even see his own hands when he looked down. "Where have you taken us?" he demanded.

A brilliant flash of light was the only answer he received from the void, causing him to rapidly blink his eyes as they adjusted. When he could see clearly again, he was back in the Spire, but not the one they had left hours ago. This was the Spire as it had been during *his* time. He was in one of the great halls that led to the Room of Convergence, where the members of The Gathering met to perform rituals. His brother, Nothias, was speaking with Festocina. Kovacik quickly looked around, and saw the others, along with Progity, just off to the side. He squared his jaw as Festocina's voice broke the silence.

"And just *where* did he go?"

"As I said, Preceptor Festocina, I do not know. He said that he wished to test out the new vessel to see that it is performing satisfactorily."

Kovacik smiled to himself. He would not have faulted his brother if he had told her the truth, but he swelled with pride as he saw Nothias stand by his word.

"Kovacik tries the patience of The Gathering. Only being your brother has spared him from judgement thus far. When he returns, that patience will have *run out*. He will be brought before us to judged, and punished."

"But, Preceptor..."

What happened next caused Kovacik's blood to boil. She sneered at his brother and gave him a backhanded slap across the face, causing him to stumble backward.

"You utter worm. I am *Preceptor*. You dare to lie to my face and insult my intelligence?!"

Immediately dropping to one knee and bowing before her, Nothias furiously shook his head. "N-No! I would never speak out of turn, Preceptor! I *swear* I do not know where my brother is, but...I will find him and personally bring him before the Gathering."

A grim smile crossed her lips as she regarded him and motioned for him to rise. Stepping forward, she spoke in a hushed tone. One that sent chills down Kovacik's spine. "You know so much more than you let on, Nothias. Come with me."

"Shouldn't I-" His body jerked as she waved a hand and uttered something unintelligible under her breath. Panic flashed in his eyes as he started to move forward, no matter how hard he fought against it.

"I said come."

The scene melted away, distorting and changing like the reflection on a pool of water. They were now inside the Room of Convergence. Kovacik was uncertain how much time had passed, but Nothias was leaning up against one of the pillars in the room, a wound in his side. The tables and mechanisms used in various magic rituals over the years were broken and tossed about. Every other member of The Gathering, save Festocina and an elder he did not know the name of, were dead. All looked like they had suffered terrible, violent ends. A bright flash of green caught his attention and brought his focus back to Festocina and the elder.

The other kin cried out in pain and his body began to turn to ash. He tried to reach for her, but she cackled in ghoulish delight, her eyes lighting up at his pitiful efforts. Before he even finished falling to the floor, he had blown away as dust.

"It's not too late to stop this, Preceptor! You've been taken by madness and will doom us all if you continue!" Nothias tried to reason with her, but it was having no effect. She completely ignored him as she looked to the heavens, powerful green flames erupting upward from her body.

"Come, Behemoth! Make me as a *god*!"

The ground began to crack and thick, brilliantly colored tentacles started to pour from the fissures, wrapping around her. She began chanting in a tongue Kovacik had never heard before as she was lifted into the air. A movement in the corner of his eye caught his attention; Nothias was struggling to move towards her, his hand gripping his side as he bled out.

There was no doubt in Kovacik's mind that he was witnessing the final moments of his brother's life. He'd made peace with Nothias' death so long ago that he'd nearly forgotten what the sorrow and grief felt like. Actually watching it unfold before him was a new torture on his soul. Everything in him screamed to leap out and save him somehow. Progity either saw the look on his face or read his thoughts, because he soon heard the god's voice within his mind.

We are not experiencing these in current time; these are but memories. We cannot affect them, much as a single pebble cannot affect the course of the raging river.

But...Nothias...

Watch.

There was a blade on the ground and Nothias leaned to pick it up. Kovacik could see his lips move and the knife began to glow a brilliant blue as he moved towards the thickest tentacle holding Festocina. It slowly unwrapped from her and she began to change, her features becoming more like a great and terrible lizard. As her body grew in size, she began to sprout wings.

Fire spewed from her mouth as she exulted, "Yes! Fill me with your power!"

Nothias lifted the blade high above his head and brought it down on the tentacle with such force that the knife was sucked into the wound, right up to his wrist. A great moaning was heard, and the whole room shook violently. The tentacle shot back up and wrapped tightly around Festocina again. She struggled as the thing squeezed, and her final breath was a scream as it dragged her down into the depths of a fissure. All was silent for a moment, and Nothias, satisfied, let the blade drop to the floor with a clatter. He swayed, his stance faltering, and then fell head first into one of the fissures as his wound finally overtook him.

They were all back in the study, as if nothing had happened. Shae was the only one to reach out to Kovacik, placing a hand on his shoulder. He reached for her hand and was surprised to find that he was actually crying. Wiping his eyes on the cuff of his sleeve, he stood and regarded Progity.

The god spoke as he retook his seat. "Res'Kel made a deal with Festocina to make her as one of us. She was to use the life force of the new races to help make his children a reality. It started to work, but your brother's interference caused Res'Kel to think he was betrayed. At the last moment, since the spell was incomplete, he was forced to use himself and the kin as the catalyst. At the time, we were not fully aware of the ramifications of these actions, nor that it was Deghat who had imprisoned us. Ultimately, what happened was of no concern to us. The conflict was finally over, so we were happy to turn a blind eye to our sibling's methods. It wasn't until much later we learned the true fate of the kin, including Festocina and Nothias."

Kovacik was confused. "But we just watched them both perish."

"Res'Kel never told us *exactly* what happened after, and we only know what you've seen because of the power involved in the spell surrounding it. What we witnessed was a memory of the *world*. Such memories are created during only the most cataclysmic events."

Progity rose, and in an uncharacteristic move, placed a comforting hand on Kovacik's shoulder as he continued. "What you need to understand, Kovacik, is that because the spell was interrupted Res'Kel wasn't able create a *new* race. Instead, he had to mutate an existing one. His race, the brinore...were *kin*."

The weight of the words and their implications came crashing down like an avalanche in Kovacik's mind, and he began to reel. He stumbled, grabbing onto the edge of a nearby bookshelf to steady himself. "The...the kin *live*?"

"Not as they were. They were mutated and changed in ways I'm not sure even Res'Kel anticipated when he sacrificed himself. All of the kin, except yourself. Something we've never quite figured out."

"It's impossible," Rhikter spoke up, "for an entire race to remain completely hidden without detection for so long. The apocrita were hidden as well, but there are records of them, sightings. There are even myths and fables of men made from stone. And yet, none of us have even *heard* of the brinore."

"Oh? Have you visited the bottom of the Black Sea recently?" Progity made a show of staring at Rhikter until the man sheepishly shook his head. He continued. "Festocina became the queen of the brinore shortly after their inception. Res'Kel did his best to hide them from us, but since we discovered their existence we've kept tabs on them. Until recently, they did nothing to warrant more than a passing glance. As for Nothias, his life force never went out, but we are not sure what became of him."

"My brother is alive?!"

"Possibly. We simply *do not know*. Nor, as I said, *did we care*. We decided to forgive our brother for this transgression. He was free of his confines, but could do little to actually influence events. Most of his time, prior to the Unbinding, was spent among his 'children' in the Black Sea."

"What does any of this have to do with the Withered King's recent actions?"

Kovacik had to concede that Shae had a point. While the tale shed a great deal of light on what had happened to the kin, he couldn't understand what it had to do with everything happening currently.

"We believe he originally intended the spell to eliminate *all* races, save his own new creations. By responding to Nothias' actions, Res'Kel inadvertently changed the spell. It altered the outcome a great deal and did *not* create a new race all his own. Something which has, I fear, become his obsession. I'm certain he did not make a move until now because he lacked the means and the ability to try again. It is why he's trying to sway more to his side. Already he's seduced another to his cause."

"*Another*?" There was alarm in Greyania's voice.

"Abtrue has joined in Deghat's betrayal. Ever the realist, he believes this is the logical and natural progression of life on this world," Progity rolled his eyes and let out an annoyed sigh.

"What happens when he has everything he requires?" Hunter asked.

"The Unbinding continues, the prisons dissolve, and Antembra continues being restructured into whatever Res'Kel originally intended for his new children. Somehow our staying confined is stopping the process." Progity shook his head and muttered under his breath. "Altered blood magic is...cumbersome and unpredictable."

Hunter was not satisfied. "This history lesson is all well and good, but it tells us nothing of what you and your siblings expect of us."

"We expect you to stop him."

In a blink, Progity was gone. The others erupted into a heated discussion over what had just transpired. The one thing that weighed heavily on Kovacik's mind, more than the truth about his race, was the fact his brother may *yet live*. If this was true, why, in all these years, had Nothias not sought him out? Surely there were ways he could have contacted him, even from the depths of the Black Sea.

"We'll find him."

He turned to see Shae's hand on his shoulder again, as if she had read his mind. He gave her a half smile. *Perhaps you did read my mind. No telling what you're capable of now.*

Perhaps. She smiled as his eyes went wide and he couldn't help but laugh and shake his head. "What do we do now? We're tasked with the impossible...finding and stopping an obsessed god. One that lives in the Black Sea, no less."

Shae looked at Kovacik for a moment and shook her head. "I don't know. None of us do. But I have faith we'll figure something out. You never did answer his question, though. Now that you know you're not the last of your race, what will you do?"

Kovacik took in a breath and let it out with a sigh. "I'm going to get a drink."

*****

Greyania had cleared off one of the tables in her study and brought out a map of the world so they could plan their next move together. Rhikter felt anxious, mostly about the fact that he had the amulet stuck in his chest.

At first, after Trinfrey and Gron'Tul had restored him, he thought the amulet had been destroyed by the blast. It wasn't until he was getting dressed in the clothes they had managed to find for him that he actually *felt* it. There was a steady pulse of energy coursing through his body, just barely enough to notice. It thrummed in time with his heartbeat, and, to be honest, he'd never felt better. He took it as a sign, and a gift, from the Gods Who Walk.

"Before we get too far into this, I need to tell you all something. It's about the vessel and the amulet," he spoke up as the map was being laid out.

Kovacik let out a forlorn sigh and shook his head sadly. "Damned shame, that. Nixturjekur won't ever be as powerful without that amulet. Even if we could fashion another, I built it *around* the damn thing."

"Actually, Viezal is still here...sort of. I believe it's inside me."

"It...it is *in* you?!" Hunter's exclamation of disbelief echoed the looks of everyone around the table and Rhikter could only nod.

"I'm pretty sure it is, yes. I feel better than I've ever felt."

Greyania extended a hand towards him, her face contorting slightly in concentration. Her eyes shot open in shock as she realized his claim was true. "It really is within him. I can feel it."

Kovacik looked at Rhikter, rubbing his chin as he studied the human. A moment later he shook his head and shrugged. "We toyed with the idea of imbuing a living creature with a gemstone, but never got it to work quite right. You can imagine the *complications*. I have no idea if the vessel will respond the same or not."

Greyania added, "It doesn't seem to be doing him any harm, and we know the vessel is still operational, despite the damage it sustained. We can worry about the side effects after we formulate a plan."

The rest of the group nodded in agreement, though Rhikter noticed Hunter did so begrudgingly. He frowned to himself; Hunter feeling guilty over the events of the day was the last thing he wanted.

Greyania pointed towards a section of the map. "What I propose is that we head directly to the Black Sea, and stop whatever the Withered King is trying to accomplish right at the source."

Kovacik agreed. "Yes. I think we need to find a way to take the fight directly to these...brinore before they can surface and help finish what the Withered King started."

"I agree, but...we're already assuming they're hostile? Also, they're your...well..." Rhikter couldn't help but allude towards the fact the brinore were still Kovacik's people.

Kovacik met his eyes and furrowed his brow before giving a curt nod. "What limited information we have indicates they are fully in league with Res'Kel. Until we discover otherwise, it would be foolish not to assume they are *all* loyal to him. As for what they were...Festocina destroyed what was left of my kind."

"How in the hells do we fight something that lives in the sea? We are unable to breathe underwater, unless some of you have been hiding something." Hunter's concern was more than valid.

The absurdity of having to fight while underwater was enough to lighten the otherwise dour mood that had been cast over the group. Rhikter couldn't help but snicker, which caused Hunter to shoot him an icy glare, but it was infectious; soon everyone, including Hunter, had a good, cathartic laugh.

Once everyone had caught their breath, Hunter continued. "But we still don't really know where to look. The Black
Sea is vast *and* it is split by the God Spine. They could be on either side."

Rhikter had all but forgotten about the mountain range
that ran nearly the full length of the dark side of the world.
The outpouring of magical energy had changed so much so
quickly, it really was a wonder the world hadn't torn itself
apart. Part of these changes were the Black Sea and the God
Spine.

When Antembra had shifted, volcanic events caused a
new mountain range to rise up from the depths, practically
overnight, flooding nearly a third of the Dark Plains. This
range came to be known as the God Spine, and it cut a path
down the middle of the new ocean. While having more of their
area exposed to constant sunlight had caused the frozen
wastes at both poles to recede, it was the sudden uprising of
these mountains that had changed things so dramatically.

"The spell imprisoned the Gods Who Walk and created
the brinore. We also know that Res'Kel had a direct hand in
how the spell was actually going to remake the world,
correct?" Rhikter had an idea forming, but he needed to be
sure. As the others nodded or murmured their agreement, he
continued, "Greyania, do you have any accurate maps of *just*
the Dark Plains?"

She thought for a moment and then nodded. "If I do,
they'll be in the next room. Several cartographers were killed
trying to map out the changes to Antembra, but a few learned
to tap into magic to do it for them. I'll be right back."

About five minutes passed before she came hurrying
back into the room with a large scroll in her hand, placing it on
the table over the other map. It was crudely drawn, and certainly not to scale, but it confirmed Rhikter's hunch.

He saw that the Dark Plains were not aptly named; instead of grassland, it was mostly mountainous, veined with dozens of rivers and dotted with several bodies of water. The largest of these was the Black Sea, which took up a sizable chunk of the southern hemisphere and was bordered by mountains. The God Spine ran vertically through the Dark Plains, through the middle of the Black Sea, and then tapered off into the southern pole.

"There, look at the left and the right side of the spine."

On the right side of the Black Sea, the mountain border was jagged, uneven, and made no discernible shape whatsoever. On the left side the border had a gentle curve, was easy to follow, and the mountains seemed evenly spaced.

"If this was all planned, wouldn't it make sense for him to protect his children, mistakes or not? If these mountains erupted randomly during the first few days in some chaotic mess, why is this part so...perfect?"

Looking at everyone, he could see his thoughts weren't crazy. There *was* an intelligent hand in this; it wasn't as random as the rest of the world may have thought.

"It makes some sense, but I'm still not sure...Kovacik?" Shae doubting him was no surprise, but her looking to Kovacik was curious. The way she gently let her hand rest on his arm, the look in her eye...*I'll be damned. That'll be interesting to watch develop.*

Kovacik nodded slowly as he pieced it together in his head. "Makes sense, actually. Both sides are a *literal* shot in the dark, but choosing the more formed side seems the logical choice."

"That settles that part. Now, how do we breathe under water?" Rhikter was not one who usually led such conversations, but all they'd been through, combined with the fact that the Viezal was right next to his heart, energizing him...he was starting to warm up to the idea of his birthright. His father, were he still alive, would be proud.

"There are spells and reagents, but none work for more than ten to fifteen minutes at a time," Greyania answered. "We will *not* be able to travel to the depths of the Black Sea if we cannot find other means."

"Maybe something in Aungermiest?" Shae asked.

"Why Aungermiest? The dwarves hardly use magic," Hunter responded.

Shae looked disappointed, but when Hunter mentioned the dwarves, Rhikter's eyes went wide.

"I think Shae is onto something. For decades the dwarves have used machines to dig through the earth and rock. Machines impervious to heat and cold..."

Kovacik lit up at the mention of machines. "Machines capable of getting us through the Black Sea!"

Hunter met Rhikter's gaze. "Rhik...you think...?"

"There's only one dwarf crazy enough," Rhikter replied.

"Chuktorik!" They both exclaimed.

SEVENTEEN

THE TRIP BACK to the city of Aungermiest was without incident. When they arrived, they left the vessel back in Hunter and Rhikter's shop, and Shae wondered as they walked through the maze of streets if she was the only one who felt so oddly about the current state of events. Here they were, back in the city, in the hopes that they could find a dwarf named Chuktorik, who may or may not have a machine that would allow them to explore the Black Sea.

She knew that being proactive in this was the only prudent course of action. Waiting for the first move to come from the brinore could end up being disastrous, and at least this way they had a chance of catching them off guard.

Back when they had first arrived at Greyania's sanctuary, and before they all realized that Progity was there, she had *felt* his presence. Much like one would feel the warmth from a flame, she could feel his distinct energy and instinctively knew what he was, and where he was. Since then she had wondered if it was because of Jek's empowerment, the fact that Progity was one of the Gods Who Walk, or something more. Here, walking through the streets of the city, she could put that notion to the test.

Reaching out with her mind, she tried to detect the life surrounding the group. A headache developed at the base of her skull, but she kept at it. There was so much to take in at once, and trying to find a focal point was causing sweat to appear on her brow. After a few seconds she could tell exactly where several dwarves were in their homes, along with much smaller forms around the edges of her detection that she assumed were rodents.

It worked! She was beside herself as she pulled her mind back, the headache from the strain easing. The only thing that concerned her about this experiment was that she wasn't sure exactly how she did it. One moment she was thinking about wanting to do it, and the next she was doing it. Was this what it was like to be a god? Simply think what she wanted to do and then it happened?

"Lost in thought?" Kovacik words interrupted her thoughts.

"Lost in...something."

"Sounds complicated." He chuckled softly.

Shae hesitated for a moment, wondering how much she should admit to the kin. The two of them had fallen a few steps behind the other three, and at the moment she felt she could trust him more than the others. Even though she had forgiven Greyania for what happened, the sting of betrayal was still fresh. As for Hunter and Rhikter, they seemed to follow their own path, loyal only to one another.

As for Kovacik, she was torn. Ever since Jek had imbued her with his essence, there was a kinship that had blossomed between them. Taking a chance, she decided he was the one to confide in.

"Not complicated, so much as strange," she responded.

She then began to explain to him, in a hushed tone, what she had felt when they encountered Progity and how she had tested the ability just a few minutes prior. His face gave away no surprise or shock, and she found it comforting. The last thing she wanted was to be regarded as a curiosity to be studied, or a freak to be avoided.

"That does sound strange. *Damn* strange. But I've found that the best thing to do in these situations is test your limits."

"To what end?" Shae inquired. "How will detecting those around us ever begin to help us in the battles ahead? I'd sooner put my trust in blade and bow."

"As would I. Even in the most skilled hands, magic can be unpredictable. However, we are headed to the Black Sea to find a *hidden* race. This ability of yours could be more worthwhile than you realize. If nothing else, exploring its limits could lead to the discovery of new powers. Just a thought."

Shae nodded. She could understand his logic. In her rush to try and test out the ability and dismiss it as worthless, she completely overlooked what it could actually be used for. His idea of testing it further to try and unlock other abilities also had merit. It was then she realized that they were both being watched by several dwarven bystanders, and had fallen several paces behind the others.

"We're being watched..." The volume of her voice drifted off to a whisper as she looked from person to person and realized *they* were not the focus of the staring, but *Kovacik* was. *My gods, that's right. They've never seen a kin before.*

"We should catch up with the others." he said, noticing he was the focus of the bystanders gaze as well.

Quickening their pace, they closed the gap just as the others turned a corner. Heading out into the main city square, a sudden brightness caused them all to blink and shield their eyes in response. It was morning in Aungermiest and the Yormsun had dawned.

Kovacik stopped and gasped, "Gods...this is...*breathtaking.*"

His voice was filled with awe and astonishment. Even with people staring at him, it was easy to forget he had never visited the city, nor seen their crowning achievement in artificial light. Shae was unsure of what made it work, exactly, but was glad for it. More than a few hours in any deep, dank cavern and she would start to grow listless.

"It's the Yormsun," Shae explained, "an artificial sun the dwarven people constructed shortly after they accepted refugees from the surface."

Still standing there, shielding his eyes, Kovacik seemed mesmerized by what he was looking at. "Such ingenuity."

"If you stare too long you'll go blind." Shae smirked and grabbed onto his arm to pull his gaze away. "I don't know where we're going and I'd rather not risk losing the others again."

Reluctantly he nodded and turned away from the sun. Then they both moved with the others, past the city pavilion and towards the industrial area.

"There's a dwarf here who's been working on excavation equipment. Stability, speed, power...the works. If anyone will have, or be able to fashion, what we need, it will be him," Rhikter was leading the way now. As they made their way through the sprawling streets, Shae longed for the surface.

Making their way down a few more side alleys and roads, they eventually stopped near a large opening cut directly into the rock, with a small building just outside. Rhikter walked up, knocked loudly, and waited. Silence answered him and seconds turned into minutes. He knocked again and was greeted by more silence; there was no movement or any sign of life. He grumbled something unintelligible and turned back towards the others.

Figuring this was a perfect opportunity to test herself again, Shae closed her eyes and reached out once more, trying to see if the dwarf they sought was there or not. Allowing herself full concentration not only also eased the pain at the base of her skull significantly, it also heightened her awareness tenfold. She could easily see a figure in the cavern, hunched over and working on something in the dark.

Without thinking, she simply willed light to fill the cavern. Just enough to see without aid. With the light, she could see that the dwarf was wearing grease-stained clothing, a tool belt cinched around his waist, and a magnifying-glass contraption over his eyes. He wore a cap, but his wild, messy blonde hair refused to be contained underneath. His thick beard was cut short, but still had two neat braids, tied off with brown string. The dwarf, startled by the sudden illumination, cursed and fell onto his backside, quickly looking in their general direction.

"Whut in tha damned blazes are ya doin'? Turn off 'dat damned light!"

Shae immediately complied, willing the light away. She stood there, stunned by what she had done. The concept was frightening; the ability to simply think what she wanted and have it happen.

The dwarf continued to yell his displeasure as he came out into the open, rubbing his eyes. "Do any of ye have a clue whut ya coulda caused ta happen!?" When his eyes fell on Hunter, his demeanor softened, but not by much. When he saw Rhikter he shook his head and stormed right over to him.

"Chuk! So good to see you again," Rhikter greeted him.

"I've told ya time'n again ta call me by mah full name, Chuktorik, ya daft twit! Ya finally come back ta pay what ya owe?"

Rhikter tensed at the dwarf's words and nervously cleared his throat. Shaking her head, Shae couldn't believe he had forgotten he owed a *debt* to the dwarf. As amusing as the interaction promised to be, she felt a sense of dread about acquiring what they needed. What if the dwarf refused to cooperate until the debt was settled?

Rhikter slowly nodded. "In a way, yes."

"Excellent. I'll expect ya ta deliver tha machine by the end of tha day."

"Chuk, you know I can't d-"

"Chuktorik!" the dwarf corrected. "Ya agreed to tha terms when we made that bargain, *Rhikter*. Ya bet yer fancy machine, and ya lost, so now I get yer suit. Few months later 'n what I woulda liked, tho'."

"You gambled with it?!" Kovacik's voice boomed, a slight echo coming from the cavern.

Rhikter bit his lip and turned to try and explain what was going on, but just then Chuktorik caught sight of the kin. His eyes widened, he dropped the tool in his hand, and immediately ran over to Kovacik.

"By tha tears o' Karak." Dropping to a knee, he bowed his head.

Kovacik was flabbergasted. "Wh-what are you doing? What's going on?"

It was obvious to Shae from the look on his face that he had never encountered a reaction like this before. Even she was flummoxed by the dwarf's actions; she had never before seen any of their kind show reverence for anything other than gem or machine.

Chuktorik uttered something to himself before rising, and looked up at Kovacik with the largest smile Shae had ever seen.

"As I live 'n breathe. *Tha Inventor*! All of ye, come inside, come inside!"

He walked so quickly that Shae had to stifle a giggle at the way his body waddled to and fro. Instead of following the dwarf, however, all eyes were on Kovacik. The confusion on his face had changed to a look of understanding.

"Well? Are you going to explain what is going on?" Hunter inquired.

"You all have to understand, I've lived a *damned* long life. It's easy to forget things."

"You don't mean to tell me you *forgot* you taught the dwarves how to build?" Greyania stated incredulously.

Kovacik replied as he started off towards Chuktorik's hut. "No, no. I never taught them how to build. Not *all* of them, at least. I *did* teach a specific clan some of my personal secrets. I was alone in the world and found I had more in common with dwarves than any other race. I befriended them for a time, and I never heard from them again after I set off on my own. They also gave me a nickname."

"The Inventor," Shae stated.

"For Chuktorik to know who I am on *sight*...they must have revered me far more than I ever imagined." He smiled as he reminisced. "I would be deep into theory and discussion of machinery with the clansmen, debating and arguing until dawn, sometimes. It helped with the new...*solitary* nature of my existence."

Shae could understand being alone, having been so for most of her life, but Kovacik's pain ran far deeper than that; he was the last of his kind. Such a thing was nearly impossible to truly understand.

"Come on, then! I've got tea!" Chuktorik was standing in the doorway, ushering them in with exuberance.

"We could use this to our advantage," Rhikter commented in a more hushed tone, so Chuktorik wouldn't hear.

Kovacik glared at him. "*We will do no such thing*! I forgot how brash humans, *especially you*, can be. You actually used Nixturjekur in a damned bet?!"

Without waiting for an answer, Kovacik stormed off towards Chuktorik. The others followed, leaving Rhikter alone.

"Hey, at the time it seemed like a sure thing!"

EIGHTEEN

GREYANIA NOTICED THERE was barely enough room for everyone inside Chuktorik's home. Crammed in shoulder to shoulder, and slightly hunched over, they all tried their best to hide their discomfort since their host looked like he was having the time of his life.

"Tha kettle should be ready soon fer tea. I'd offer somethin' a bit stronger, but I drank tha last o' mah ale fer breakfast."

"Tea will be just fine, thank you," Kovacik stated appreciatively.

"I still kenna believe yer here. Tha Inventor, as I live n'breathe."

Chuktorik began to mumble as he busied himself with preparing the tea for his guests. Greyania made her way over to where Shae and Kovacik were trying to make themselves comfortable near the far wall.

"You must have made quite the impression on his clan."

"Like I said outside, I honestly can't remember the exact details. All I recall is I taught them how to..." His voice trailed off and his eyes grew wide. "Chuktorik!"

"Aye?"

"How many vessels has your clan crafted?!"

All eyes fell to the dwarf as the weight of the question hit the rest of the group. Chuktorik looked thoughtful and acted as though the question were as commonplace as asking him what ale went with what kind of meat.

"Oh, hrm. Since tha time o' yer disappearance...I'd say 'bout five'er six."

My gods...five or six more vessels. Greyania was floored by the revelation. That many vessels could easily turn this ordeal in their favor, providing they could find them.

"You *happened* to forget you taught a dwarven clan how to craft *vessels*?" Greyania couldn't help but glare at Kovacik.

"Five or six? That's all?" Kovacik ignored her accusation, unconvinced by Chuktorik's number.

"Ha! Five'er six *hundred*. That's just from the Fenster clan. Tha others may 'ave more. Dunno. Tha clans n'er kept records o'er tha years."

Greyania's emotion went from annoyed to angered as she addressed Kovacik. "Why didn't you tell us this sooner?!"

Kovacik looked at her and grinned sheepishly. "I didn't teach them how to build Behemoth Vessels, not like Nixturjekur. I just gave them fundamentals, theories. Besides, without any Behemoth essence to gather, there was no way to make them as powerful. Hells, I can't be sure even *I* could build another Behemoth Vessel."

"Anything else you're forgetting?!" Greyania was exasperated.

Ignoring her again, he asked Chuktorik, "Did your clan find a way to power them efficiently without gemstones?"

There was a twinkle in Chuktorik's eye as he grinned wide. "Aye. We got quite creative wit dat problem."

Kovacik moved awkwardly through the rest of the group to get closer to Chuktorik. His demeanor had changed completely and he seemed quite excited as he talked with the dwarf. Greyania was still taken aback by the sheer amount of possible vessels that remained in the world. Even under-powered, they could be a huge boon.

Kovacik's voice was tinged with excitement. "You mean to tell me you found a way to...?"

"Aye. We tap directly inta tha ley lines."

"The overloads?"

"Instead o' tryin' ta avoid em, we turned 'em inta tha *main power source!*"

"Ingenious!"

Both were so wrapped up in their back and forth that interjecting any questions or comments to their conversation was pointless. Greyania motioned for the others' attention so they could discuss these new developments.

Shae spoke in bewilderment, "Hundreds of vessels. This is..."

"Unheard of," Hunter replied. "Rhikter and I only knew of his because of his family name and birthright. How in the world did the dwarves keep something like this from being common knowledge?"

"They're dwarves. *Sharing* technology isn't their strong trait," Shea stated pointedly.

"Something to consider, everyone: he said that many had been *built*, he didn't say how many still exist, operational. For a dwarf that's a *definite* distinction." Rhikter folded his arms and leaned back against the wall as best he could.

The statement tempered the mood, and the astonishment and excitement over new vessels decreased. Rhikter had a point: unless they could confirm their existence, it was pointless to debate on what more vessels could mean.

Greyania added, "You're right. Discovering more vessels can wait until we solidify our plan of infiltrating the brinore in the Black Sea."

The others nodded their heads in silent agreement.

"N'tha damned thing exploded in his face!"

Chuktorik ended his story, both he and Kovacik howling with laughter. The kettle began to whistle and he moved to tend to it, wiping a tear from his eye as he continued to chuckle to himself. This seemed to be the cue for the others to interrupt and ask if the dwarf had what they needed.

Greyania moved to Kovacik and placed a hand on his shoulder as she leaned in to tell him of the group's decision about the vessels.

He agreed. "Rhikter and I can go search for them once this is over and done with. I've no love for the Behemoths, but the Withered King is too dangerous."

Cups of steaming tea were passed out to everyone. Greyania took a sip and nearly spit it out. "My gods, I forgot even your tea is alcoholic."

Chuktorik grinned as he sipped. Hunter had already downed his and was going for a second cup. Greyania pushed her cup into his hand. He smirked as he took it.

"Let's get down ta business, den."

"Yes, let's," Kovacik nodded. "Obviously you know I can't let you have Nixturjekur."

Chuktorik nodded, "Aye. Wouldn't be right, you bein' tha Inventor n'all. Rhikter can find me another payment. A dwarven vessel. Maybe get tha Grimstone clan ta help fashion it. Dey developed a way ta smith gemstones like metal!"

Kovacik's brow rose and he looked as if he were about to question that statement when Greyania shot him a look, hoping he would understand its intent: no time for distractions. He looked slightly crestfallen, but did not push further.

Then she injected herself into the conversation. "Fascinating. However, I wish to discuss why we sought you out. Rhikter and Hunter have told us that you develop machines that can drill through solid stone."

"Dat dey ken. Even workin' on one dat ken go right through magma!"

"We need one capable of exploring the Black Sea."

Rubbing his bearded chin, he thought for a moment. "You'll need one dat ken not only getcha deep enough, but dat ken handle tha cold, too. *All* oceans are cold, see? But tha Black Sea? It's tha coldest. Surprised tha water don' freeze, honestly. Must be all dat salt...Maybe magic; I e'rd ley lines run all through dat area."

His penchant for going on tangents was starting to annoy Greyania. She tried her best not to let it show and tried to get him back on track and focused. "Exactly. One capable of going to the ocean's depths as well as being to withstand the bitter chill. Do you have such a machine?"

"That I do. That I do. Yer in luck, actually. It's in tha cavern right now."

"Perfect! How soon can you teach us to use it?"

"I could teach all ya right now."

"Let's get started then!" She rose quickly, nearly hitting her head on the low ceiling.

Chuktorik remained seated and held up a hand. She slowly lowered herself again, dreading what was coming. The stoic look on his face was not promising.

"Ya kenna take 'er, though. She's mah finest machine'n she's not fer sale."

Greyania pressed. "There must be some sort of agree-"

"Not. Fer. Sale!" He was adamant, but he continued in a softer tone. "*Though*, if ya take me wit ya, ya ken use 'er fer free."

"*Absolutely not*. This isn't some game, Chuktorik. We are on a mission of the utmost importance, and we cannot afford to be distracted by your presence." Greyania was just as adamant as she stared down at the dwarf.

He folded his arms and leaned back in his chair, his smug appearance saying so much more than his simple verbal reply. "Guess ya won't be gettin' mah machine."

"Do not make us take it by force, Chuktorik."

It took Greyania a moment to realize that the words had come from Hunter. He'd been quiet through most of this, and his direct threat was alarming; would they really be forced to act as thieves to get what they wanted? How far would any of them be willing to go to see this through, then? Chuktorik's face hardened, but not because he was offended or angered by the words.

"Yer an orc of honor, Hunter. 'ave been fer as long as I've known ya. Fer ya ta speak sucha thing ta mah face...this really must be serious." The dwarf scooted out of his seat and moved to the kettle, pouring himself a fresh cup. He sipped at it, staring into the liquid for a few moments in silence. "Mah terms still stand. If'n ya want mah machine, ya needs ta take me wit' ya." He looked up, locking eyes with Hunter. "All mah life I've built. I've made machines like this tunneler fer men far greater'n more adventurous dan m'self. Tha only regret I've 'ad was n'er going beyond this city'n out inta tha world."

He looked over at Kovacik, and the men smiled at one another in what Greyania could only assume was some kindred feeling; both men were inventors and probably understood each other more than anyone else here could.

Chuktorik continued. "Ta explore with tha Inventor, though...I could die a happy dwarf, dat I could."

The group exchanged glances as Chuktorik got back into his seat and finished his tea. Belching and disrupting the silence, he pat his stomach in satisfaction.

There was no point in arguing further; the looks from the others, especially Shae and Kovacik, were pleading. Even though the sensible move was to refuse his request, the others would have no part of it. Now was not the time to fight them on this, especially since she was still trying to regain their trust in her judgement and leadership.

"We seem to have no cho-"

The sound of a massive explosion interrupted her, as the ground quaked and threw everything, and everyone, in the room to and fro.

Someone yelled, unintelligible words flying through the air as the furniture made a ruckus. Greyania felt her back crash against the edge of a table. Wincing in pain, she cried out as she was then thrown across the room into a wall. Something small and hard hit her. Glancing down, she saw it was Chuktorik, curled into a ball. *Dwarves can get smaller?*

Stopping suddenly, the room and even the city outside, went eerily quiet. She felt where she had been struck by the table, and her hand came away warm and wet. She was bleeding, but it didn't feel like more than a superficial wound.

"Is everyone alright?"

Murmurs greeted her, followed by a hiss of pain. Kovacik was favoring his left arm, and even from across the room she could see part of a bone in his forearm threatening to push through the skin. Everyone else, aside from minor cuts and bruises, was fine.

Chuktorik coughed and stood, dusting himself off and sighing heavily at the mess. "I jest cleaned dis place."

Shae was tending to Kovacik's arm, speaking a healing incantation, but she stopped mid-chant. Her eyes grew wide and she stared right at Greyania. "Can you hear that?!"

Greyania strained to hear. The city was quiet, aside from distant cries of panic. Not wholly unusually after a cataclysmic event. She was just about to give up when she *did* hear something.. A moment later she could tell exactly what it was: water. *Rushing* water.

Shae ran outside. Falling to her knees, she began to sob uncontrollably. "I can feel them!" She turned back to the others as they followed her out, tears streaming down her face. "I can feel them on the other side of the city, drowning!"

"Der's no way water ken get inta Aungermiest. We aren't *near* any!"

"Is it possible you're mistaken? An underground lake you never accounted for?" Kovacik was still holding his arm gingerly.

"I'm telling ya, der's no way!"

"We can argue about it later. We have to do something to help!" Hunter gestured towards the center of the city.

"Gods, no..." Shae grabbed the sides of her head, and then screamed long and hard, before collapsing. Greyania rushed to her side as she pushed herself up, weakly, on one arm.

"The King's here."

*****

Despite his misgivings, thing were going according to plan. Deghat and Abtrue were with him, as were a contingent of brinore. His two brothers had managed to open the way to Aungermiest, and the flooding was a pleasant side effect. It would keep the city busy while they took what they really wanted: Yormsun. Such an unimaginative moniker, but that was the result of letting the dwarves get their hands on it.

"We're through. Close it," he commanded.

"Res'Kel. Cannot. Remains. Open."

"*Eldric'Kel* now, brother."

Yes, I like the sound of that one. It had been decades, and he'd never felt the need to call himself anything. Recent events were forcing him to find a name he preferred besides the Withered King. Most just made him uneasy, sounding too foreign to his conjoined mind. Eldric'Kel seemed to please both sides of his joined consciousness.

This duality of his had been disconcerting originally and made him feel at odds with himself. The two minds were joined so closely now though, that any attempts to separate them would result in both being destroyed. Had he know the melding would have been *this* complete, he was unsure he would have agreed to it. Neither part of himself would have.

"Name. Does. Not. Effect. Portal."

The brinore were the ones responsible for keeping it open, and it would be an easy thing to tell them to stop. He had no clue why Abtrue would refuse his command, but it was such a minor thing that he found he ultimately didn't care.

"Fine. We're here for Yormsun. Once we have it, let the city flood."

"Very. Well."

Abtrue's demeanor was never easy to judge, and his monotone cadence was grating at best. How the others could stand him had always been a mystery. Letting his mind wander, Eldric'Kel watched the brinore fan out into the city, establishing a foothold as they prepared the next part of the attack.

"Brother, wouldst thou be so kind as to explain why it is we are here to take the sun of the dwarves?"

"Isn't it obvious?" Eldric'Kel motioned towards the Yormsun. "Do you not recognize it? It's one of the Matriarch's devices. The fact that the dwarves are using it as no more than a candle in the dark is sickening."

Deghat regarded Yormsun for a few moments before his eyes went wide in astonishment.

"Brother, I've followed the path thou hast forged. Even after thine...transformation, I chose to follow thee once more and have done mine best to support thee in thine endeavors. This new course leaves me mystified and in a stupor; what possible need have we for such a thing? The Matriarch is...gone. What could this device give us that we doth not already enjoy?"

"Deghat, Abtrue knows when to keep his mouth from running. Learn from him."

Eldric'Kel turned away from his brother and back to the armies moving through the flooded streets. His words were curt, but he had no time to explain every facet of his plan to Deghat, nor anyone else for that matter. He was trying to rebuild this world into perfection. A perfection suitable for his children. The discovery that the Matriarch, the being that created he and his brethren, had left devices in Antembra had changed things drastically.

Brinore. The name brought revulsion as he spoke it to himself. They were *not* his children, merely a mistake. The fact that they used to be kin mattered little to him. They were mutations, perversions of what he envisioned his *true* children to be. The thought of it all angered him. If only the rest of his siblings weren't so short-sighted, then none of this would have to happen.

The waters rushed through the streets, and he could hear the screams and cries of those below as either the water or his soldiers overtook them. Closing his eyes, he took in another deep breath and let it out slowly. It was like music to his ears. The symphony of the end of this world. His *true* children would flourish in the new one.

A nagging remorse at the edge of his consciousness made itself known. The brinore *did* regarded him as a god. The fact that he would ultimately betray them to create his true children never sat well, especially since the two minds had become one. It was unpleasant, but necessary; the kin suffered for their hubris, and their race ended long ago. They were now the brinore, mere stepping stones to his ultimate goal. Through them he would perfect his vision.

"Withered!"

Sneering, he looked down. Festocina had demanded to be part of this excursion. He had always regretted letting her live, but she commanded the loyalty of the rest of the brinore. To destroy her would turn them against him, and he had use of them yet.

"You, *witch*, will call me by my name, Eldric'Kel." He lowered himself to her level, near the surface of the water.

Time, as well as the transformation, had been kinder to Festocina than most of her cursed race. While her torso and face were still quite kin-like, the rest of her body was that of a crustacean. She had the body of a lobster, but with jelly-like tentacles in place of legs. Bony protrusions, akin to scales, covered each one.

A coy smile played on her lips. "Is that what you're calling yourself now? Why not Human-God? It would be *just* as subtle."

Her tone infuriated him, "What is it you want? Your task is overseeing the forces as they take the city."

"It is being done as we speak. I just thought you would enjoy knowing that your little *pet* is here in the city as well."

Without waiting for his reaction, she turned and swam away, yelling orders at a creature more claw and sinew than humanoid. Her revelation was no surprise;. he had felt Jek's presence the moment they passed the threshold of the portal. If the elf was here, so were the others.

"Abtrue!" Looking to the stone god, he barked out a command. "They'll come to the portal. Distract them."

A moment of silence, and then Abtrue nodded and was gone. Whether he went to find them before they arrived or was waiting in ambush didn't matter. All that was important was acquiring the Yormsun unmolested. He was so close.

"Brother, is it really necessary to use Abtrue as a watchdog?" Deghat sounded concerned.

"You question me often, brother."

Deghat closed his mouth and looked back towards the portal. He muttered to himself, but Eldric'Kel heard. "So much destruction..."

Eldric'Kel also looked to the portal. Even though the forces of the brinore had all come through, the water still flowed forth; an unending torrent. That nagging remorse again. *No matter. We'll be done soon enough.*

*****

"We need to fix his arm!"

"People are dying, it can wait!"

"What's happening?!"

The whole world seemed to stop for a few moments after Shae had collapsed on the ground, and Rhikter could barely hear his own thoughts in the ensuing chaos. Greyania and Kovacik were arguing over his arm, Shae was still shaky, and Hunter had the same look in his eye that he had in the desert. He wanted blood.

"I must stop him!"

"Hunter! What are you doing!?"

Before the last word left his lips, Hunter had disappeared. Rhikter wasn't sure if it was some sort of teleportation ability or speed, but in the blink of an eye his companion and brother-in-arms was gone.

"Godsdammit!" Turning to Shae he shouted, "Can you do anything to stop this?" It came out far more pleading than he intended. For a moment their eyes locked, and Shae looked unsure. She tried to get up but her face contorted with pain and she fell back to the ground. She weakly shook her head.

You did your best. Even if she couldn't hear his thoughts, he was sure the look on his face conveyed the message. Turning to Greyania and Kovacik, he wanted to give them some direction, but he didn't know what to say. Both were far more experienced in leadership than he could ever hope to be.

Hells, by all rights he should be dead. It was only divine intervention, a twist of fate, that had put him back into the game. *The gods' game...we're all just damned pawns, but I'm going to reach the other end of the board.* He just had to survive that long.

"I need to go after Hunter. I can't let him face the King alone."

The sound of water coming from the other side of the city was his only indication of where Hunter could be. Grimacing, he cursed to himself as he realized that was also where the shop was. Where Nixturjekur was.

"Greyania, can you open a portal to-"

The sound of thundering metal footsteps on stone filled his ears and he looked towards the source. *Gods, what now?* Eyes growing wide, he couldn't believe what he was seeing: Nixturjekur, dripping water, was running through the streets right towards him.

"How is this happening?" The disbelief in Kovacik's voice echoed Rhikter's thoughts.

"The Amulet! Viezal is still *inside* Rhikter!" Greyania called out.

Only after she called attention to it, did Rhikter realize he'd been scratching at his chest. The same spot the amulet was stuck under his skin. Nixturjekur stopped a few feet in front of Rhikter and, looking at it up close, he noticed that it looked drastically different.

The exterior was leaner, and there were more spikes and armored plating at the joints. Even the faceguard had a sharper, more war-like appearance. The crest billowed with brilliant blue fire, mimicking ornate plumage. There was no time to speculate how or why its appearance had changed, though, not when there was so much work to be done. The hatch opened, without him even touching the vessel, and he hopped in.

Inside, it was also noticeably different. Whereas before it had been an uncomfortable fit, with him being too small, now it felt like it had been custom made for him. Another effect of the amulet's power?

"You can't just go after him again, not after what happened last time." Kovacik was still struggling with his arm as he made his way towards Rhikter and the vessel. The kin's reaction to the vessel's changes was obvious. His jaw dropped and his eyes went wide.

"I'll be fine," Rhikter insisted. "You three need to save as many as you can before the whole city is flooded."

"We can't do anything as long as that water is still pouring in."

Shae had a point. Anything they did would be an exercise in futility unless they could stop the water right at the source. Everything in him was screaming to go help Hunter, but maybe the four of them could...*Four? Where's Chuk?*

A rumbling started beneath their feet, and a moment later the ground began to crack and split apart over near Chucktorik's workshop. A massive drill erupted from the earth, attached to a large metallic box with thick, heavy wheels made of metal treads and spokes. A second later, a hatch on the side opened and Chuktorik stuck his head out.

"What are ye waitin' fer? Git in! We'll go at 'em from below!" The dwarf's eyes were wild, and full of excitement. At least someone was finding enjoyment in all this. Everyone just stood there, frozen. "What do ya want, a gilded invitation? Ah said git in!"

With that, he dropped an ill-fitting gas mask over his face and dived back into the machine. The others looked hesitant, but Rhikter knew there was really no other choice.

"Take the machine to the source of the water. If we're lucky the King and Hunter are there, and we can come at him from all sides. If not, then you worry about stopping the flood, and I'll worry about Hunter. Got it?"

The others agreed and quickly made their way over to the machine, stuffing themselves inside. How on earth Chuk thought everyone was going to fit was beyond Rhikter. At least he didn't have to squeeze in as well.

Turning back to the sound of the water, he broke into a run. The vessel had changed, and he eagerly wanted to see just how much.

NINETEEN

FLIGHT WAS STILL something Hunter found unnerving, but it was currently serving him well. The first few seconds had been rocky, especially at the speed he was going, but he had quickly righted himself and was now steady as an arrow. From this height he could easily see where he needed to go.

The water was pouring from what looked like a hole in the air. It was a portal, no doubt, but Hunter could not understand why they had not closed it behind them. It had to be taking a tremendous amount of concentration and energy to keep it open.

The damage it was causing was devastating. The area nearest the source was nearly submerged, with water flowing through the tightly wound streets and alleyways like a rushing river. At the rate it was going, all of Aungermiest would be submerged within hours.

Arriving at the portal, he knew there was nothing he could do to close or stop it. The portal was not what he had come here to find, anyway. He stayed there, hovering, looking for the King, or even a sign of the dark deity.

"Withered. Gone. To. Sun."

Hunter was mid-turn to face the voice he recognized as Abtrue, when a stone fist connected with his jaw and sent him flying. He crashed into a nearby building, hard enough to burst out the other side and skip along the water like a stone on a pond. Flying back up into the air, he could taste blood in his mouth. Spitting, he gazed up at the emotionless god and smirked.

"My quarrel is not with you, statue. But if you seek to fight, I will meet with you gladly."

Force built up behind him and he shot towards Abtrue like a demon rising from the hells. The more he fought with these abilities, the more second nature they became. Being an Avatar of Yorm was to feel endless rage tempered with the clarity of intense meditation. It was a surreal feeling of hanging on the knife-edge between pure bloodlust and inner peace.

His knee connected with Abtrue's midsection. He pulled back a split-second later, grabbed onto either side of the god's head, and forced it down onto the same knee, hard.

"GrrrrrUUUURRAAGGGHHH!!!" A guttural warcry overtook him as he felt the stone crack. Hunter was unstoppable. He was more than an Avatar of Yorm; he was fury incarnate. "NOTHING CAN STO-"

Abtrue's stone hand shot up far faster than anticipated and grabbed Hunter by the head, squeezing hard, before flinging him down into the waters below. As he surfaced, the god slammed his foot into Hunter's back. A rib cracked and he cried out in pain, causing water to fill his mouth.

"Avatar. Not. God."

His overconfidence and underestimation of his opponent would be his undoing. Hunter tried to surface, but a stone hand pushed his head back under the water, attempting to drown him. Panic filled him as he tried to free himself.

"Where's Res'Kel, ya pile o' rubble?!"

Even underwater Hunter could hear the words as clear as a bell. Try as he might to see who had yelled, he couldn't. He then heard the muted sound of metal striking stone, and Abtrue's hand was gone. Quickly surfacing and taking in a desperate breath, he flew up to the top of a nearby building and watched what was happening.

It was Karak, and while he still wore the plain armor from before, his battle axe was breathtaking. The blade was made of what appeared to be a single diamond with obsidian accents along the cutting edge. The haft was made from a smoky, dark green crystal. Coughing, Hunter tried to regain his strength as the dwarven god called over his shoulder at him.

"Yer daft, boy. Yorm picked a good one fer his Avatar, but ya ken't go off like a loon! Use yer head, unner'stood?"

Grinning wildly, Karak turned and rushed at Abtrue, his axe moving with a swiftness Hunter could barely follow. Chunks of rock from the statue's body were knocked off in rapid succession until an entire arm fell to the water below. Abtrue stumbled back, holding up his other arm to stay his brother's attack.

"Always wonn'ered if der were gems in ya, Abtrue!"

"Brother. Stop."

"*No!*" Karak yelled. "Ya came after mah city. After mah *children*. Dis has gone on fer long enough!"

"You. Left. Cell."

"Damn right I left dat self-imposed prison! Yer a fool ta think I'd sit idly by like tha rest o' them while ya destroy *my city*!"

"Illogical. Choice."

"Bah!" Karak had enough talk and raised his axe to finish the job. Hunter saw movement in the water and tried to call out, but a jolt of pain from his injuries prevented him from uttering more than a hoarse cry.

Abtrue's severed arm had reformed and broken free from the surface with a splash, striking Karak from underneath, and sending the dwarf flying into the ceiling of the cavern. It grabbed him before he could fall and slammed him down into the water below. His weapon went flying.

"Upper. Hand."

Gritting his teeth, Hunter rose. He would have to do his best to fight past the pain. He had underestimated Abtrue once before, but he was not going to make the same mistake again. The god's advantage was his bulk and power. Going at Abtrue in a frontal assault would likely result in the same outcome as before. This required careful strikes. Not as brutal as Hunter would have liked, but wearing Abtrue down was the only way to truly overtake him.

Floating up into the air, he faced Abtrue, the god's expression still devoid of all emotion.

"Come. Avatar."

Preparing to launch his second assault, the water started to bubble and churn below them. A massive form rose, spraying water in every direction as it broke the surface. It was the head of a snake, the scales made of thousands of different gems and stones. It enveloped Abtrue in its massive jaws and pulled him under the surface, causing a giant wave to wash over Hunter and send him flying. Karak the Burrowing had saved his life.

The churning waters stilled, and there was no sign of either combatant. Soaked, beaten, and bloodied, Hunter managed to make his way to a rooftop and collapsed. He began to concentrate on healing himself just as the light in the cavern flickered.

"No...it can not be..."

Turning toward it and shielding his eyes, he watched Yormsun as it went out and plunged the city into darkness.

*****

"Ya all comfy? We should be der soon."

As awed as he was by the dwarf's contraption, Kovacik was anything but comfortable. The conditions were cramped, the air had an oily stench to it, and his arm still had not been mended. He was seriously second-guessing the decision to ride in this fashion.

"Where exactly are you going to take us in this thing? The area at the center of the flooding is going to be completely submerged." Kovacik questioned Chuktorik. "Can this thing even surface?"

"Aye, I think it ken."

"You *think* it can?!" There was no hiding the doubt in Kovacik's voice.

As he questioned Chuktorik, Shae started to try mending his arm again. He brushed her off; she needed to regain her strength, not worry about his arm. There would be plenty of time after they stopped Aungermiest from becoming an underground lake.

She still looked drained. He had a notion that it was her ability to feel those around her. There was so much death and panic running through the city, and she could probably feel every second of it. It was a miracle she could even sit upright, let alone attempt to heal his arm.

"Greyania can do this. You need to rest."

Without an utterance of protest, she closed her eyes tightly and leaned back in her seat as best she could. Twisting slightly so Greyania could get a better look at his arm, he hissed as they hit something hard and the whole machine jerked backward abruptly.

"Sorry! Musta hit a rock'er sumthin'."

"She's going to push herself too hard, and I'm afraid there is nothing I can do to stop her," Greyania spoke aloud as she tended to his arm. It was unclear if she was actually speaking to him, or just trying to get out what she was feeling, but he responded regardless.

"That's the strength of her character. Something I imagine she learned from you."

"Perhaps."

Greyania inspected his arm closely, and frowned. A second later she uttered a few words of healing, and the pain eased. However, the damage remained.

"Is it too far gone?"

"No, but we don't have the luxury of time I'd need to properly heal this." She tore off part of her robe and fashioned it into a sling. "Try not to move it and aggravate the wound further. If we all surviv-"

"*When*," Shae interrupted, without opening her eyes.

Greyania smiled at the elf and continued, "*When* we all survive this, I'll be able to heal it properly. All I can do now is ease the pain."

"Fair enough. I know a few spells to help in that regard as well," Kovacik added.

"As long as you don't cause your arm to get any worse, do what you can. We may need the extra help closing whatever portal they have opened."

"Are you so sure it's a portal?"

"Yes. I can feel it," Shae interjected again. This time her eyes were open and she reached forward to grab Chuktorik by the shoulder.

"Surface here. We're very close."

Kovacik could feel the machine slow as Chuktorik looked at several dials and lights on the console. "I'll be damned, yer right. I woulda missed it by half a click! Hold on!"

The sound of grinding filled Kovacik's ears again as they lurched forward, quickly going near-vertical as they made the ascent to surface. Another jerk and he could feel almost no resistance, just a sensation of rocking. They had to have hit the water.

"A'right. She'll hold steady in tha water, but I've n'er tried ta make her surface in these conditions."

"You better. We can't close the portal from here," Greyania stated.

With a nod, Chuktorik turned back to his console, hit several switches, and turned a few knobs. A hiss filled the cabin and it felt like they were slowly floating upward. Just what had this dwarf created?

The sensation of rising quickened, and Kovacik felt his stomach bottom out as they jumped up and then smacked back down onto the water's surface. "Gods, it actually worked," he exclaimed.

"O'course it worked!"

Reaching to undo the hatch, Kovacik looked out. They were surrounded by water, but the portal was visible. It sounded like they were at the base of a massive waterfall, and the water wasn't slowing down by any means. The district they were in was so crowded, the buildings clustered so closely together, that it was acting as a kind of crude dam, stemming the flow of water. They needed to close the portal, or the city would be lost.

"Alright, I know what to do."

"Are you positive? I've spent my life using magic," Greyania questioned him. "You originally built vessels."

He shot Greyania a look and shook his head. "All kin used magic. While I'm not as skilled as most, I have knowledge of what we need to do here. Portals like this are *held* open. We just need to find who, or what, is channeling the damn spell and destroy it."

Shae pushed past him, looking out at the portal. At least, he initially thought she was just looking at the portal. Looking more closely at her face, he could see she was searching for something in the water near it.

"There!" Shae pointed. "They tried to mask their lifeforce, but over there, that's the source of the portal."

He followed her finger towards a group of what he guessed were brinore in the water. From this distance he would have assumed they were just flotsam, but after a moment he caught sight of a face that looked far too kin for his liking. This was what his race had become; lapdogs for a mad god.

Shaking it off, he brought his head back into the machine. "I can't swim with my arm like this. You two are going to have to deal with them while Chuktorik and I try and figure out a way to drain the city."

Greyania frowned, but was resolute. "We have no choice. It would take too long to counter the spell...we have to kill the casters."

Shae seemed hesitant, and Kovacik had a good idea why. She'd feel their lifeforce snuff out, and experience it. She was *still* feeling it all around her. There was no way she was at her full capacity right now, but she took a deep breath and nodded her agreement to the plan regardless.

"I'll hit them hard and fast." She moved past both he and Greyania and dived into the water.

"Guess I'm the distraction then." Her eyes going white, Greyania spoke a few words and floated out of the machine.

Kovacik desperately wanted to be out there with them, with Shae, but with his arm in the condition it was, there was nothing he could do. He silently wished them luck and closed the hatch to the machine.

He secured the door and turned to Chuktorik "Tell me you know where an underground cavern or abandoned mining operation is."

"Why?"

"We need to drain the city. All this water has to go somewhere."

*****

Greyania was nearly on the group of brinore spellcasters when Yormsun went out. It drew her attention long enough for something to leap up out of the water and grab onto her. Twirling in the air, reacting before it could drag her beneath the surface, she stretched out her hand. A steady stream of fire engulfed her attacker in crimson flames until the appendage grabbing her ankle let go. The squid-like form screamed all the way back down to the water, where it splashed with a sizzle and did not resurface.

She could barely see, but after that display there was no doubt that the brinore knew exactly where she was. Greyania just hoped Shae was alright. While the elf could hold her breath far longer than anyone Greyania had ever known, even without enchantments, there would be other brinore she'd have to contend with in the water before she was able to reach the spellcasters.

An arc of lightning flashed toward Greyania from the surface, nearly striking her. She tossed a fireball back, but it sizzled as soon as it hit the water. The fight was one-sided before it had even begun.

She dodged quickly to the side, but an incoming shard of ice grazed her arm, slicing into the flesh. Gasping as the mixture of cold and pain hit her senses, she tried to see how badly she'd been injured. The light was so dim it was impossible to tell, and she hoped it was no more than a scratch.

A glow appeared in the water to her left. It was moving faster and faster, and with each passing second the intensity of the light increased as well. As it grew brighter Greyania could see the group of spell casters, just under the surface. That glow had to be Shae.

By the time the light reached the group it was bright enough to illuminate them entirely, and Greyania couldn't believe what she saw. While the water distorted her vision some, she could clearly see that the brinore were more monster that humanoid, and no two of them looked the same.

The water surrounding them began to churn and bubble, as if brought to a rapid boil, then all was still and silent. Before the light blinked out, Greyania could see the bodies of the brinore floating listlessly. Shae had done it, but why hadn't she surfaced?

"Shae! Shae, answer me!" Greyania cried out, daring to move closer. A single humanoid figure bobbed in the water, motionless. Ignoring any possible remaining danger she rushed in and saw it was Shae, floating face down. A stab of panic hit Greyania's core as she scooped the elf out of the water. Turning her over, she tried to see if she was still breathing. She was, but it was shallow. "Oh thank the gods," Greyania exclaimed, lifting them both to a relatively dry rooftop. There, in the silence, Greyania could hear the sound of Shae's heartbeat along with the gentle lapping of waves against the few buildings that were not fully submerged. She could hear it *all* now. Looking towards where the portal had been, she smiled. There was no longer a waterfall suspended in the air; the portal was closed.

"Excellent work. Just late."

She immediately turned to attack whomever was speaking to them and was shocked to find Deghat floating there behind her, his bulky arms folded.

"Traitor," she spat out.

"Not all is as it would appear, m'lady. Dost thou know for what purpose thou wast summoned?"

Of all the gods, she disliked speaking with him the most. Aside from his monstrous appearance, he managed to make every word sound like a riddle. Frustrating wasn't even the half of it.

"I know why Gron'Tul summoned me all those years ago, and why she continues to summon me. If you've come to hurt Shae or myself, Deghat, it won't be easy for you."

"Nor shoulds't be. I come to thee with tumultuous tidings; Eldric'Kel, the Withered King, hath been distracted by his own desire. Go now and end this farce, so all may return to normal."

"You would betray him?"

"One cannot betray that which thou never pledged to fully. Go to the Yormsun."

There was no reason to trust him, but since he was not attacking or making any other moves towards the two of them, she quickly moved past him as Shae stirred in her arms. Coming to, she murmured something Greyania could not hear, then drifted back into unconsciousness. Leaving Deghat behind, she made her way towards Yormsun, hoping this would all be over soon.

Deghat watched them go. "Forgive me, brother."

TWENTY

"WHAT'ER YA THINKIN', Inventor?"

"Can we re-submerge?"

"Aye. Quick'n dirty way is ta throw dat lev'r derr'n it'll release tha buoys. But, if ye do that, we won't be able ta surface like dis again. One way trip ta tha bottom."

Kovacik placed his hand on the lever, and looked Chuktorik dead in the eye.

"I asked you before, do you know of any caverns or large mined-out areas that can hold the water?"

The dwarf took a moment to think, tugging at his beard as his brow furrowed. Nodding slowly to himself, he responded. "Der may be somethin'. Due east are tha ruins n'an old mining colony. Close enough ta get derr'n back, I reckon."

"Will you be able to plot a course?"

"Ya insult me, Inventor! I use tha same schematics ya gave mah ancestors ta plot *all* mah courses. We'll find it, straight'n true."

"Brace yourself then."

Gripping the steering lever tightly, Chuktorik faced forward, his body tensing. Kovacik pulled the lever and felt the whole cabin rock as the flotation devices were jettisoned from the machine. Immediately they began to submerge. Soon the entire compartment shuddered as they hit the bottom with a thud.

"Right. Get up 'ere wit me. I'll need a co-pilot fer this next part."

Moving as quickly as he could through the tight quarters, Kovacik took the small seat next to Chuktorik. Obviously it had been meant for someone of dwarven stature, and he felt cramped. Frowning, he saw there were two sets of controls; with one arm seriously injured, there was no way he could operate them effectively.

"I can't do this, Chuktorik. My arm was never fully healed. I can barely move it, let alone operate this contraption."

"Eh, it's all in tha wrist." He paused, shooting Kovacik a smirk and then continued. "Still, yer right. I dunna need ya to operate it, though, jes navigate me tha way tha charts direct'n we'll be fine."

That he could do. It had been years since he used navigation such as this, but he found it was an old and comfortable feeling as Chuktorik fired the engines to life and started moving forward.

The changes to his original designs were ingenious; the charts could map out caverns and show their relative distance from a focal point. To achieve this, the contraption tapped into the energy cast off by the ley lines of the world and redirected them back, effectively making a magical echo location. This design was far more refined than his, and gave a far more detailed reading. It was also displayed across a mirror-like surface, which looked more reliable than his scrying pools. "This is remarkable."

The dwarf beamed at the compliment. "Thank ya. I found a way ta refine tha way tha energy bounces from tha focal point'n used liquid silver instead'a water."

How Kovacik wished he could sit there and fiddle with Chuktorik's design. He could easily spend hours learning from it. *If only the circumstances were different.* He scanned the reading for the largest cavern he could find, and thankfully there seemed to be one directly underneath them.

"What about this one right here?"

Chuktorik leaned closely to inspect the mirrored surface, lifting his gas mask and scrunching his face. "Ne'er seen dat one befer. Could be jes what we're lookin' fer, or it could be a magma pocket.

"The city is that close to active magma?"

"How do ya think we heat tha damned place?" He pointed with a stubby finger at another location. It was much farther away and only half as large.

"This here is tha ruins. Der was a mining excavation der recently, too."

While it was the safer of the two options, it was so far away that Kovacik wondered if they would take too long in getting there. Then the craft rocked as something struck it from the side.

"Tha hells?"

There was another strike from the opposite side, this one powerful enough to leave a slight impression in the hull. Cursing, Chuktorik gunned the engine, sending the machine shooting forward.

"It's gotta be dose damned fish folk!"

"Brinore!"

"Do I look like I care if'n I insult 'em?! Which cavern are we going fer?"

Kovacik had to make a choice. The farther cavern was the safer bet, but the closer one was larger. Since they were under attack there was no telling if they could make it to *either* destination before their attackers managed to breach the craft.

"Below us! It's our best chance!"

Nodding curtly, Chuktorik yanked on a lever, twisted a dial, and Kovacik felt the machine lean forward abruptly. It must have caught one of their attackers off guard; he swore he heard the sounds of a muffled, watery scream just before the drill started up. A second later he felt the familiar rumble as they dug into the earth.

"I dunna need ta tell ye what'll 'appen if'n that's magma down der."

A grim look came across Kovacik's face as he nodded solemnly. If there was indeed magma filling that cavern, and they introduce this much water to it, the resulting explosive reaction would not only kill the two of them instantly, but destroy all of Aungermiest. Instead of saving the city, they would be its doom.

"We should be der'n ten minutes, if all goes well."

A troubling thought crossed Kovacik's mind. "How will we keep ourselves from falling into the cavern?"

"Well, we kenna go at 'er from a side. We're too vertical and the cavern's too large ta move ta one o'er sides. *But*, if we're careful den we can stop just as tha drill penetrates. Back up'n head in a differn't direction, lettin' gravity'n pressure do tha rest!"

The idea was sound, logical, and had every hallmark of having been thought through. "This isn't the first time you've done this, is it?"

"First time'n a more practical settin'."

Chuktorik's response did little to fill Kovacik with confidence, but it was their only shot at getting out alive. The thought of his own death was something that hadn't occurred to him in decades, if not centuries. Foreign and uncomfortable, a gnawing fear grew in the pit of his stomach. A slam against the back of the drilling machine caused the feeling to grow.

"They're not letting up. Can we go any faster?"

"Aye, but only if ye want ta burn out tha drill. We've already put it ta task going through all dem rocks before."

"Well, we may not have a choice!"

Grumbling, Chuktorik pushed the lever to his left forward all the way, locked it in place, and twisted several wheels counterclockwise as he slammed a button. The machine lurched forward, but there was an audible whine.

"Godsdammit! I knew it would be too much fe-"

A pipe burst in the back, steam escaping with a high-pitched wail.

"We're gonna lose pressure! We need ta redirect dat flow, now!"

Jumping out of his seat, Chuktorik ran over to where the pipe was damaged, and grabbed the valve on it. Howling in pain, he let go just as soon as he touched it.

"It's hotter'n Yorm's balls! We'll ne'er get it shut off!"

Kovacik got out of his cramped seat, and made his way to the valve. He could withstand temperatures most could not, but even he found the valve uncomfortably hot. He was also unable to turn it with just one hand. Another slam against the back of the machine and the hull dented inward.

"Damn it all! NnnnARRRRGH!!"

There was no time to wait for another attack. Kovacik grabbed onto the valve with both hands and, despite the pain, tried to turn it. His left arm was useless, but he angled it so that he could hopefully use it as lever. It worked; he could feel the valve give and begin to move.

Just as he finished however, he felt a snap. The pain was excruciating and he had a feeling there was no way his arm would ever heal properly now, even with magic. Falling back against the floor, he panted and dared to look at the wound.

The bone was no longer poking against the skin; instead, it had torn through and was fully exposed, silver blood leaking slowly from the tear. Judging from the way the arm hung limply at the site of the first break, he'd now broken clean through both bones of his forearm. It was ruined. Gritting his teeth, he tried his best to get it back into the sling.

"Inventor, are ye..."

"Just make sure we make it to that damned cavern! If we fail now we're *all* dead!"

Chuktorik turned back to the controls for the machine, pushing it even harder than before. The steady whine turned into a deafening screech the further down they went, but the attacks had subsided. *It seems the Behemoths* are *looking out for us...*

Breathing heavily, he leaned as best he could against the hull, reveling in the few moments of peace they had. As he sat with his back against the metal, he noticed how warm it was to the touch. Dread coalesced in his gut as he struggled to get to Chuktorik. "Do you have any means of gauging the temperature outside?"

Silence was the only reply. Chuktorik continued to man the controls, took in a deep breath and let out a heavy sigh. Finally, the dwarf spoke. "Aye. From dis readin's der's no doubt in mah mind dat it's magma."

Crestfallen, Kovacik slumped into his seat. No wonder their pursuers had given up. "If we keep going..."

"Ah'yup. We'll probably blow tha whole godsdamned city ta bits."

Their progress slowed to a halt, a good two-thirds of the way down to the cavern. Kovacik desperately scanned the readouts for something else nearby, but there was nothing. Their only option now was to level out and head towards

Chuktorik's recommended site. Slamming his fist down, he cracked the glass of the readout, causing Chuktorik to curse under his breath.

"We were so close!"

The dwarf nodded as he adjusted the controls, ready to send the drill to the next location, when he stopped. Kovacik recognized the look on his face: inspiration.

"How good are ya at magic?"

"Being kin, I've got a better handle on it than most. Why? What are you getting at?"

"If'n ya can use yer abilities ta cool tha magma down der..."

Following his train of thought, Kovacik finished his sentence, "...Then it could lessen the explosiveness of the reaction. The venting steam wouldn't build up as much pressure!"

Could it work, was the real question. Even if he managed to solidify the upper crust of the magma pocket, it would still be able to vaporize the water. But would it be cool enough to boil the water off harmlessly without exploding? Could he even muster enough energy to accomplish such a feat?

"I can teleport myself into the cavern, and attempt it."

"Ya 'ave any idea how hot it is down der?! Ya'll be cooked in seconds!"

"I've told you, Chuktorik, I'm far more resistant to heat than you realize. This is our only chance. I'll go in and attempt to cool the magma. If it works, I'll send you a message to continue. If you hear nothing after a few minutes, continue towards the ruins."

"How'll ya get back?"

"If it works, I'll figure out a way. If it does not, then I'm dead."

Shaking his head, the dwarf reset the controls so they would continue down towards the cavern again. Licking his lips he took in a shaky breath. "If'n I dun see ya af'er dis...been an honor, Inventor. Ne'er could I 'ave imagined meetin' ya in tha flesh."

Using his good hand he patted the dwarf on the shoulder and squeezed it firmly. "You're a good man, Chuktorik of Fenster."

Eyes misting slightly, Chuktorik grinned and turned back to his task. "What'll be tha sign? How'll I know?"

"You'll know."

Standing as best he could considering the size of the compartment, he spoke a few words of Kintare as he focused on the cavern below him. "Arrvi fyr'gux et noke."

He blinked out of the cockpit of the drilling machine and into the magma cavern. A blast of heat assaulted his senses, making it difficult to breathe. He needed to clear his mind, so as not to descend into panic and lose focus when he cast the spell. Kovacik closed his eyes and slowed his breathing; a trick he'd learned eons ago to lessen the effects of more hazardous environments on his body.

Opening them again, he let out a gasp of surprise; the cavern was indeed filled with magma, but the top layer had already crusted over. While the cavern was still dreadfully hot, he was confident the plan could work now, and the risk of an explosive buildup was minimal. Reaching out with his mind, he sent a single word and image back to Chuktorik. *Drill!!*

A moment passed, then another, and there was no sign of movement coming from above. No slight tremors or even the faintest noise. Afraid his message had not gotten through, he was elated when he saw something break through the cavern's ceiling on the far side, a metallic glint catching his eye.

We did it! Kovacik moved quickly over to where the dwarf had broken through, and waited. The drill backed up and disappeared, no doubt to right itself, and soon the water would pour through as gravity and pressure took over the rest. He heard a loud clang and the drill was forcibly pushed back through the hole it had made. It was sticking out much too far, and Kovacik used magic to try and help move it back, but there was a strong force pushing against it from the other side, actively trying to make it fall.

Horror spread across his face as he felt his mental grip on the drill slip and falter, giving whatever was pushing against it enough leeway to force it all the way through. There was nothing he could do as he watched the machine fall helplessly through the air, water gushing out right behind it. As it did, a tentacle burst from the flow to wrap tightly around him and yank him back through.

TWENTY-ONE

WHAT THE HELLS am I doing? Doubt was flooding into Rhikter's mind, as he and the vessel stomped through the streets toward their destination. They were up against *gods* here. Gods! Greyania and Kovacik had their control of magic, Hunter had the powers bestowed upon him by Yorm, and Shae apparently had the essence of one of them inside her.

What did he have? A near-death experience, a magical gemstone lodged in his chest, and a Behemoth Vessel that he barely understood. Still, he ran. Even if the fight was futile, Hunter needed him. Shrugging off his hesitations and doubts, he tried to focus on the task at hand.

Hunter had to have headed off in this direction. As he moved, the sound of rushing water became louder, indicating that he was going in the right direction, but he noticed something else as well. Creatures that looked like a nightmare amalgamation of marine life were stalking through the streets now, their numbers increasing as he grew closer to the source of the water. This wasn't just the Withered King, this was an army. The brinore were here with him.

Slowing to a stop, his feet splashing in the few inches of water on the ground in this area, he knew he had to make a choice. A few of the creatures had noticed him and in his mind he knew it would take minimal effort to plow right through and ignore them on his way to Hunter. Taking a quick survey of his surroundings, however, told him that here was where he was needed most. A group of dwarves, humans, and a lone elf were fighting against another of the creatures as it used its reach and speed to pick them off one by one.

Gritting his teeth, he made his choice and said a silent prayer for his friend and the others. If only he had a weapon, he thought. His forearm itched and, instinctively, he looked down at it. A bright blue flame was extending from his right hand. Fascinated, he couldn't turn away as it changed shape, from a simple jet of flame to a single-sided great axe. Not his first choice, but effective.

There was no time to wonder if the strange flame would actually be effective against the brinore though. Rhikter caught a glimpse of movement out of the corner of his eye, breaking him out of the flame's trance. He swung his arm reflexively as he barely dodged a wicked looking claw. "The hells?!" He exclaimed.

The axe had somehow coalesced into a solid piece of obsidian. The only flame left was a fine trace dancing along the edge of the blade. When the weapon connected with the claw, it sliced through it like butter. Along with the screams of pain from his attacker, he could hear a faint, brittle cracking noise. Frost was spreading from the wound as a clear liquid, possibly blood, leaked out.

"*Cold...fire,*" he whispered to himself.

Remembering the hapless group, he turned just in time to witness the brinore they were fighting kill one of the dwarves by slamming the small body against the street. It was most gruesome, and the rest of the group was starting to pan-

ic. The sheer violence of the act made Rhikter's blood boil.
These brinore were obviously stronger and faster, but to kill in
such a brutal manner showed nothing but malevolence. Ignoring the two he was facing, he rushed at the third before it
could latch onto another victim with a tentacle and tackled it
into the side of a nearby building.

From deep inside its body he heard a snap, and it
screamed at him as he felt something grab onto his back and
yank him away. Regretting not keeping track of the other two,
he sailed through the air and slammed to a stop against another building. Picking himself up off the ground, he saw that he
now had the full attention of all three brinore. The rest of the
group being attacked just stood and watched in shock.

"RUN!" he bellowed as he got to his feet, causing the
survivors to scatter.

Squaring off against the trio, he finally got a decent
look at each one. The first he had attacked had half of its claw
severed, rendering it useless for grabbing, but the larger part
of the claw still looked to be sharp and deadly. The rest of its
body reminded Rhikter of Kovacik, even the face. Its partner
had no arms, only a single large tentacle coming out of its
back. The lower half of its body was a giant slug-like appendage and its face was a hideous mishmash of teeth and
muscle. The one that had been attacking the group had long
tentacles for arms and its eyes were on either side of its head.

"I could *really* go for a good plateful of fish. Some
lemon, a pat of butter...absolute heaven." He smacked his lips
loudly, taunting them. An angry opponent was one that made
mistakes. The one Rhikter had injured seemed to be taking the
bait; it yelled as it lunged at him.

Then the lights went out. At first Rhikter thought
something had gone wrong with his vision. Before the accident caused him to absorb the amulet, it had been like looking
at everything through the helmet of a suit of armor. Now, it

was as if Nixturjekur's eyes were *his* eyes. When he heard an awful gurgling noise he knew it wasn't the vessel having an issue; the brinore were laughing. Glancing upward, he saw that Yormsun had gone out. Wondering what had happened wasn't a luxury he had time for at the moment. Even as his eyes adjusted, he knew they could see far better in the darkness than he ever could.

The axe in his hand started to glow. He saw the injured one move, about to strike in the darkness but it paused as the glow grew more and more brilliant. The axe's form was still there, he could feel its heft and weight, but it was fully engulfed in flames now. The vessel's response to his subconscious was something he didn't think he would ever get used to, but he was infinitely thankful for it.

He lashed out with zeal as he rushed at the injured one, swinging the axe over his head with far greater ease than he would have expected. In fact it was so much easier that he over swung and missed his intended target, the thing's head, and lopped off the rest of its clawed arm. Barking a surprised laugh at this newfound strength, he let his guard down for a moment too long and a thick tentacle wrapped around his midsection, pinning his arms to his sides and causing him to drop the axe.

Held fast, he struggled against the grip, but it would not let go. Pulling him in close, the mangled, ugly face bent into what he could only guess was a smile as the thing spoke in a raspy, gurgling voice. "Not so hungry now, are you?"

He felt the grip tighten and squeeze. There was no way to know if the vessel could withstand being crushed like this and he had no intention of finding out, but nothing happened no matter how he fought against the pressure. It felt as if he himself were being constricted, and he struggled even harder as a jolt of panic shot up his spine.

"Any day now!" Rhikter called out, hoping the suit would respond.

Just as something near his hip began to buckle, he caught sight of his reflection in the eyes of his opponent. The vessel's eyes blazed with brilliant blue fire. A moment later the rest of the vessel followed suit.

The brinore tried to let go, screaming in agony as it did, but for some reason its tentacle remained wrapped around Rhikter. The same brittle sound he'd heard earlier filled his ears, and he realized why. The thing was actually *freezing* to the metal body of Nixturjekur. He tried to move his arms again, and this time the tentacle shattered like an icicle thrown onto the street. He brought both of his hands around and boxed the sides of the brinore's head, crushing it and ending its agony. Turning to face the other two, he gave a battle-cry as he rushed at them.

The flames on the axe had died down by the time he reached the one with tentacles for arms. The thing grabbed him, using its tentacles to try and pull his arms apart. Smirking, Rhikter twisted his hands and grabbed onto them, pulling back as hard as he could. They popped off surprisingly easily, leaving the brinore to fall back against the pavement, writhing in agony. Rhikter leaned to pick up his axe, and ended its life in a quick, decisive blow.

This left the one he had squared off against originally. Standing there in the middle of the street, it stared at him with fear in its eyes, and Rhikter thought for a moment it was going to run off. Instead, a low growl emanated from deep in its throat, and it sped towards him. Rhikter could only feel a small amount of pity as he swung the axe, granting it a swift death.

He wondered if brinore culture mandated going down in battle instead of retreating. Perhaps he had injured it far more gravely than he first realized and it knew it was going to die anyway. Answers to such questions were beyond him though, and he mentally shook his head, focusing more on what was going on around him than philosophies wandering through his mind.

Sounds of continued battle came from all around him now. There was no need to go searching for where he was needed most; the fight was coming to him, and quickly. At least the water was no longer rising. It was only about halfway up his shins now, and he was certain if it got any higher he'd barely be able to move at all.

Wading towards what appeared to be a pavilion, he saw several brinore fighting with a small contingent of the city guard. This bunch looked far more prepared and better equipped than the group he had saved earlier, though, and he looked around to see if any others were in more desperate need.

His stomach began to feel slightly uneasy and he realized he was beginning to float up out of the water and into the air. Was flight some new function of the vessel as well? No, spinning helplessly in the air caused him to doubt this was some new ability. The feeling was cemented when he felt his whole body become immobilized.

High above the tops of the buildings, and almost to the ceiling of the cavern that housed Aungermiest, he continued to fight against the invisible bonds that held him. If he got free, he was certain he would survive the fall. Mostly certain. From here, even without the light of Yormsun, he could see that the portal was closed, and that one section of the city had been completely submerged.

His body was whipped around several times and he was flung in the opposite direction from where he had been looking. When he finally stopped, he was face to face with the Withered King.

"Rhikter?!"

Greyania's voice sounded from somewhere on the ground to his right, but he found himself unable to even turn his head.

Frowning, the Withered King yelled, "Deghat! Abtrue!"

No reply. Keeping Rhikter suspended, he turned just in time to wave off a ball of fire that was hurtling towards him as casually as brushing off a mosquito. Rhikter struggled even harder against his bonds.

"He's got me held fast! Throw everything you've got at him!" he called down to whomever was on the ground.

Cracked lips curling into a snarl, Eldric'Kel called out, "Festocina! I don't care what you're doing, come and deal with these annoyances!"

He turned back to face Rhikter, and the volume of his voice was barely audible as he replied to a voice Rhikter couldn't hear. Gods, how he hated telepathy.

"*I said I don't care*. Finish with him after! Just make sure the one who's got Jek in her head remains alive." He paused. "You forget your place, witch."

The Withered King took in a deep breath and let it out slowly as he moved quickly away from the extinguished Yormsun, dragging Rhikter along just behind him.

"I think it's time we finally talk, boy."

*****

Knowing he had to get back into the fight as quickly as possible, Hunter sat on the rooftop, took in a deep breath, closed his eyes, and willed his body to heal itself.

Meditation had never been his strong point; there was a reason Rage was his title. Now, however, he had no choice. There was no other way he could continue to fight without being in the way and a burden. They were up against a mutated race and several gods. His foolish and brash attack would have cost him his life if not for the intervention of Karak.

If you can hear me, know you have my thanks.

There were no implicit instructions for what he was attempting. All he knew from the legends were that the Avatars of Yorm could fully heal themselves, even from death's door. He hoped it wouldn't have to come to such an extreme before the ability manifested itself, though.

Quieting his preoccupied mind was proving more difficult than his encounter with Abtrue. He watched, helpless, as Greyania and Shae closed the portal, and had seen their brief encounter with Deghat. He couldn't hear their conversation, but the fact that no blows had been exchanged and that he allowed them to go towards Yormsun was curious. What was Deghat trying to do? Play both sides? As monstrous as his outer appearance was, it belied a sharp cunning.

Kovacik and Chuktorik had to still be in that machine of theirs as well. He had watched it as it submerged again and wondered where they were heading off to. Rhikter was out there as well, no doubt on his way here to help.

After several long minutes of nothing happening. Hunter opened his eyes and cursed the futility of it all. He stood, ready to head back into battle, even if his wounds were not healed. As he moved towards the edge of the roof, though, he realized that his strength was quickly returning, and the wounds and cuts on his body were mending at an amazing pace. Whatever he had done was working. Smiling to himself, he was ready to fly off in the direction Greyania and Shae had gone when he noticed the whirlpool in the water.

Growing larger and faster, something was draining the water from the area. His mind immediately went back to the dwarf's machine. Could they have found a way to drill the water away? It was an amazing feat, and he was impressed by their ingenuity.

Mesmerized by the swirling water, he was about to turn away when he noticed a shape swimming against the current, barely visible in the dark. With Yormsun out, the ambient light of the dwarven city was all that remained. Hunter was surprised he had even seen it at all. As it got closer to the surface he could see the form grow larger as well. Whatever it was, it was powerful enough to swim against the draining current with an uncanny speed. Had Karak returned?

When it broke free of the water, he knew immediately it was one of the brinore invaders, but this one looked nothing like the others. While the attackers all resembled some form of marine life, even in an amalgamated form, they still retained some portion of their kin heritage. This one looked *nothing* like a kin; numerous tentacles and growths erupted from its oblong and deformed body. There was no visible area he could tell was its head or torso, nor its legs. It was a wriggling, disgusting mass of claw, bone, and sinew.

"Pitiful creature," Hunter muttered under his breath, as he watched it sail through the air. One of its larger tentacles was gripping something.

"Kovacik!" he cried when he realized what the creature was carrying.

Jumping from the roof and into the air, he flew as fast as he could to snatch his friend out of the grasp of the beast. Before it could react, he grabbed the tentacle holding Kovacik and tore it free, causing it to scream in pain and swing at him with a bladed claw. It missed, if barely, and he was able to fly to a nearby rooftop with Kovacik.

Coughing violently and gasping for breath as the remains of the tentacle fell away, Hunter was happy to see the kin was still alive.

"You and the dwarf drained the water?"

Still breathing in big gulps of air, Kovacik nodded. Hunter saw him favoring his arm, and even he could see how badly injured it was now. Even if they found a healer more skilled than Greyania and Shae combined, it would never be enough to completely repair it. He set his jaw and gave a nod.

"Well done. One of those things pulled you out. Do you know why?"

Kovacik shook his head. "The others gave up when we neared the magma pocket...too hot. This one came from out of nowhere and...Chuktorik..."

The look he gave Hunter told him everything he needed to know.

"At least he died saving his city. There is no greater honor than protecting one's people in sacrifice."

"My, how touching."

An unseen force knocked Hunter from the roof and into the air, where he quickly righted himself. Snarling, he turned to where the voice had come from and was surprised to find a brinore woman crawling up the side of a building, looking like some kind of crustacean centaur. If not for the fact she was more sea-creature than woman, he would have found her beauty striking.

"Fes...Festocina?!" Kovacik cried out in surprise.

"Come now, Kovacik, your surprise is insulting. Did you really think I would miss this? My time has *finally* arrived."

Hunter moved closer, cautiously. The creature he had attacked earlier was also hanging back. He was still unsure where its head and face were, but from the way it was floating in the water, he knew it was focused solely on him.

"You betrayed our people! Wiped them out! Doomed them to...*this*!" Kovacik waved his good arm towards the thing in the water, tears beginning to stream down his face.

"Doomed? I *elevated* them," She pointedly looked at his injured arm. "Here, allow me to help you."

As she opened her mouth, Hunter could see it was moving in an odd way, and it took him a moment to realize it was bifurcated, like the orthoxson. Before Kovacik could move out of the way, Festocina spat out a glob of green material which hit his right arm.

"What have you-NAAAAGGGHHHH!!!" Cutting himself off with his own scream, Kovacik fell to his knees, clutching at his arm.

Hunter flew forth to challenge Festocina, but the thing in the water leapt up and collided with him midair, causing them both to fall and tumble onto a rooftop, breaking down into the home below.

Still hearing Kovacik's screams from above, Hunter faced off against the thing. Here, in drier conditions, he could see that its eyes were on either side of its body, but there was still no discernible mouth.

Stepping forward, he raised a fist and brought it down hard on the hide of the creature, surprised at how spongy the flesh felt as his fist bounced back. A tentacle wrapped into a ball and shot out towards him, striking him in the chest and knocking him back. It was followed by a claw slicing through the air, grazing his chest. It left a gash that started to seep bright blue blood.

Feeling his rage build, he knew exchanging glancing blows like this was a waste of time. He had to find an opening that would allow him to deliver a more decisive strike. When the claw came around for another slicing attack, he managed to grab onto it and yanked as hard as he could. It separated from the body with a sickening tearing noise, but the thing uttered no sound as it jumped up through the hole they had created in the roof, escaping from him.

Hunter followed, but could see no sign of either it or of Festocina. Kovacik had stopped screaming, but he lay curled into a fetal position on the roof. Hurrying towards him,

Hunter checked to see if he was still alive. Kovacik's chest rose and fell with steady, even breaths, which was a good sign.

"Kovacik, are you alright?" Hunter asked as he moved closer.

"Stay back!!"

"You need to let me see the wound, perhaps I can help you."

Reaching out, he turned Kovacik over. The kin gave no resistance and Hunter gasped as he saw what Festocina had done. He had expected to find the arm missing, or horribly burned. Instead, the wound had healed, and a series of barna-cle-like protrusions covered his forearm, which now ended in a tri-tipped claw of some sort. The barnacles were spreading slowly upwards, and Hunter could only watch in horror.

"She...she's somehow turning me into one of them."

The creature had returned, silently, and now it knocked Hunter aside in one quick swipe. It overtook Ko-vacik, but to Hunter's surprise it did not attack. It seemed to be cradling Kovacik in its arms, holding him, one of its large eyes watching him intently. When it still did not attack, Hunter realized what it could be. *Who* it could be.

"By everything that is holy...I believe that thing is your brother, Nothias!"

As he spoke its name, it turned to him, recoiling as it set Kovacik down.

"Nothias!?" Kovacik choked on his brother's name. "Oh my gods, brother...what did she do to you?!"

The creature did not respond, and Hunter wondered if it even could. There was no question in his mind that this form was some sadistic punishment from Festocina or the Withered King. Perhaps both. Why Nothias was willingly helping them now was baffling.

"What *happened*?" Kovacik asked of his brother.

The creature before them said nothing in reply, and made no movement save to blink slowly at them. How much of Kovacik's brother was actually still in there? Another moment passed before it slipped over the edge, into the water below, and quickly disappeared.

Kovacik stood there, looking after his brother, wiping at his eyes with his good hand. Clearing his throat he turned to Hunter.

"We need to find the others."

"Your arm..."

"We'll figure it out after this is done. I'm still a damned kin, and I intend to *stay* one."

"Do you have any idea where the others are?"

Kovacik looked over towards the artificial sun. "Before Festocina left, it seemed as though she were talking to someone unseen. I can only assume the King called her to his side, and I'm pretty sure they've got to be at Yormsun."

"Then what are we waiting for?"

TWENTY-TWO

SHAE CAME TO feeling incredibly weak, and she hated it. All this power inside of her, and she could barely lift her head up. Something was wrong, it had to be. Was Jek's essence truly inexhaustible, or had she pushed herself beyond her limits? Watching the Withered King head off with Rhikter in tow was infuriating because she knew there was no way she had enough energy to do anything about it.

Jek, if you're in here with me and can understand, I need more. I need to be able to help him!

No response or respite, no second breath was forthcoming. Cursing to herself, she wished she had her weapons with her. Then she could be of some use.

"Damn it all to hells," Greyania said, watching as the two figures disappeared around the other side of the dead sun. "We need to find a way to get the Yormsun working again."

A strange green blob flew past her head, narrowly missing her. Whirling around, they both faced off against a female brinore. Without hesitation Greyania threw a fireball, which hit their opponent right in the chest, scorching the armor she wore, but doing little else. The brinore laughed it off.

"Was that your best, Behemoth *pet*? It's no wonder they now choose to aid the Withered. Their champion isn't even suited for parlor tricks." Moving her hands quickly in a preset motion, she shoved them forward and shot a blade of ice at Greyania. Shae reached out with her mind, deflecting it to a wall nearby, where it shattered. "Ah, the pretender," the brinore's face contorted in a sneer as she regarded Shae. "You've got something I *need*."

Shae could feel a force on her, pressing against her skin but nothing more. The brinore's mood soured as she moved her arms more furiously. Still, nothing happened.

"Fine. If I can't extract it from a distance, I'll rip it from your corpse!"

The brinore raised her arms high above her head, her body beginning to glow with a green fire. Just as the intensity of the flames was beginning to increase, Hunter slammed into her side, sending her flying down the street and into the side of a nearby building. Shae had never felt so relieved to see anyone.

"Hunter!" Greyania ran over to him, embracing him tightly.

Even in the heat of battle, Shae couldn't help but smirk slightly at the two. She then noticed Kovacik and ran over to him, but he held up a hand, urging her to stay back. Confused, Shae slowed to a stop. Then saw his arm. "What did they do to you?!"

"Festocina." He motioned towards where the brinore had been thrown. "It appears to be spreading...Could be some sort of mutagenic magic, and I have no idea what will happen if anyone else touches it."

Ignoring his warnings, she rushed to his side, and placed her hands on his arm, uttering every word of healing she knew. She also tried to channel the power within her, but could only feel it ebb sporadically. It felt like Jek's essence was fading.

"Godsdammit," Kovacik muttered, "I wish you weren't so stubborn."

"If I wasn't, you wouldn't like me so much." Shae grinned at him, and if he could blush she was sure he would be at that moment.

Kovacik kept quiet as she continued to work on his arm. A surge of energy flowed from her, unprovoked, and right into his arm, causing him to cry out. A bright flash and she fell back, even more exhausted.

It had worked, somewhat. His hand was still in the shape of a strange claw, but the growths were gone and he was otherwise fully healed. He regarded the claw with visible disappointment.

"How in the hells am I supposed to build with *this* damned thing?"

"NO!" Festocina's voice echoed around them. "You don't get to walk away unscathed, Kovacik!"

Festocina had freed herself from the rubble, and Hunter rushed to attack her. Greyania threw her hands towards the two, causing bits of nearby debris to lift off the ground and hurtle towards the brinore. She was able to easily deflect the larger pieces, but some of the smaller ones made contact, chipping away at the shell of her carapace and causing just enough distraction for Hunter to land a hit to her midsection, causing it to break into pieces.

Enraged, Festocina pulled herself from the ruins of her shell, revealing that it wasn't part of her body, but was being worn as armor. Her actual body was gelatinous and translucent, like a jellyfish. Organs and strange glowing bits that Shae had never seen before floated in the mass. Her tentacle legs pulled her body quickly away from Hunter before he could land another blow. *She's vulnerable!*

That was when the ground began to rumble. As the sound increased, Kovacik got a worried look on his face.

"No...no no no..." he repeated.

"What? What is it?" Shae demanded.

"The magma was too hot!"

"What are you talkin-"

Shae was unable to finish her question as the ground cracked and a jet of steam shot out. Similar fissures were popping up all over the place.

"Watch out!" Kovacik yelled just as a fissure erupted between them, obscuring everyone from her view.

In the steam and fog, a force grabbed her and flung her backwards, twisting her body around so she was face to face with Festocina. The brinore was frowning as she regarded Shae, hatred flowing in each of her words.

"I can *feel* him in there. You don't deserve it."

Festocina slammed her hand onto Shae's chest, and Shae could feel energy rocket through her frame as the wind was knocked from her. The pain was intense, and it felt like her soul was being ripped out. Festocina was trying to extract Jek from her, forcibly.

Weakly, Shae tried her best to resist, but there was no use; Festocina was too strong for her, and it didn't feel like Jek was fighting at all. The pain grew more intense and she looked down, seeing a brilliant ball of white being pulled from her breast.

"Hush, little elf. In a moment *nothing* will bother you ever again."

"SHAE!" Kovacik jumped onto Festocina's back, shoving his clawed hand deep into her body and grabbing onto something that appeared vital. He squeezed and Shae saw it rupture into a ruined mess. Dropping her and screaming in pain, Festocina attempted to throw Kovacik off her back.

Shae couldn't focus. The extraction process had been halted, but the world was fading in and out. She could still feel Jek within her as she stumbled, trying to stand on legs as heavy as lead but as wobbly as jelly.

As Hunter came into her field of vision, she blacked out.

*****

"You still have no idea what is really going on, do you? With any of this?"

Rhikter didn't reply. The King held him as a captive audience, but he wasn't going to give him the satisfaction of conversation. Not while his friends were fighting below.

Glancing down, Eldric'Kel shrugged before looking back at Rhikter. "Nothing you can do to help them. Must be torturous." He pause and then sighed exasperatedly when Rhikter continued to be defiant and refuse to speak. "Well, since you are being as stubborn as an ass, I'm going to explain a few things to you."

The King waved his hand, and the hatch that allowed access to Nixturjekur was opened. Rhikter was roughly pulled from its confines. He glared at the King in defiance.

"I wasn't about to tell all of this to a suit of armor." The vessel was released from whatever grip the King had on it, and it dropped out of the air like a stone.

"No!"

"*Now* he speaks! Maybe he will listen, also." Gesturing towards the blackened sun, he continued. "Pay attention, Rhikter. This dwarven sun is a *lie*. Did you know that? They never created it. The filthy creatures *stole* it. From me, no less."

"*What?*" That couldn't be possible. The stories of how Yormsun came to be were common knowledge. There was never even a hint that any of it was false.

"They use it as nothing more than a light in their piti-ful, dark lives! This, boy, is far more than that. It's a power source. Well, more accurately, a conduit for power. The ener-gies I need to create new life are massive. This just makes it...easier."

"There's no way that is true. If it was, why haven't you used it yet?"

"I must give credit where credit is due. The dwarves hooked it up to a network of machines, made it follow their crude commands, forced it to operate like a mere sun. Remov-ing their mess without damaging the device has proved to need a more delicate hand than I anticipated."

"You should find a different magic ball to use in your mad conquest, then."

A dark laugh erupted from his lips, shocking Rhikter.

"A sense of humor. I see we share more than just a name and blood."

"What are you talking about?"

"The main reason I brought you here, Rhikter," his face cracked into a wider smile as he spoke, "is to tell you that as a human my name was Eldric. Eldric *Lehmann*. *You* are my di-rect descendant, and you *are* going to join with us."

It was now Rhikter's turn to laugh. "You really are the fool of the gods if you think that."

The smile faded from Eldric'Kel's face as he stared at Rhikter. He stayed there, floating motionless with his arms folded, for a long moment, until Rhikter met his gaze and fi-nally broke the silence.

"Well? Either release me or kill me. I'm not going to become whatever you are."

"Perhaps. Perhaps not. Just a moment."

Deghat was making his way towards them, rubbing his hands together and speaking as soon as he was close enough.

"Ah! Eldric'Kel. Everything is in a state of ever-present motion. However, Abtrue is currently locked with Karak in a battle most dire. What act dost thou wish me to perform in thy service?"

Smirking, Eldric'Kel held out a hand. "I want you to serve as my first example, you duplicitous bastard."

Deghat dropped all pretense, growing arrogant and defensive towards Eldric'Kel, "Tread lightly, dear brother, for thou knowest I am far more powerful than ever thou wert."

"This won't take long, I assure you. Rhikter just needs a demonstration."

Deghat's bravado faded away and a look of concern washed over his face. Rhikter could tell he wasn't looking at Eldric'Kel now, but past him. He was scrutinizing Yormsun, and his eyes grew wide.

"Thou hast activated it!" Deghat cried out in surprise and he tried to flee.

The King closed his outstretched hand into a fist. Deghat was yanked back and slammed into the side of Yormsun, jarring it loose. Struggling against invisible bonds, there was true fear in his eyes as he began to plead. "Brother, thou knowest not what thou does! Release me from this contraption afore thine actions cause thee regret!"

"Regret is for the weak, Deghat."

Rhikter could hardly believe his eyes. It looked like Deghat was actually *melting* into the device. Instead of struggling harder, a look of acceptance was on his face as he stared right at Eldric'Kel

"Thou hast lost thy way, brother. I pray thou findest it once more."

Saying nothing more, Rhikter and the King watched as Deghat disappeared into Yormsun, which trembled slightly and then was still.

Eldric'Kel spoke. "Yormsun, as the dwarves call it, was originally used to create *us*. It can also be used to absorb us as well. Converted into energy to be reused as I see fit."

"You...killed him."

Eldric'Kel paused, and his voice caught as he agreed with Rhikter's assessment of what he had done. "Fratricide...is a small price to pay to bring about a new world. He was never truly going to help me. He'd become too browbeaten by the others, by making playthings for *their* children."

"Was Abtrue's fate to be the same?"

"If he did not fall into place, yes. I only need a few of the gods, not all. It matters not which ones."

"If you're so obsessed with creating a new race, seems you should put yourself in there."

Shaking his head, Eldric'Kel scoffed at Rhikter's suggestion.

"Such a small mind to have come from my bloodline. Think, boy! Who would create my children if I was gone? Besides, I already tried self-sacrifice once, and my body was destroyed when Festocina botched the ritual due to the interference of that damned kin. If she had killed him in the first place, then everything would be different now."

Yormsun began to stir, showing signs of coming back to life, only the light it gave off was no longer a brilliant white. Instead, a sickly, purple glow seemed to *ooze* from it. It hurt Rhikter's eyes to look at it.

"Deghat, you fool. Even in death you challenge me." He clenched his hands into fists and quickly turned back to Rhikter. "I should have known it wouldn't be so simple..."

Rhikter laughed,and when he spoke, his tone was mocking and dismissive. "You planned to use this device to trap the gods, but never tested it?! What kind of fool are you? It's no wonder the brinore look as they do."

Eldric'Kel smirked and flicked his wrist. Rhikter heard a loud snap, and pain bloomed in his leg. Without even looking he knew it was broken. It took everything in him not to cry out.

"You're fortunate I need you, or I would've torn your head off for such a remark. You're a an impetuous braggart, Rhikter. Like a mewling child screaming for a teat. You want, but you have no idea why."

A commotion came from below, as familiar voices called up to them.

"Rhik! Hold on!" Hunter's familiar voice was a godsend.

Eldric'Kel frowned. "Festocina is even more useless than I thought. No matter, we're leaving."

"You shall go nowhere, *Withered!*"

Festocina crawled around the surface of Yormsun, the light playing off her translucent body and throwing eerie shadows in every direction. Her own body was beginning to glow green. Whatever she was up to put a knot in the pit of Rhikter's stomach; he was right in the line of fire.

"You traitorous sea witch! After all I've given you!"

"You gave me empty promises! Cast me down like a broken doll after that fool attacked you. You promised me that I would become a god. Well, now I've found the way."

"Enough of this!" The King roared. "I WILL NOT BE DENIED AGAIN!"

Throwing his arms out, dark tendrils erupted from his back and thrust forth at Festocina. Hoping that his divided concentration would loosen the King's hold Rhikter struggled against the bonds again, trying to free himself. It was no use; he was still held fast.

The vessel, however, was not held back. It flew up from where it had fallen, and moved between Eldric'Kel and Rhikter. The position Nixturjekur took broke the King's line of sight, and Rhikter felt the invisible restraints loosen and dissipate. Glancing down he panicked as he realized there was no way he could survive a drop from this height.

As the hold fully gave way, the vessel caught him and he managed to get inside, despite the pain in his leg. Looking at the King, his hands ignited and he reached out, grabbing one of the tendrils before him.

The scream was deafening, but he held tight, watching the frost spread quickly along the dark mass. Digging his fingers in, he tried to climb up, towards Eldric'Kel's body, but he was being thrashed about left and right as the King tried to sling him off. He was barely holding on.

"If you've got a plan, now's the time!" he yelled to the others below.

*****

Greyania had hoped *he* would have a plan. Shae had blacked out again, and their fight with Festocina had exhausted them all. Even Hunter, who had more power in him than she could fathom, looked beaten. At least the fissures had stopped belching steam.

Ignoring his exhausted state, Hunter gave a war cry and jumped towards the King, fists flying in a flurry as he attacked while Rhikter appeared to be holding on for dear life. Kovacik was trying to keep Festocina distracted as well, firing at her with a strange contraption that he had carried on his back. He looked like he was having difficulty adjusting to using it with the claw, as most of the projectiles it shot were well off their mark.

Making sure Shae was safe, Greyania joined in, throwing all manner of magic into the battle, hoping some way, somehow, it would be enough to bring down not only the god, but his minion as well. They needed a miracle, and she wasn't sure how they would get one.

Festocina managed to slam the tentacle she was fighting against Yormsun, and to Greyania's surprise the sphere began to absorb it. *Just what had the dwarves built?*

"No! NO!!"

"Your fight is over! I've WON! If you won't make me a Behemoth, I'll do it myself!"

Greyania and the others stopped attacking and watched in fascination as the Withered King struggled against being sucked into the device. Try as he might, he was pulled further and further in, screaming all manner of curses at Festocina, who began cackling with glee.

Rhikter let go of Eldric'Kel, and Hunter caught him before he fell to the ground. As the others continued to watch, Greyania knew that whatever was happening, the outcome would be dire.

"You think I actually trusted you?" Eldric'Kel sneered. "Why do you think I brought you?"

Dark energy whipped out from his sides, slicing the tendrils from his body, and they were quickly sucked into Yormsun. The energy then coalesced into something solid and he thrust it outwards, like a spear, pinning Festocina to the surface of the device. She screamed out as he hovered over her. She spat poison at him in a futile act of defiance; her aim was so badly off that he didn't even need to deflect it.

"I think it's time I make good on my promise."

The King glared down towards Shae and outstretched his hand. Balling it into a fist, he twisted it slowly. "Romvas." Shea cried out in pain as her body began to convulse. Greyania ran towards her quickly, but stopped short as a ball of light was extracted forcibly from Shae's chest.

"You're killing her!" Greyania yelled.

Ignoring her plea, Eldric'Kel yanked his fist towards his chest. With a final spasm, the ball of light was ripped free and flew up towards him. Shae lay motionless.

"No...gods no!!" Greyania cried out as she scooped Shae up in her arms. "She's still breathing!"

"We need to get her out of here. There's no telling what's about to happen!" Kovacik's clawed hand was on her shoulder and she nodded quickly.

"Everyone, we need to go, now!" Greyania called for the others.

She tried to open a portal to her laboratory, but it wouldn't happen. She tried again, starting to panic now, but still nothing happened. The look on Kovacik's face meant he couldn't do it either.

"No one goes anywhere until I've finished!!" Eldric'Kel bellowed.

Jek's essence, the piece of it he'd pulled from Shae, was floating before him. With a wave of his hand he produced the other half that he'd taken directly from Jek. Immediately the two parts melded together, and Greyania could have sworn that the light they made once they were reunited seemed...happy.

"Time to become a god, *witch*."

Taking the newly joined ball of light in his hands, he shoved it into Festocina's chest. She cried out in pain at first, but then she began to revel in it.

"Yes...Yes! This power! It's phenomenal!!"

Even as she rejoiced in being granted her wish, Greyania could see that Festocina was being absorbed by the device much like Deghat had been. By the time Festocina realized what was actually happening to her, it was too late.

Her eyes ablaze in fury, she spat out a final curse towards Eldric'Kel, "You will never see your world come to pass! All you cherish will wither and rot!"

Then, she was gone.

TWENTY-THREE

EVERYONE WAS STUNNED, especially Kovacik. He had no love for Festocina, not after what she had done to his people, but he would not wish such an end on anyone. The King just hovered and stared at the place where she had been absorbed.

"We need to get out of here," Kovacik stated.

"If we strike now, all of us, we might be able to take him out once and for all. All we need to do is get him to touch the Yormsun again!" Rhikter sounded hopeful.

Kovacik knew they were in no state to mount an offensive. Shae was holding onto life by a thread, Hunter needed time to rejuvenate, and Greyania was in no shape to continue her attacks. Even he wasn't in the right frame of mind, still reeling from what had happened to his arm earlier.

"If we don't leave now," Kovacik stated again, "chances are we'll all die here."

On cue, the ground rumbled beneath them. Twenty or thirty yards away, something erupted violently from the earth. Afraid that it was more steam venting from the magma cavern, Kovacik yelled for everyone to brace themselves, but then he saw the drill and cried out in joy and amazement.

It was singed and beaten to hell, but Chuktorik's machine was in one piece. The side door flew open and the dwarf stuck his head out. A cut was bleeding over one of his eyes, forcing it shut, but he otherwise looked no worse for wear.

"What're ya all waitin' fer?! Get in 'ere!"

Kovacik quickly ushered Greyania and Shae towards the machine, but the King slammed into the ground, cutting them and the machine off from the rest of the group.

"Get Shae out of here!!" Kovacik yelled.

Eldric'Kel looked unperturbed that she was getting away. "I no longer need the elf."

Kovacik found that he was thankful for the dismissive words, and hoped Chuktorik would help get Shae far, far away.

Looking right at Rhikter, Eldric'Kel continued. "Come. *You* I need."

A bright flame erupted from Rhikter's arm, and an axe made of some dark substance formed itself into existence. That was *not* something he had originally designed into the vessel. Just what the hells had happened to it, and to Rhikter?

"No. I am not your puppet. We share a bloodline, *nothing more.*"

Share a...gods, what did I miss?! Kovacik glanced over at Hunter and it looked like he was just as surprised by the revelation.

"I am older and far more powerful than bloodlines, *boy*. I am the end of this world and the harbinger of a glorious new one."

"Enough talk!" Rhikter rushed forward, brandishing his axe high above his head. The King waved a hand and the head of the axe snapped off, but it reformed immediately as pure blue flame, and Rhikter brought it down across the King's chest.

The blow barely grazed him, but caused him to hiss in pain and left a growing spot of frost behind it. Kovacik saw there was no avenue for escape. He nodded to Hunter, and they both joined the battle. As the orc lunged forward to rain blows down where Rhikter had cut, Kovacik managed to brace his rifle against his clawed arm, helping to steady his aim as he fired in rapid succession.

The combined attacks seemed to be weakening The Withered King, causing him to stagger backwards. Just as it seemed they were overtaking him, he lashed out, his dark energy striking like a scorpion's tail.

Kovacik tried to dodge, but was stabbed in the shoulder. The blow tossed him onto his backside, and he skidded away. Hunter had grabbed onto one of the tendrils and was grappling with it as it tried to strike him in the face. His body began to glow like it had in the desert and Kovacik cried out to him.

"No! You'll kill us all!"

Thankfully, Hunter exhibited more control this time, and the glow did not increase. If he was going to explode with power again, Kovacik wanted to be far, far away. Looking up he saw that the drilling machine was gone. *At least they got away*

Rhikter was wielding a sword now, along with the axe, slicing and hacking every tendril the King threw at him with a masterful efficiency. He wondered if Rhikter was that good of a swordsman, or if the vessel had augmented his natural ability. Even as the creator, he realized he had no idea what it was *truly* capable of. The amulet was a mystery, now more than ever.

"This ends here, Eldric! I won't let you destroy what's left of this world!"

"Let me? *Let* me?! You presume far too much, boy!"

Suddenly, everything felt off, wrong. Kovacik could feel his body lifting off the ground and he found himself levitating just a few feet in the air. Hunter seemed to be floating just as helplessly as his power began to fade. The world around them began to crumble; cracks appeared in the ground, and whole buildings were swallowed.

"I can do as I wish, when I wish, *and how I wish*! I am a GOD. *And you will show me the respect I deserve!*"

Eldric'Kel then ripped off his own arm, a tentacle unlike any other quickly growing in place of the stump. It was a brilliant turquoise color, and glinted like it was made from gemstone. Rhikter tried to attack it, but he too was floating and couldn't get enough heft in his swing. He missed as it wrapped around his midsection.

"Rhikter!" Hunter's voice seemed so far away as Kovacik watched the King lift Rhikter up and then slammed him into the ground. The end of the new tentacle arm grabbed at the chest of the vessel, breaking it open like an egg shell, exposing Rhikter's body.

"I control *everything*! The others will *never* stop me because they are weak, frightened children! *ONLY I KNOW THE TRUTH!*"

"What truth is that? That you're delusional and acting far more like a human than a god?!" Rhikter spat at him.

The King flew into a blind rage and he slammed Rhikter against the ground several more times, becoming increasingly erratic. "NO! I was Res'Kel, the Wandering Dream. I...I was Eldric Lehmann, Last Crowned Monarch of Humanity. I *am* Eldric'Kel, the Withered King. *AND I WAS THE FIRST!*"

Rhikter continued his defiant attitude as he egged him on even more. "What's the matter...mommy didn't hug you enough?"

You damned fool! Kovacik knew it was all for show, but why was Rhikter so insistent on rushing headlong to a swift death? The kid had luck in spades, for sure, but it was quickly running out. Kovacik watched Eldric'Kel rip Rhikter's sword from his hand and raise it high, even as the blade started to freeze his own hand and arm. The King was ready to deliver a killing blow and Kovacik could only watch in helpless horror.

"You need me, remember?" Rhikter yelled confidently. "I'm the last of our line!"

"*NRRRGGGAAAAAHHH!!*"

The sword came down with such force, there was no way for Rhikter to avoid, let alone survive, such a strike. From Kovacik's viewpoint, the sword went into Rhikter's chest all the way down to the hilt.

"RHIKTER!!!" Hunter cried, struggling to move.

Eldric'Kel raised his hand to withdraw the blade. But as he pulled up, all that came was the hilt. Frustration and confusion colored his features as he jerked his hand to the side to toss away what was left of the blade. His hand, being fully frozen, broke off and flew through the air as well.

A new hand grew back immediately, and Eldric'Kel scoffed, ignoring what had just happened. Looking up at Yormsun, he reached out with his power. The device stirred, then ripped itself from the ceiling, showering the ruined city with dirt and debris. Yormsun floated there for a moment and then was gone.

"This...has not been a favorable day."

The King disappeared before Kovacik could even blink. Both he and Hunter fell to the earth, he himself narrowly missing falling into one of the newly formed cracks. Both men quickly made their way over to Rhikter, and peered into the vessel.

"Rhikter!"

Though it made no sense, the blade was not jutting out of his chest as they had both expected. In fact, there was no sign of the blade at all, and Rhikter lay there, smirking up at them with a bloodied mouth.

"H-how?!" Hunter asked as he placed a hand on his friend's shoulder. Rhikter stirred slightly, trying to sit up but falling back.

"Guess my own sword knew it would be in bad taste to run me through. The blade just...*disappeared* as he shoved it in."

"You're a damned idiot, kid. Are you *trying* to get yourself killed?!"

"He wanted to posses me! You'd want to get a few insults in too."

Kovacik shook his head. Even though he was glad Rhikter was alive, he couldn't shake the feeling of dread as he looked to the gaping hole where Yormsun had been.

"He's got the power of at least two Behemoths in that thing now," Kovacik stated.

Hunter reached down and grabbed the hilt of the sword. The hand was still attached but fell free and disintegrated before it hit the ground. He tossed it back to Rhikter, and Kovacik was amazed it hadn't damaged his hand with the frost.

"I suppose it likes you, Hunter," Rhikter observed.

"We are brothers. Nixturjekur knows this." Hunter smiled as he helped Rhikter out of the vessel.

"We have a lot of work to do. Gods know what he intends to do next, and we still need to find the brinore."

"Speaking of which, it seems they lost their lust for battle once their queen fell."

Hunter was right. Kovacik could see many escaping through their own portals throughout the city. He only hoped his brother had found a way out as well. *I will find a way to help you, Nothias. I promise.*

Looking down at the badly damaged Nixturjekur, he sighed deeply. "There's a city to rebuild, a vessel to repair, and a mad god to stop. This is *exactly* why I've been a hermit for a millennia."

EPILOGUE

ABTRUE STOOD BEFORE all that was left of their pantheon: Gron'Tul, Karak, Yorm, Progity and Trinfrey. Gron'Tul just stared at him, wondering what they were ultimately going to do. What was occurring now was unheard of.

"Never in our existence have any of us attacked the others in such a fashion, let alone *killed* them. Jek is gone, Deghat is gone..."

"Ya nearly destroyed mah city!"

"And *you*, Karak, nearly destroyed all Antembra with your rash actions! The balance was already skewed because Deghat, Abtrue and Jek had left their cells. You nearly gave Res'Kel exactly what he wanted," Progity admonished Karak.

The dwarven god slammed his fist against the table. "Ya ken all stand aroun', making yer decisions, but I'll do what needs ta be done!"

"Which is what, exactly? What are we to do with our brother?" Gron'Tul asked of them all.

"Execution."

A silence fell over the rest of those who were assembled and all eyes fell to Abtrue. He raised his head slowly, looking from one member to the next, before meeting Gron'-Tul's gaze and repeating what he had said.

"Execution."

She shook her head vehemently. "No. We did not convene to discuss your death. As much as what you did pains us, you are one of us, and as such, we will *not* end you."

Karak threw his hands up in exasperation and was about to speak when she interrupted him. "No matter how much some of us may disagree."

"He. Comes. Joining. Logical. Betrayal. Warrants. Punishment."

"You don't get away from usss that easssily, ssstone brother," Trinfrey spat out, venom thick in her voice. Gron'Tul noticed that so far Yorm had been silent, his arms crossed as he looked off into the distance.

"Yorm? Your thoughts?"

"This is a farce. Two of our brothers are dead, and we talk about keeping another as prisoner. We are *all* prisoners, Gron'Tul. What we do no longer matters. Res'Kel will change the world with or without us."

"He's right. Though, I prefer to be called Eldric'Kel now."

Gron'Tul jumped out of her seat when Eldric'Kel suddenly appeared next to Abtrue. He casually put his arm around the stone god's shoulder and smirked at her.

"Calm down. I'm not really here. Since our last encounter you've done an excellent job of preventing me from doing much more than projecting myself. I just wanted to let you know that it is only a matter of time before I finish what I started one thousand years ago."

"Every victory for you seems so backwards, brother. Each win is so narrowly achieved that it can barely be called a win at all," Progity pointed out.

"Perhaps." Eldric'Kel then walked around Abtrue and stood between him and the others, stating, "I'm giving you all one last chance to join me in this. You know exactly what is at stake here, and why I'm fighting so hard for this. Will you not *finally* give me your blessing?"

Yorm laughed and shook his head, standing and making his way from the table.

"Something amusing, Yorm?"

Looking over his shoulder he replied, "The Matriarch is never going to come back. No matter how much you want it to happen, no matter how much you try. Were you actually here I would challenge you again, but all you wish to use are words, and I am sick of your voice."

As Yorm left, Progity got up and silently followed after him. Karak sneered at the dark god and left in a huff. Trinfrey looked at Gron'Tul and then Eldric'Kel.

"I will never join you, brother. But I will wisssh that you ssstop this obsssesssion before it consssumesss you fully."

This left Abtrue, Eldric'Kel and Gron'Tul alone. Neither spoke for several moments until Gron'Tul let out a sigh and shook her head. So much weighed heavily on her mind.

"You have broken so many of the covenants we held with one another. There is no going back. Once we discover how to be truly free again, there is nothing on Antembra that will be able to stop us from ending you, Res'Kel, not even the Matriarch."

Eldric'Kel folded his arms. "I told you my name. And it doesn't have to be like this, Gron'Tul. The others aren't dead, you know."

"What?!"

"Yormsun, or whatever the pitiful dwarves called it, is actually a device of the Matriarch. The one she used to make *us*. I'm certain it can unmake us as well, but I didn't use it like that. Jek and Deghat are still within."

Gron'Tul balled her fists and fought back tears as she stared him down.

"Go. Now. I won't allow you to use them as bargaining chips against us. Pray that you can beg our forgiveness when we finally move against you without reservation. Abtrue, you may choose to leave with him, but the same goes for you: if you leave, you *will* end when next we meet."

Eldric'Kel seemed stunned by Gron'Tul's reaction and opened his mouth to say something further, but slowly closed it again without speaking. His form disappeared, but Abtrue remained, looking at her. He stared at her, and his eyes were suddenly filled with sadness. She was taken aback by the visual emotion on his face, something she had never witnessed before.

"Matriarch. Made. You. Best."

In a blink he was gone, leaving Gron'Tul by herself in their pocket dimension. Finally and truly alone, she felt overcome with emotions. Like a human.

"Why, mother? Why did you have to leave us?"

Falling to her knees, she wept.

ABOUT THE AUTHOR

C. M. W. Hawkins is an American writer who lives in Alberta, Canada, with his wife and son. Imported back in 2004, he's come to view the country as his adopted homeland, and now can't imagine living anywhere else.

The Gods Who Walk is the first in a planned trilogy, but is the author's second book. The more adult-themed horror novel *Fear in the Blood* is available online and through order at book stores everywhere.

When not writing about gods, walking or otherwise, he enjoys reading, game nights with friends, video games with good stories, and sometimes a few rounds of Hearthstone™ in-between edits.